Everyone is wanting *Moore!* – praise for the *Follet Valley series* and Ian Moore

'A joyous read!' Alan Carr

'A writer of **immense wit and charm**' Paul Sinha

'A very funny page-turner. **Fantastique!**' Adam Kay

'Ian is **one of my favourite writers**; this is hilarious and a great mystery too' Janey Godley

'**Good food and a laugh-out-loud mystery**. What more could anyone want in these dark times' Mark Billingham

'**Like going on a joyous romp** through the Loire Valley with Agatha Christie, P.G. Wodehouse and M.C. Beaton. A delight' C.K. McDonnell

'Ian Moore is a **brilliant, funny writer who perfectly captures the foibles of rural France** but judging by this book I will never be visiting his bed and breakfast' Josh Widdicombe

'**Beautifully done. Very funny indeed**. I can't imagine how one plots something like that. Tremendous work' Miles Jupp

'I'm so **punchdrunk from the sheer entertainment of it** I've got a sore jaw. Encore!' Matt Forde

'This is like **two great books in one**, a tricksy whodunnit, and a really, really funny story' Jason Manford

'Such a brilliant read, smart, funny and **his sharp writing captures the nuances of "Anglo-French" relations beautifully**' Zoe Lyons

'This book is **a fun and funny read** and I'm very much looking forward to the next one' Ian Stone

'**Funny, pacey and very entertaining**' Robin Ince

ALSO BY IAN MOORE

Death and Croissants
Death and Fromage
Death at the Chateau

Death and Papa Noël

DEATH IN LE Jardin

A FOLLET VALLEY MYSTERY

IAN MOORE

First published in 2024 by Farrago,
an imprint of Duckworth Books Ltd
1 Golden Court, Richmond, TW9 1EU, United Kingdom

www.farragobooks.com

Hardback ISBN: 978-1-78842-498-1
Ebook ISBN: 978-1-78842-499-8
Trade Paperback ISBN: 978-1-78842-500-1

Cover design and illustration by Patrick Knowles

To all those who need a smile

Chapter One

'Ah, spring!' Richard Ainsworth said out loud. He was trying to inject the right note of optimism and hope that the word spring was supposed to provoke. Then he took a deep breath, said '*bloody* spring' under his breath and ventured outside into the fresh morning. Richard had views on spring and they weren't entirely positive. In fact, he was downright suspicious of the whole thing.

Spring was a mantrap which rolled around once a year looking to catch the optimist off guard with its promise of regeneration and new life. As a rule, Richard was quite some way down the street from optimism but was wary nonetheless. It was a glorious, warm day but as if guarding against an enemy, Richard kept his jumper on over a buttoned-up polo shirt, muttering to himself under his breath as he pulled on his stiff Wellington boots. It wasn't that he was against regeneration and new life *per se*, just that those things brought with them the burden of responsibility and inevitably, backbreaking hard work.

Every year. *Every year.*

Like clockwork, the bleak Follet Valley winter would just suddenly end and, within the space of what seemed like hours, new shoots, rampant and vigorous, would sprout everywhere, going off like floral fireworks. Weeds would grow through his gravelled driveway literally before his eyes, his leylandii hedges would break free of their finely edged shackles and look like an untrimmed beard. And the grass, oh the grass, he moaned, that would need cutting on an almost daily basis. He had of course tried to embrace the recent fad of leaving your garden to grow wild, thereby encouraging nature to look after itself and promote the insect population, but it wasn't his style and wasn't necessarily his choice to make anyway. He ran a high-end B&B, a posh *chambre d'hôte*, and generally his clientele liked their nature to look shipshape, its borders smart and its insects preferably at somebody else's arm's length.

None of this would really matter if the garden was small and manageable of course, but it wasn't. It was just under a couple of acres and Mother Nature regarded it as a large blank canvas just to be Jackson Pollocked with flora whenever his back was turned. He sighed and took in the view. *What were they thinking?* he thought to himself, not for the first time, *what were they on?*

'They' were he and Clare, but it was mainly him. Wounded by redundancy, booted out of a film historian job he loved by the rampaging desire for digitalisation and the internet, specifically the world-ruining IMDb.com, he had salved his ego in the purchase of the biggest bloody property they could afford. Which in rural France meant very big indeed and, in comparison to southern England, at dirt cheap prices. Clare had warned him that the maintenance would be too much, that he'd regret it in the long run, almost as if she knew then that she herself wasn't going to be in it for the long haul. And she'd been right on all counts. Not that he

2

would ever admit that to her, even now, now that they were separated and she was living back in the UK.

'Me?' he'd said, a brash confidence papering over fragile wounds. 'I am a man of the soil.' And off he had gone to buy a ride-on lawnmower, one more fillip for the male ego. His heart sank at the memory. The ride-on mower. His enthusiasm for the machine had lasted perhaps two of the early spring cuts. It was the most uncomfortable contraption he'd ever ridden and after a couple of hours of admittedly rapid grass-cutting he'd stagger off the thing and feel like he'd spent the afternoon trapped in a tumble dryer. Clare had been right about that too.

'You're just not a gardener, dear,' she said, every time she heard him swearing somewhere on the property. 'You don't have green fingers.' She would then back this theory up by claiming that because there were so few films about gardening, he had nothing to draw any heroics from, no grounding in the subject. She would then turn the page of whatever glossy magazine she was perusing and take a triumphant sip of an early evening cocktail.

'Not true,' he'd argue. '*The Spanish Gardener*, Dirk Bogarde, 1956. *I Confess*, Hitchcock, 1953. Peter Sellers, 1979, *Being There*…'

'For which he should have won the Academy Award, yes, yes, dear, so you say. Top me up will you?'

Clare. The letter was still sitting in the kitchen, unopened after ten days. It was an official-looking brown envelope with Richard's name and address typed on the front. Anyway, he assumed it was from Clare because the sender's address was stamped on the back. 'Forshaw-Banks' it read in pale blue print, 'Solicitors'. Followed by an address somewhere in Woking. Only bad news travelled by old-fashioned mail these days so he was guessing that Clare, not for the first time, had taken charge of the situation and the inevitable grinding wheels of divorce were turning. Well it could wait, was his barely considered opinion. If it was a divorce petition then he knew it would all be fairly amicable, they were still good friends after all, communicating often; and if she wanted half of everything she was welcome to it, in fact she could have the whole lot of it in his opinion, just as long as he didn't get custody of the ride-on mower.

'She has a new boyfriend,' their daughter Alicia had warned him, the tone in her voice more than hinting at disapproval. 'He has a sports car like the one your girlfriend has.'

It had taken Richard some time to work out who she meant by 'your girlfriend'. He was pretty sure that if he had a girlfriend he would have known about it, but it was now the assumption of pretty much everyone they knew that he and Valérie d'Orçay were what used to be called 'an item'. They weren't, but like owning a ride-on mower, the prestige of the assumption was good for Richard's delicate male psyche so he affected a sort of 'gentlemen never tells' type air and hoped no one would actually ask him a direct question.

From a distance it was, he had to admit, an easy assumption to make. Valérie and Richard behaved, on the face of things, like a couple. Or at least what had become Richard's notion of a couple. She bossed him about and he more often than not did as he was told, secretly happy to be bossed about. What social life there was to be had in rural France was passed together; Richard's friends had become her friends. They even, in theory and certainly to the outside world, lived together since Valérie and her pampered Chihuahua Passepartout had taken up permanent residence, though in the largest of the B&B bedrooms, not the main house. For free too, but as they were now business partners as well, he was putting that down as a tax break.

Business wasn't booming though, he ruminated as he dithered his way to the dreaded ride-on lawnmower shed. In fact they hadn't had a job in months. Granted, private investigations and personal security work was always going to be a tough sell in a quiet agricultural French backwater like the Follet Valley, but Richard – and he would never admit this to anyone, probably not even himself – missed the excitement of their adventures. It was fair to say that his initial foray into the world of personal security had got off to a rocky start; three deaths on his watch wasn't the launch anyone was looking for, but it all seemed a long time ago now. Two whole seasons in fact, and while he had kept the reduced capacity B&B going, it had all become a bit dull, a bit safe. No doubt, Clare would say, a bit Richard.

Valérie on the other hand kept a professional hand in on her own full-time job as a bounty hunter and likely assassin; the facts of the latter had never been properly established and Richard had never felt like addressing it full on. Every so often she would disappear for a few days, sometimes to visit her apartment in Paris which was still for sale, sometimes for work and always leaving strict instructions for Passepartout's personal menu. Richard could piece together her work movements by checking on the internet whether a fugitive on the run had been captured or a rogue tin pot dictator had disappeared. She offered him no further information than that and he was far too English to ask for any. He was just relieved when she returned.

He stopped by the chicken coop to check on his hens. 'Morning, ladies,' he said with genuine warmth and was greeted with a comforting chorus of contented clucking in reply. 'Sleep well?' He opened the gate and went in to check on their water as they fussed happily around his feet. Clare's letter, Valérie's dangerous profession, money worries and the dull descent into a sedentary middle age, from an admittedly not very great height, could all be forgotten when he was with his hens. They were his happy place, his balm. Joan Crawford and Lana Turner pecked at his feet while Olivia de Havilland lagged behind, eventually joining the others though clearly limping as she made her way over to Richard. He bent down to pick her up, putting the calm bird on his lap as he sat down on the hen coop bench.

'What's up, old girl?' he asked gently and she cocked her head in response. 'Why are you limping then?' She flattened her back as he stroked her and he saw the culprit immediately as a small section of bramble hung aggressively off her right foot. He pulled it off gently, making his own clucking noises as he did so, trying to comfort the animal. The bramble was a rogue element of a larger bush that had sprung up right next to the coop ladder. 'Bloody spring!' he said loudly, and after placing Olivia back on the ground, he stood up ready to attack what he now saw as the epitome of his seasonal nemesis, Mother Nature herself.

'Bloody spring!' he repeated, almost as a battle cry, as he cupped his hands like a murderous strangler ready to choke the life out of the floral invader and injurer of his beloved Olivia.

'Richard, what are you doing?'

Valérie's mixture of concern and bemusement, a look echoed with frightening accuracy by the nestled Passepartout, momentarily put Richard off his stride. Though not enough to actually stop his act of revenge on the bramble which went ahead anyway and with predictably painful results.

'Ow! Bloody hell!' he cried, and staggered backwards, a look of horror on his face as blood began to drip from a cut on his right index finger. 'I'm bleeding!' he said redundantly.

'Yes,' was the equally useless reply. Even Passepartout seemed to nod in confirmation.

There was an awkward silence as Richard sucked childishly on his torn finger and Valérie, who had no mothering instinct whatsoever beyond that for tiny dogs, tried to look away as Richard crumbled into a man child.

'Bloody hell!' he repeated, though now it was more a whine than a rage.

'Richard, I am worried,' Valérie said eventually.

'Pah.' He shrugged. 'I'll get over it. It's just a bit of blood.'

Again a look of confusion crossed her face. 'No,' she said quietly, 'not about that.' She pointed at his stricken hand so he folded his arms in a gesture of embarrassment, hiding his finger. Richard didn't consider himself a scruffy individual but Valérie always made him feel like one. She wore beige jodhpurs, a cream turtle neck jumper and a tweed jacket; her brown suede Chelsea boots looked brand new. She looked like she was off to a society gymkhana.

'Have you lost your horse?' he asked attempting a casual air to distract from his bramble tantrum. She narrowed her eyes in response, looking at him now not only with no sympathy whatsoever but with an expression that indicated her confusion had now been replaced by the obvious conclusion that Richard was an idiot. 'Never mind,' he added quickly, as usual internally admonishing himself for trying humour on her. She took life too seriously for such frivolities as jokes and sarcasm.

'I am worried about Madame Tablier,' she said eventually. 'I have not seen her this morning.'

In his anti-spring fever Richard hadn't realised that his *femme de ménage*, and permanent fixture since he'd moved to France, wasn't there. There had been no guests staying the previous evening so he hadn't had to prepare breakfast, but Madame Tablier was always, always there and now he felt guilty for not noticing. Even if there was nothing to do, no reason for her to be at the B&B at all, she would have been there anyway having taken on the role of Richard's protector. Richard didn't need protecting in his opinion, but Madame Tablier thought otherwise having concluded almost on first sight that Richard was a danger to himself.

'I'm sure she's OK,' he said unconvincingly.

'Well, we are worried aren't we, *mon petit*?' Passepartout didn't look overly concerned to be fair.

They were interrupted by the throaty roar of a large-engine motorbike as the aforementioned Madame Tablier, in full cycling leathers, pulled up beside the couple, scattering the hens.

'I'm late,' she said in what Richard knew passed for an apology from the doughty old woman. 'I've been to a funeral,' she added quickly. 'My brother-in-law.'

Richard and Valérie looked at each other wondering how to respond. Madame Tablier didn't do schmaltz or platitudes.

'I didn't know you had a brother-in-law.' Valérie was testing the water.

'I don't anymore.'

'Well, you don't have to stay today, Madame Tablier, if you want to be with your... er, family.' Richard thought he may as well play at being in charge, ridiculous notion though it was.

'No. No need. There's nothing can be done now he's in the ground, is there?' She wandered into the chicken coop.

'How did he die?' Valérie asked, presumably showing a professional curiosity.

'Ha!' snorted the old woman. 'He went and got his head chopped off, didn't he?' She bent down and ripped up the bramble bush that had caused Richard so many problems, then realised that jaws had dropped and eyes were staring so she looked up. 'What?' she asked innocently.

Chapter Two

This startling revelation, introduced in Madame Tablier's usual gruff, take it or leave it fashion, had rather stunned Richard and Valérie into silence, and they had all moved silently inside, trying to take stock. 'You're bleeding,' Madame Tablier said matter-of-factly, throwing a brief look of suspicion Valérie's way as she did so. It was only then that Richard noticed his finger had bled into his cream jumper and the stain was rapidly spreading out, making it look like he had a knife wound. Events had rather overtaken his own thorny problems for the moment, however, and he sat down at a table while Madame Tablier grabbed a broom for no reason other than cause of habit. She remained standing, happier now that she had her accoutrement to lean on. Valérie stood at the breakfast bar having placed Passepartout in one of his many beds.

Richard looked at his finger which was now covered in dried blood. He knew that the subject of Madame Tablier's brother-in-law's decapitation would need to be handled delicately. She was wont to clam up if she felt pressured. She was an earthy woman of the country, there were no emotions anywhere near the surface and though she had taken on the job of looking after Richard, especially so since Clare had left, it didn't mean she trusted him. He still didn't even know her first name. No. Tact, diplomacy and caution were the way forward.

'My dear, Madame Tablier...' he began gently.

'Oh this is absurd!' Valérie could hold it in no longer. 'How can a man just lose his head?'

Madame Tablier gave her a look that said men were capable of losing just about anything given half a chance. 'Showing off,' she said harshly. 'How else?'

She looked no less indomitable out of her bike leathers. Her grey hair was pinned tight to her head and under a net, a perfect copy of the equally indomitable old British actress, long since dead, Irene Handl. Her light blue floral sleeveless apron was equally forbidding on her stocky frame and she wielded her broom like it was Excalibur. She wasn't happy, clearly, but then Richard had known her for nearly six years now and wasn't sure he'd ever seen her happy as such.

'Madame Tablier,' Valérie threw a disarming smile at the room in general, and it acted like a light being turned on. 'Camomile tea, *fruits des bois*, or mint? I'm having camomile.'

The older woman stopped in her tracks. She wasn't used to being waited on and certainly not being offered a menu of herbal variety teas so the offer took her by surprise, throwing her completely. She sat slowly at a table opposite to Richard's not taking her eyes off Valérie as she did so. 'Mint,' she said suspiciously. The kettle boiled almost on cue and Valérie poured the teas. Richard wasn't offered a choice but took his mug of camomile, which he would have chosen anyway.

There was an awkward silence as Madame Tablier looked from one to the other, a proud, almost aggressive look on her face like a suspect in a police interview. 'When you say showing off...' Richard said eventually, 'what happened exactly?'

The old woman looked down into her mug, obviously weighing up whether to say anything at all. In the years that Richard had known her she had often made pointed remarks about being ignored, or relegated to the background but her obvious unease at now being the centre of attention told a different story and though she would have beaten Richard to a pulp with her broom at the suggestion, she looked vulnerable. He decided to change tack before Valérie took an impatient wrecking ball to the tense atmosphere.

'I thought that you weren't really in touch with your sister?' he asked, trying not to sound too heavy, and sensing that Valérie was tensing at the roundabout start to proceedings.

'We're not close,' was the terse reply. 'But she's all I have left, so I keep an eye out, she always needed looking after. Especially now.'

'You never liked her husband?' Valérie pounced on the opening.

Madame Tablier looked from one to the other, narrowed her eyes briefly and then seemed to come to a decision. 'Have you heard of Duval Cuistot?' she asked eventually. There was no warmth in her voice at the mention of the name.

It meant nothing to Richard whose knowledge of French culture, high or low, was slim at best. The odd appearance of Sacha Distel on the Saturday evening variety programmes of his childhood aside, he had little else.

'Duval Cuistot?' Valérie rolled the name around hoping to perhaps jog a distant memory, though Richard suspected her cultural knowledge didn't go much wider than his own. 'It does ring a bell…' she added, too stubborn to give up.

Madame Tablier snorted at their ignorance, 'I knew it,' she said disdainfully. 'He was quite famous for a while. Years ago.' She stopped, leaving this scant knowledge hanging there.

'For what?' Valérie asked impatiently, when it seemed like the woman had clammed up.

'For showing off!' was the speedy reply. 'I told you.'

Even Richard was beginning to lose patience with this game. 'Madame Tablier,' he said, trying to sound calm. 'Who is, sorry was, Duval Cuistot?'

She shook her head again. 'He was a big noise forty years ago or so. A stunt motorcyclist.'

'Like Evel Knievel?' Richard interrupted, finally feeling they were getting somewhere, though it was clear that neither Valérie nor Madame Tablier knew who he was talking about. That's the fickle nature of fame, he thought. Evel Knievel had literally broken his body into pieces trying to set daredevil stunt records in the 1970s, yet now it seemed he was just an ignored footnote of male ego and rampant show-offery.

'There was a time,' Madame Tablier continued, and Richard noticed a slightly wistful look in the eye, perhaps, though surely not, bordering on admiration, 'that he held the world record for a motorbike jump. Ramp to dirt.' She nodded again with the memory. 'Like I said, he was a big noise.' She seemed suddenly to feel that she was revealing too much about herself and her manner changed immediately. 'Then someone else broke the record a week later.'

'And this is your brother-in-law?' Valérie couldn't hide her surprise.

'He was.' Again Madame Tablier clarified the situation. 'He owned a restaurant and my sister worked as his *femme de ménage*, then he tried to re-take the world record…' She shook her head sadly at the memory. Clearly things had not gone to plan. 'My sister…'

'Sorry,' Richard couldn't help himself. 'What is your sister's name?'

'Madame Cuistot,' was the cold response.

'Ah.'

'She stayed with him. Ran his restaurant for him, nursed him back to health… I mean, he couldn't walk for a year.' Her tone wasn't admiration in any way, it was purely matter-of-fact. *C'est normal* as the French would say, it's just what you do. 'When he was fit, eventually, my sister was going to move in with me. We were going to share my place.' She stopped as if that were explanation enough.

'And…?' Valérie was having none of that. 'She married him instead.'

'No.' Madame Tablier said very definitely. 'He married her.'

Richard, and quite obviously Valérie, had no idea of the distinction between the two but it was equally clear that Madame Tablier certainly did. Duval Cuistot had perhaps ruined her plans for a family reunion and the old woman had not forgiven him at all.

'Is that why you didn't have much contact with your sister?' Richard asked. 'From when they were married?'

'I'm not one to stick my nose in where it's not wanted,' she said proudly. 'And he didn't want it.'

'And Madame Cuistot?'

'She was working too hard, never had time off, did she? She ran the restaurant, then it became a *chambre d'hôte* like here and she ran that for him too. He only married her so she'd do everything for him.'

'And what did he do all this time?' Valérie asked, a touch of sisterly indignation in her voice.

'Pah! He did what he'd always done and showed off! Women, and drink and WOMEN!' she shouted, clearly vexed at the treatment of her sister.

'And your sister did not want to leave him, this man?'

Madame Tablier looked at Valérie, again there was a look of stoic pride on her face. 'No,' she said quietly. 'You don't, do you? Life is for life, no matter what.'

Richard was shocked that Valérie was quietly nodding in agreement to this statement when, at the last count and if his figures were correct, she wasn't far off double figures in the marriage stakes. If Valérie was actually a disciple of the 'life means life' approach to marriage then it was that of the short-lived life of a mayfly. Madame Tablier, however, seemed to appreciate the support and the two women, as different as two examples of womanhood could possibly be, seemed to bond briefly.

Richard felt that they should get back to the initial thrust of the conversation. 'So how did he lose his head then?' he asked.

'I wouldn't blame your sister if she'd chopped it off herself!' Valérie wasn't letting go of her umbrage but the suggestion ruffled Madame Tablier.

'She didn't!' she said angrily.

Richard jumped in again. 'So what happened?'

The fire of outrage in her eyes died as quickly as it had risen. 'Showing off,' she repeated quietly. 'Every year, the restaurant would have a grand re-opening to mark spring. It never actually closed in the winter, he wouldn't have let my sister have the time off, but it was a chance for him to put on a show. The long garden out the back of the restaurant is quite steep and he would take his ride-on lawnmower and race it down the hill and he would jump the *terrasse* like he used to do bikes over buses.'

If Madame Tablier and Valérie d'Orçay were opposite poles of womanhood, he could have said the same about himself and Duval Cuistot. The man sounded like a lunatic.

'But something went wrong?' Valérie could not hide a fervent excitement.

'My sister begged him not to do it. He had had a fall the previous year and had been bedridden for weeks, he didn't have the strength for the stunt. The landing alone might have killed him. Oh, she pleaded with him.' She snorted then shook her head sadly.

Valérie was getting impatient and said 'And?' but directed it at Richard as if he knew the answer.

'Well, he agreed not to do it. I don't know how, but she got him to change the stunt, make it a joke. He could ride down the hill, but slowly and then a ramp would be at the bottom and the lawnmower would jump over toy buses.'

'And he agreed to that?' Richard felt like it was something of a comedown for the French Evel Knievel.

'Not happily,' was the reply. 'But I think he knew he had no choice.'

'But it didn't go to plan?' Richard asked.

'No. The lawnmower had no brakes.'

'Ah.'

'Well, it had brakes but no brake fluid.'

'The line had been cut?' Valérie's palpable enthusiasm for the grisly was unnerving, even to Richard who had become somewhat used to it.

'No. Not cut. Just the reservoir was empty. He hadn't checked beforehand. Silly man.'

'So…' Richard tried to visualise the scene. 'Monsieur Cuistot came down the hill too fast in the end, unable to stop. He hit the ramp and…' He left the sentence hanging, probably not unlike the doomed Cuistot himself.

'The lawnmower hit the ramp. He let go of it and flew into the *terrasse* sign, L'Auberge Cuistot. Took his head nearly clean off it did. Died instantly.'

'How terrible!' Even Valérie reined it in for this detail. 'Your poor sister.'

'And she had still lunches to serve too, everyone was there, you see? The whole town. Even I was there. It was her birthday.' She briefly looked at the floor, unusually for her avoiding eye contact.

'She still served lunch?' It seemed, to Richard's eyes, an unnecessary responsibility given that you've just seen your husband's head separated violently from his body. He knew that Madame Tablier's generation of rural French womenfolk were made of strong stuff, but even so.

'Not straight away! It was mainly salads so it kept.' Richard felt she'd missed his point. '*Mort par imprudence*, that's what the coroner said. Death by showing off, I say.'

Passepartout interrupted this by growling at the door, his lips curled in rare aggression. Whether it was via telepathy or training Richard couldn't tell, but Valérie reacted immediately. 'It's OK, *mon petit*, come in Henri!'

There was an unnecessary knock at the salon door and a shy-looking Commissaire Henri Lapierre entered. The policeman, the highest ranking in the Follet Valley, was still wearing a winter coat and, improbably, a black porkpie hat. He was also sweating profusely. '*Bonjour*,' he said, a little sheepishly. '*Mesdames*, monsieur.' He remained standing at the door, then was bustled through further by an eager-looking police woman in uniform. 'Ah, this is Commandant Delfort.' After some awkward introductions, Lapierre cleared his throat. He was clearly quite nervous.

'Erm, Madame Tablier, I am here to arrest you for the murder of Duval Cuistot.'

Apart from tutting loudly, the old woman showed no emotion whatsoever. In fact, Richard had the distinct impression that she'd been expecting it.

Chapter Three

'Don't be ridiculous, Henri!'

'I,' the now pompous policeman said, 'am not being ridiculous, Madame d'Orçay.' His attempt to deploy formality as a tactic may have worked on a less determined individual but seeing as Valérie was, and Richard still had enormous trouble getting his head around this, the Commissaire's ex-wife, it failed miserably.

'You are arresting her on what grounds?' She ventured forward menacingly and for a moment Richard felt a second arrest might be on the cards.

'Madame.' It was a serenely calm Madame Tablier who broke the tension, an air of the Sydney Carton at the guillotine about her. 'Please. Let the Commissaire do his job.' She walked out of the door alone, then popped her head back in after a few seconds and told the dithering Commandant Delfort to sodding-well get on with it as she didn't have all day. *She'll be all right*, Richard concluded.

'On what grounds?' Valérie repeated. 'And take that so silly hat off.'

The Commissaire ripped his hat off angrily, pursed his lips and waited for the inevitable questions. He stoically stared ahead rather than catch Valérie's eye directly and Richard couldn't help but feel some sympathy for the man whose hat had been hiding a dressing on a shaved patch right on his crown.

'It was a fishing accident,' he said, trying to give it an element of heroism.

'So is the arrest of Madame Tablier,' Valérie snapped, her sarcasm taking Richard by surprise. 'Now put your hat back on, Henri. You look absurd.' He did so gratefully.

Richard had had enough of this by-play. 'I'd like to know,' he said grandly, standing up as he did so, 'exactly why you have arrested Madame Tablier? I was under the impression that Duval Cuistot's death was accidental.'

'What do you know of this affair, monsieur?' The Commissaire, hat back in place, had regained his composure.

'I know enough,' Richard bluffed, refusing to back down.

'And who gave you the impression that Monsieur Cuistot's death was an accident? Would it by any chance be the woman who has just been arrested for his murder?'

'Madame Tablier, yes.' He tried not to let a brief dip in confidence show.

'I see.'

'It was not accidental then?' Valérie's question was rhetorical, but the Commissaire decided to score the point anyway.

'Obviously.'

Richard and Valérie both began asking questions at once, clamouring for details while the Commissaire, as implacable and emotionless as a public building itself, remained impassive until even he, a servant of the state and therefore trained in the art of giving nothing away, could take no more.

'*Ça suffit!*' he shouted sharply, ripping his hat off again. 'That will do!' he added unnecessarily. 'There is new evidence...' Richard and Valérie started up their assault once more. 'THERE IS NEW EVIDENCE,' the Commissaire shouted above their noise, quietening them in the process. He tried again. 'There is evidence. I am not at liberty to give all the details just yet; all will become clear in due course...'

Valérie was on the verge of exploding. 'Oh shut up, Henri! You are talking like an official.'

'I am an official!' he countered. 'An official in charge of this investigation.' Finally this seemed to put Richard and Valérie under some sort of control but, just to keep his physical and metaphorical distance, he walked slowly to the other side of the breakfast bar. Richard watched Lapierre as the policeman calmly poured himself a small coffee from the percolator. The confidence of the man was infuriating and in contrast to most of the other times Richard had had dealings with him. Hitherto he'd been happy, well happy-ish, to allow Valérie to take a lead in any investigation, unofficially of course, giving him the chance to concentrate on his fishing and his oft-spoken ambition of a quiet life. This new-found self-belief was worrying and it showed that in his mind, this case, the now apparently non-accidental death of Duval Cuistot, was pretty much sewn up.

'This new evidence...' Richard began.

'As I have said, monsieur...'

'Yes, yes, yes. Not at liberty to say and so on. But whatever it is, it's come to light very late hasn't it?'

'And your point is what?'

Valérie cottoned on to Richard's train of thought. 'So the funeral was this morning, Henri. It could have only gone ahead because the coroner had already declared death by misadventure.'

Lapierre lifted his espresso cup slowly to his lips, narrowing his eyes as usual when he felt he was being hunted. 'It is true,' he started slowly, 'that this, er, this new evidence, has come to light later than I would have liked.'

'So you were never happy with your original conclusions then?' Despite the seriousness of the situation, if asked, Richard would have admitted to thoroughly enjoying himself, he felt like he was in a classic court-room drama. 'You went back over old ground then, as it were?'

'That's very conscientious of you, Henri,' Valérie said, and got a nod of gratitude for the compliment in return. 'Not your usual style at all,' she added, enjoying herself as much as Richard.

Commissaire Henri Lapierre flushed with anger and put his coffee down with exaggerated care. 'I was never fully happy with the original investigation, that is true. That place, that town, it is one of the strangest towns I have ever known, it is peculiar even for the Follet Valley.'

'What do you mean?' Richard asked.

The policeman gave it some thought. 'I do not know exactly. Just that it does not seem real.' He threw his hands in the air. 'I cannot put my finger on it at all. Nobody helped, nobody wanted to help. There was the death, the very strange death of one of their own but all they could talk about was the town. Like the death, and I know how this sounds, was like a sacrifice to the service of the town.

The town is more important than life, almost like La Chapelle-sur-Follet, the town, is alive itself. So you see, this nose,' he flicked the end of said nose, 'it knew, it knew something was not quite right.'

Richard had seen enough low-budget, hastily scripted horror films in his former career to recognise the voice of portent when he heard it, and normally he'd run a mile in the opposite direction. If it wasn't for the arrest of Madame Tablier he would have done exactly that.

'Are you saying that while everyone was at the funeral this morning, you took the chance to have another look around?' Richard agreed with Valérie and clearly thought this was out of character. 'Are you supposed to do that when an investigation is officially closed?'

'Brilliant, Richard!' Valérie cried excitedly.

Again Lapierre blushed. 'I received an anonymous tip-off late last night which led, after some further investigations on my part, to the discovery of solid physical evidence linking your Madame Tablier to the death of her brother-in-law Duval Cuistot!' He pointed his finger upwards with a *j'accuse* flourish. 'Solid physical evidence in his *garage!*' he repeated. 'Namely,' he looked from one to the other, 'her wedding ring!' His triumph immediately dissipated when he realised he had given away far more than he had intended.

'Hang on, there's a number of things here. First, she doesn't wear a wedding ring. She told me years ago that she had to have it removed because it was cutting off the blood circulation and second, it's all a bit convenient, isn't it? Someone slips a note under your door late at night and says "go back to the garage, you may have missed a bit"? I don't buy it,' Richard concluded. 'It's a set-up in my opinion,' he added with a Bogart twang. He was aware that Valérie, despite her obvious fury with Lapierre, couldn't take her eyes off him.

'A *set-hup?*' The policeman exaggerated his English mockingly. 'No, monsieur. I received a telephone message, an anonymous text, telling me there were rumours of a falling-out in the Cuistot household. From there, you see, I know where to check these rumours, I am professional, I made a further search. That is when I found the wedding ring, inscribed "*Tablier Toujours*".'

'Oh really, Henri, and what is the motive?'

'Ah.' His eyes lit up. 'Jealousy!'

Richard couldn't help but burst out laughing. 'Jealousy!' he cried. 'Madame Tablier? Our Madame Tablier in murderous love triangle shock? No wonder you wanted to keep that quiet!'

'What do you really know of the woman?' Lapierre asked, implying he knew a great deal.

'I know that she's not a murderer.'

The Commissaire straightened his hat and turned for the door. 'Nevertheless. I have evidence, I have a motive, I have a suspect, and I have made an arrest!' His finger of triumph shot up in the air again and he turned to leave but bumped straight into a returning Madame Tablier.

'Can we get a move on, Commissaire?' The old woman was awash with frustration. 'Stop showing off. You know what happens to people who show off.' It sounded like a badly timed threat, which wasn't lost on the Commissaire, who once again looked with triumph at a now seated Richard while Valérie stood beside him. Then Madame

Tablier addressed them both. 'Stay out of it,' she said without any emotion whatsoever. 'Please stay out of it.'

She hurried Lapierre out of the door and closed it behind her leaving just the two of them in stunned silence. Valérie put a hand on Richard's forearm. 'I know what you will say, Richard, but I do not think we should be staying out of it.'

He stood up briskly, sliding his chair back noisily as he did so. 'You're damn right we're not!' he said, his jawline rock hard, staring at the closed door. 'We're going in.'

Chapter Four

In Valérie's experience Richard Ainsworth was a 'slow' driver. He used driving almost as a source of relaxation and would pootle about the Follet Valley, happily obeying the – in her eyes – asphyxiatingly slow speed limits, tapping his fingers on the steering wheel to some imaginary tune and with a look of vacant contentment on his face. He was exactly the kind of driver she hated to be stuck behind. So usually their driving duties were divided along 'need to' lines. If it was a journey that had a fixed time of arrival, Valérie would drive her classic 1979 soft top Renault Alpine, and Richard would close his eyes. If it was a trip to the market, Richard would get behind the wheel of his battered old 2CV and Valérie would be a pent-up ball of frustration in the passenger seat thinking, not without justification, that she could walk to the market quicker than Richard drove.

It was something of a surprise then that Richard had headed straight for the Renault Alpine driving seat and demanded Valérie's keys. It was also something of a surprise that Valérie had given them to him. Richard's tone of voice, one that she had not heard before, convinced her that it was the right thing to do. She was also learning, after months of watching him at close quarters, that he needed the occasional boost to his confidence. He wasn't a weak man, far from it in her opinion, just a little lost sometimes. Not frightened of the world, just weary of it and wary too.

But this was a different Richard that was driving her powerful sports car, throwing it into the infrequent hairpin bends, his jaw still clenched and his knuckles as white as chalk as he gripped the steering wheel hard enough to rip it out.

'We are going to La Chapelle-sur-Follet?' Her question was more of a confirmation as they had barely spoken since leaving the house.

'Yes,' was the terse reply, barely audible above the booming V12 engine.

'You don't believe Madame Tablier is guilty then, do you?' She was trying to get him to open up a bit, aware that he rarely made his true feelings known. He wasn't exactly the silent type but he was English after all. In her experience, he wasn't keen on silence, awkward or otherwise, and tried to fill it whenever possible. But his mind was elsewhere after Madame Tablier's arrest; she hadn't seen him like this since the mafia had assassinated his favourite hen. He was taking the arrest personally.

'Of course not!' He sounded affronted and briefly took his eyes off the road, something he never did even at a red light. 'Do you?' he added quietly, a small sign of his more usual diffidence.

'Of course not!' she repeated. They carried on in silence as Richard put his foot down even harder, Valérie pretended not to grip the inside door handle and Passepartout, used to fast cars more than most, buried his small head into his dog blanket showing that he had less confidence in

Richard's road-handling ability than he did in that of his mistress.

The road between Richard's adopted home town of Saint-Sauver and La Chapelle-sur-Follet was as French as it could be, and it stretched out in front of them, making it feel like a longer journey than the fifteen minutes it actually took. Though of Roman design and mostly straighter than a snooker cue it was lined with plane trees on either side, just as Napoleon had ordered so as to keep his troops in the shade as they marched. It undulated too, pleasingly, as the powerful classic Renault practically flew over anything that wasn't flat.

Duval Cuistot would have been proud, Richard thought, though in fact he was terrifying himself and was not altogether enjoying being slightly out of control. Something he never was. The French roads though are mostly single carriageway. Overtaking was therefore a constant hazard due to farm traffic especially, and Richard's jaw, which had been set in determination since Lapierre had taken Madame Tablier away – or was it the other way around? – was now clenched in something bordering on self-inflicted terror. He was worried that at the next acceleration past a dawdling tractor and over a blind hump, he may even end up biting his own tongue off. But he had started on this course, and he was going to see it through. In all honesty, he was still in shock that Valérie had let him have the keys in the first place; he hadn't *really* expected to be driving.

He slowed down at a roundabout which indicated that La Chapelle-sur-Follet was the first exit on the right. Richard still had to concentrate on French roundabouts.

It was always tempting to veer left, the English way, and it had taken him a long time and many near misses to get the hang of them. It was only when he did so that he realised that the French didn't understand their own roundabouts anyway, and that they were to all intents and purposes a traffic free-for-all and that if you did venture to indicate, you were taken for the lame gazelle at the back of the pack and ripe for picking off. Once away from the traffic island and down a steeper incline than they had encountered thus far, they emerged from a shorter, tree-lined road into a lush valley. The red-bordered road sign read 'La Chapelle-sur-Follet' and underneath another sign had been added; 'Village Jardin' it read in green italics and they were immediately hit with a wide variety of colours and scents as the sheer majesty of the floral collections in front of them took over their senses.

Valérie was quickly tapping away on her phone as Richard parked in a half-empty car park on the edge of town.

'I am looking up what it means, this village jardin,' Valérie said without lifting her eyes from her phone. 'According to Wikipedia…'

'Village *Jardin Remarquable* status was awarded to La Chapelle-sur-Follet in 2011,' Richard began, not taking his eyes off the amazing sight in front of him. 'It was the first time the honour had been bestowed on an entire *commune* and not just a single garden. In short,' he added, turning to Valérie, 'the whole place is a garden, curated by the inhabitants. Almost literally a commune, in the English sense. A sort of gardening kibbutz, if you like.'

She paused before answering. 'You have been here before then?'

'Twice. It's quite famous locally, and the guests like it.'

'Only twice?'

'Yes,' he replied, as though it pained him. 'Both times with Clare. Once on the way up, once on the way down as it were.' He tried a weak smile. 'Shall we?'

Finally, and with difficulty, he managed to unfurl his fingers from the steering wheel, surprised to find that he hadn't actually left indentations on it. Valérie watched him closely, which made him even more uncomfortable as he stepped out of the car gingerly, his body still tense with stress.

'Do we need a cover?' she asked, clipping on Passepartout's lead. Richard stood, hands in pockets, and said that he didn't think it was necessary. *Nobody will be interested in us*, he thought, knowing from experience.

'I just want to speak to Madame Cuistot,' he said. 'Something isn't right.'

'Well, I think we do need a cover,' was Valérie's considered opinion, and she slipped her arm through Richard's to make them look like any other tourist couple in a tourist haven. Richard, though slightly awkward with the closeness, was frankly grateful for the support, his body still shaking with the adrenalin of the drive. He gave her back her car keys. 'Would you drive back?' he asked, a slight smile returning to his face.

'Of course, darling!' she replied loudly and without subtlety, taking the 'couple' cover to extremes. 'You deserve a rest!'

Richard, despite his obvious tension at the situation with Madame Tablier and various other current points of stress in his life, couldn't help grinning. Valérie, in her capacity as in-demand bounty hunter and possible international assassin, was not used to working as a team. She was a lone wolf in effect, relying solely on her own wits and talent. She had no need of a partner and it actually reduced her effectiveness. Maybe, it struck him for the first time, it was the reason her numerous marriages were so brief?

Following this train of thought Richard was able to relax despite the tactile nature of their 'cover'. Because he knew it was just cover he was under no obligation; his brain had regularly told him it was an obligation to feel under pressure. To feel nervous that he might 'ruin the moment' in some way. This wasn't a moment, this was work.

Exiting the car park arm in arm, they followed the signs and turned left towards the centre of the village. As it was, the signs were redundant as the church spire, the centre of any French town or village, dominated the not very distant skyline. It rose almost incongruously above the small, aged houses that made up the village itself. And if the intention had been to attract the onlookers' eyes away from the mundane and up to God, then it was fighting a losing battle with the village itself.

It was a stunning sight. If Richard had issues with spring it was clearly the *raison d'être* for the inhabitants of La Chapelle-sur-Follet. The work that must go into producing a floral display on this civic scale was beyond both their understanding and they stood, almost breathless, taking in the view along the street.

Every garden was a teeming waterfall of colour, each crafted so carefully that it seemed each separate plant and flower had centre stage. The whole place was like a static carnival, a riotous horticultural Mardi Gras and the only noise was the gentle buzz of busy insects, bees especially, joined by multiple varieties of butterfly. There were slate plaques in each garden, explaining the flower types and sometimes there were gardening epithets too. Inspirational quotes the type of which always made Richard cringe. The 'Bad news is time flies, the good news is you're the pilot' variety of psychological gibberish. Each garden had its own, all in the same handwriting. He tried not to react to 'Gardening adds years to your life and life to your years', though he was surprised that Valérie couldn't hear him tut loudly even if it was in his head. He concentrated instead on one garden that had an Audrey Hepburn quote, 'To plant a garden is to believe in tomorrow.' It cheered him enormously to see Audrey Hepburn's name alongside the glorious displays.

Richard had always been fairly agnostic about such cultivated gardens. Yes, he put in a certain amount of effort at his own place, the bare minimum in truth but to his mind gardens were to be relaxed in. All one really needed was a decent lounger, an effective parasol, some wine and a bucket of ice. Anything else hinted at a greater effort and that dreaded word 'maintenance'. Even so, and even though he had seen this before, the first time he had been to La Chapelle with Clare, it was a breath-taking sight. He felt like Ronald Colman approaching Shangri-La in the 1937 version of *Lost Horizon*; it was a paradise he didn't know existed, or that he needed. It was overpowering, though for his own reasons he was trying to fight against it.

An impressed Valérie stopped to take it all in as well, before handing Passepartout's lead to Richard as she went back to her phone, hoping to find something else beneath the surface of this perfection. 'To plant a garden is to believe in tomorrow,' she said solemnly. 'That garden slate is pictured on the Wikipedia page.' They walked on in silence for a while, through the garlanded streets, the whole place immaculate and unreal, like an exhibit, which in effect it was.

They passed a *brocante* which had various rusting, antique garden implements hanging on the wall outside and beneath them a wrought-iron bench bookended by enormous terracotta pots with yellow climbing roses working their way upwards and through the hanging decorations. There was a painted wooden sign on the door, 'Christophe de la Cour – Antiquities/Brocanteur'. It was closed, and a further sign said it was only open at weekends, bank holidays or 'By Appointment' with a mobile phone number listed for those presumably in urgent need of a rusty hoe or the ubiquitous *Pastis* water jugs.

The church was on the right, but they decided to carry on down the road as if dragged by the scent and the never-ending display.

Stopping by a stream that went under the main road and which had on its bank an immaculate wooden *lavoir*, Valérie gave further scrutiny to the Wikipedia entry. Richard took in the idea of the *lavoir*. Clothes washing as a centre of the town, a social event. Any town or village with a flowing river or stream would have a *lavoir*, an old way of washing your clothes, but this looked too new, too immaculate, like an artefact in a museum that couldn't get hold of the original.

'What does it say about the *lavoir?*' he asked, failing to hide the note of scepticism in his voice.

She looked up as if she'd forgotten he was there. 'Oh, nothing,' she said, refocussing. 'But that slate we saw, the quote from this Audrey Hepburn that's the same one that is on Wikipedia. That's interesting. Maybe they never change the, er…' She was briefly lost for words.

'Exhibits?' Richard proffered.

'I was going to say display.' She fixed her eyes on him and he looked away, down at the trickling stream. 'You are not yourself, Richard. Do you suffer from hay fever, is that it?'

'No,' he replied with a forced smile. 'I'm just not sure I like this place, that's all.'

'You have happy memories of coming here with Clare, I think.'

Well, he thought, *memories anyway*. They walked on until they came to a half-empty restaurant *terrasse*, covered in a canopy of flowering lilac-coloured wisteria. Above the entrance was a sign that said 'L'Auberge Cuistot', only the sign was split down the middle, presumably where Duval Cuistot's head had hit it and it sagged badly as a result, so that Auberge had become separated from the word Cuistot. It was a brazen reminder of why they were there.

A silver-haired woman was clearing one of the wooden tables as they approached. Was this Madame Cuistot, Madame Tablier's sister? It didn't take long to find out.

'If you're looking to eat,' she snapped, without looking up, 'you're too late. We stopped serving ten minutes ago.'

Chapter Five

Richard and Valérie couldn't take their eyes off the woman now standing in front of them, and standing, it must be said, like a nightclub bouncer who's heard it all before. It wasn't her attitude as such that was, though Richard kept it to himself, rather typical of French customer service. As in there were too many customers demanding service and that they got in the way. No, it was that Madame Cuistot was the absolute spitting image of her sister, except that she wore make-up and her hair was obviously cut by a professional. Her shape – the stocky, wide-shouldered feet-apart stance – was pure Tablier, as if chiselled from granite. And though she dressed more elegantly there was something different about her and he couldn't put his finger on it.

Suddenly the woman broke into a wide grin and her face softened; it was then he noticed the laughter lines around her large green eyes and around her mouth. That'll be the difference, he thought, she enjoyed life. It was perhaps an unfair comparison and he had to remind himself that he was here to help his treasured Madame Tablier, but it was like she was Dorian Gray's painting while the woman in front of him had been having a whale of a time.

'But I suppose we can squeeze in the eminent Dr Ainsworth.' She smiled. 'And you must be Madame d'Orçay?' She held out her hand. 'I am Madame Cuistot.'

'How did you know who we were?' Valérie wasn't keen on being recognised.

'Oh, ducks, I've heard all about you two!' she giggled infectiously. 'And not all of it good!' Richard saw the frown cross Valérie's face at that. 'Come in, grab that table in the corner and I'll join you in a few minutes.'

She bustled off, shouting instructions to her staff indoors as she did so, leaving Richard and Valérie to take their seats. 'How did she know who we were?' Valérie asked, still upset by the idea of it.

'Does it matter?' Richard asked, probably naively to Valérie's mind, but he couldn't recall ever being recognised anywhere before, and he rather liked it. They sat down and Valérie rummaged in her handbag before producing what looked like an inflatable travel pillow.

'Can you blow this up please?' she handed him the package.

'Have you got a sore neck?' he asked, wondering if she'd mentioned it and he had forgotten.

'No,' she answered, a look of confusion on her face.

'Oh.' He was as confused as she was now. 'Has Passepartout got a sore neck then?' Which confused her even more.

He began to blow into the air nozzle and before long realised that what had looked like a small inflatable travel pillow was actually a cunningly folded dog bed. It wasn't an easy job either, and though he didn't want to look like he was incapable, he couldn't help notice the other diners giving him odd looks as it appeared like he was inflating a small dinghy. Red-faced and trying hard not to sweat, he placed the finished bed under the table and the mollycoddled Chihuahua hopped daintily in and lay down.

Madame Cuistot returned shortly with an ice bucket, a chilled bottle of rosé, three glasses and, more urgently for Richard, a jug of iced water which he practically threw down like a marathon runner.

'I have to say,' she began as she sat down. 'I'm really touched that you would come all this way just to pay your respects to my dear husband.' She poured out three glasses of wine and Richard was about to ask the obvious question of 'Haven't you heard about your sister?' when just in time he saw the look on Valérie's face and also swiftly moved both of his legs under the table therefore narrowly avoiding one of her 'stop talking' kicks to the shin.

While acknowledging that her methods could be brutal, he would have admitted that she was right in this case. He knew, at least he thought he knew, certainly he hoped, that Madame Tablier was not guilty of the murder of her brother-in-law. The more information that could be gathered then, before word got around, could be vital in proving that.

Valérie gave him a slight nod indicating that they were now on the same wavelength. 'How did you know who we were?' she asked through a forced smile as though it really didn't matter.

Let it go, woman! Richard thought. *There are more important things to find out, surely?* And he threw Valérie a look of frustration.

'Oh, she's always talked about you, Dr Ainsworth. She won't say it, but I think she really admires you.'

'Really?' He tried to brush it off as if it meant nothing. 'And call me Richard, please. What does she say exactly?' he asked, leaning in convivially and avoiding Valérie's arch expression.

'Oh well, you know…' He became aware that Madame Cuistot was rowing back from her original enthusiasm on the subject. She even looked nervously at Valérie.

'No.' Richard's tone had changed slightly.

'Well, that despite being totally unsuited to the life, out of your depth, lonely, and a borderline alcoholic whose only real friends are chickens – *who you give names to* – she likes taking care of you.'

Richard sat back realising that something else that ran in the family, besides rugby player shoulders, was a complete lack of diplomacy and tact. The sisters said things exactly as they saw it. Some found that refreshing, Richard wasn't at all sure. He smiled though and caught Valérie's surprised expression, not that she was an expert in sensitivity and *politesse* either, but his smile was genuine. He had always known that Madame Tablier had appointed herself as his watchdog and as for the list of his faults and summation of his life as it currently stood, he couldn't really argue with any of it. In fact, it felt like the kind of snappy, affectionate put-down that Katharine Hepburn would say to Spencer Tracy and that made him feel quite good about himself.

'And she has talked about me as well?' Valérie asked, with no hint of caution in her voice.

'Yes, madame.'

'Call me Valérie,' she replied, leaving the warmth out until she'd had the results of her enquiry. It was also noticeable that Madame Cuistot hadn't returned either invitation, something else that ran in the family.

Smiling, she said, 'My sister has come to accept you, madame, and that your motives are genuine.' Madame Cuistot made it sound like her sister was a prospective mother-in-law interrogating her son's new girlfriend. There was a slightly awkward silence following this while both Richard and Valérie tried to fathom out just what any of it all meant.

'Au revoir, Madame Cuistot.' A tall young man, possibly about twenty years old with a mop of curly hair bent down to kiss her cheeks as he came out of the restaurant. 'Just what I needed as always,' he said with a rather sad smile.

'Ah, Marcel, I'm so pleased. Do give my love to your mother.' Madame Cuistot held on to the young man's hand as if imploring him.

'I will,' he replied seriously, and then addressed Richard and Valérie, 'Au revoir, madame, monsieur.'

Madame Cuistot stared affectionately after him as he left, and shook her head. 'So sad,' she said, toying with her glass. 'Such a tragedy in that family.'

This was enough bait for Valérie. 'Something has happened, madame?'

The older woman was still distracted by the disappearing young man, but answered anyway. 'Yes, I mean it was a while back now, Christmas time, but it's all so sad.' She turned back to the table and leant forward, looking about her quickly for potential eavesdroppers, the classic gossiper's pose. 'That lovely young gentleman is Marcel Bouchard and he shouldn't really be here!' The end to her statement was delivered with such dramatic emphasis that Richard and Valérie leant in more closely too, and also couldn't help looking about them for snoopers.

Madame Cuistot though was clearly a master of the tittle-tattle and paused for full effect.

'Well?' Typically Valérie was having none of it.

'He should be back in America,' she said, unperturbed at being hurried. 'That's where he should be.'

It suddenly all sounded quite mundane and Valérie sat back, huffing in frustration.

'What do you mean he shouldn't be here?' Richard asked, hoping there was more to this scuttlebutt than just a missed flight connection.

Madame Cuistot continued to shake her head, apparently oblivious to the question, and then suddenly clapped her hands as if to wake herself up. 'He should be back at university,' she said. 'Somewhere in America, I'm not sure where.'

'Yes, you said that.' Richard could tell that Valérie was trying to be patient. 'But why is he not?'

Madame Cuistot turned to Valérie as if she were surprised that she was there. 'His mum and dad,' she said, like whatever it was was common knowledge. 'They gave everything to this place, years of service, building it from scratch practically.' Her eyes were beginning to water. 'Then they took a holiday, their first for years, a cruise to America it was. Awful.' She carried on just shaking her head, leaving them in suspense.

Richard and Valérie looked at each other, their exasperation close to boiling point.

'What was awful?' Richard decided it was best if he took the lead before Valérie caused a scene.

'Food poisoning,' the old woman said. 'Awful. Florian died…'

'Florian is the father?'

'Yes. Sorry, yes. Florian Bouchard, the heartbeat, the soul of La Chapelle. He died out there, in America and Liliane, Marcel's mother, she survived but had a stroke. She's bedridden now and poor Marcel gave up his studies to look after her. Awful. I mean we had a small bout of food poisoning here a couple of years ago, but nobody died. Really awful.'

There was no denying that it was indeed awful, Richard could see that, but it wasn't relevant to why they were there.

'Awful,' he said quietly and then left what he felt was a respectful pause. 'Madame Cuistot, about your husband…' Valérie leant in at the change in conversation.

'Ha!' Madame Cuistot immediately cheered up. 'Silly old sod! I told him to check everything on the mower, but no, he always knew best.' Her eyes were moistening again and she looked up at the broken 'L'Auberge Cuistot' sign. 'A silly way to go, I know, but it's what he would have wanted.'

'So it was an accident then?' Valérie wanted the confirmation.

'Oh yes!' She took a sip of wine. 'Of course it was.'

Again Valérie and Richard shared a look and privately came to a decision.

'It's just that your sister has been arrested for his murder.' Richard might not have put it quite so bluntly, but there was no denying that it got the point across. In mid-sip Madame Cuistot started coughing violently in response.

'What are you talking about?' she said eventually, her face bright red.

'Madame Tablier was arrested this morning for the murder of your husband,' Richard said gently. 'The police say they have found new evidence.'

'What evidence?' Madame Cuistot scoffed.

'They found Madame Tablier's wedding ring in the mower shed.' It sounded even more damning to Richard when he said it out loud.

'But she didn't wear a wedding ring!' He looked at Valérie in triumph at the confirmation of what he'd said earlier. Then his jaw nearly hit the table as Madame Cuistot added. 'She wasn't married.'

'But Monsieur Tablier…?' he stuttered.

Madame Cuistot leant in closely and spoke quietly. 'There was no Monsieur Tablier,' she said. 'There was a Monsieur Mordant, but they weren't married. They lived in sin. Well, there was no sin actually, they just lived. She cleaned for him and then he got ill and she moved in to look after him.'

'But she's often mentioned the late Monsieur Tablier, her husband. It doesn't make sense.'

Madame Cuistot shrugged. 'I am telling you, they were not married. He'd been married before and his wife had run off, no trace of her. So he couldn't marry again if he couldn't find her.' Richard was trying to take all this in. 'She called herself Mordant when he was alive, but went straight back to her own name when he died. Knowing my sister – and we didn't speak for years – she wouldn't have wanted to look sinful, so she pretended. He left her the house too.'

'But the police said they found a ring and it was engraved with "*Tablier Toujours*".' Valérie had certainly recovered her enthusiasm.

'Oh that!' Madame Cuistot laughed. 'Tablier is our family name. My husband gave her that ring. They were engaged, didn't you know?'

Chapter Six

Richard, and to a lesser extent Valérie, left Madame Cuistot and her brasserie dazed. He felt almost drunk the shock was so great. 'You think you know someone,' he repeated on a loop, sitting heavily on the low stone wall they had passed earlier. He had had to leave it to Valérie's clearer mind to ask any follow-up questions like How, Why, Where and Bloody Hell, really?

They had met at the height of Duval Cuistot's fame, Madame Cuistot had explained, a young Madame Tablier had been a talented motorbike mechanic who also had ambitions to be a stunt rider herself. To stop this from happening Cuistot had asked her to marry him, that way he could better control her ambition and douse the flames. There was room for only one stunt bike superstar in France and it certainly wasn't going to be a woman.

The horrible thought that came into Richard's mind at that point could be encapsulated in one word: Motive.

'But didn't your sister object to *your* marriage to Monsieur Cuistot?' Valérie asked.

'Oh yes! Like I said, we didn't speak for years, then when Duval became ill early last year… I needed her help and I had no one else to turn to.'

'You think you know someone.' Richard shook his head again. There was a lot he still didn't know and should have asked, but he needed to recover from the shock first, get his thoughts in order. Valérie put her hand on his shoulder, though unusually he didn't seem to notice.

'I must admit,' she said gently, 'it all seems very out of character for Madame Tablier, but what do you know of her really? Do you even know her first name?'

He looked up at her and shook his head almost guiltily. 'No,' he mumbled, embarrassed. He had always paid her cash so there was no official documentation of employment; it was just how the local economy worked. It had initially gone against Richard's naturally cautious nature to weigh on the 'black economy', but that's just how things were done here; he wasn't even sure where she lived. He was sure of where she was now though, in a police cell in Saint-Sauver and she hadn't just gone there willingly, she'd practically asked to be taken. Richard would be the first to admit that he had a pretty rotten history of character assessment; he always related new acquaintances to two-dimensional classic film characters forgetting there was another deeper, much more complicated third dimension that he rarely sought out.

That aside, he simply wasn't having it. Madame Tablier was innocent of the murder and he was determined to prove it. Standing up with a sudden burst of fortitude, he looked Valérie straight in the eye and said, 'She didn't do it. Madame Tablier did not do it.' He gave the statement as much black and white celluloid heroism as he could summon up, and felt better for it.

'OK.' Valérie was less convinced. 'Madame Tablier did not kill her former fiancé and brother-in-law for destroying

44

her career and her personal life in an act of long-held, pent-up revenge?'

Richard sat down again. 'I know you're playing Devil's advocate,' he said. 'And I understand the need for cold-eyed objectivity but…'

'And there is evidence, the ring, that she had been in the shed.'

'Yes, I know that, but…'

'And that she is an expert mechanic who could easily have tampered with this ride-on mower?'

'Look, whose side are you on?' Richard asked after a lengthy pause.

'I am on your side, Richard, but we must know what we are up against. And we are up against evidence, motive and opportunity.' He looked crushed. 'But,' she added, 'if you believe that she is innocent, then I do too. After all, you know Madame Tablier much better than I do.'

'That's the thing,' he spoke softly. 'I'm not actually sure that I do now.' He stood up again, and they began to walk purposefully back to the car. 'Where do we start?' he asked.

'I think we should start with Madame Tablier herself.' Valérie was immediately business-like. 'And Henri of course. Where did he get this tip-off? Who from?'

Richard stopped next to the same garden they had looked at before. 'Audrey Hepburn,' he said quietly, and read the quote again on the slate. Just saying the name put something approaching a smile back on his face.

'Is it really a quote from her?' Valérie asked with some validity. The internet had managed to ascribe the most ridiculous quotes to the most ridiculous people, and in truth it didn't really matter to him. 'To plant a garden is to believe in tomorrow,' sounded like something the gentle queen of the cinema would have said, and that was good enough for him.

'You know, all the beauty in this place, the colours, the drama of the gardens yet for me just seeing those two words, Audrey Hepburn, cheers me up no end. I'm not surprised this is the one that's used on Wikipedia. You know, to me, Audrey Hepburn was like a flower, delicate, radiant and…'

'Richard!' Valerie hadn't raised her voice to silence his reverie, but to get his attention. She gave him her phone to read and he put his glasses on.

'What am I looking for?' he asked.

'The quote on the website has changed. It's not Audrey Hepburn anymore!' She took the phone back. 'I'll read it to you. "Even the prettiest flower can be poisonous!" You know what that means?'

'Not entirely…'

'Well, obviously it is a warning!' Her eyes were wide, the excitement suddenly lighting up her face, like switching from an ordinary TV channel to High Definition.

'Are you sure?' It wasn't that Richard didn't agree, but that if he were honest he found her zeal quite discomforting. Attractive, but discomforting.

'Of course it is!' She was in no mood for doubt. 'Whoever has done this is warning that something is wrong here, in this place. What did Henri say? That this place was *strange*. I think he meant unnatural, he is not always articulate. Well someone thinks it is more than that! Someone thinks it is poisonous!'

Richard turned back to the floral drama in front of him. 'Are you sure it's the same slate board?' He still wasn't entirely convinced.

'Well the flowers look the same to me. It is the same arrangement. The same corner of the house here, look.' He put his glasses back on again. 'I wish I knew about flowers,' she said with frustration. 'The picture is older, the flowers not so grown… but I am sure it is the same.'

They stood next to each other taking in the vibrant garden in front of them, breathing it in, looking for a sign of poison even, but they were at a loss to know what any of the flowers were called. There was, as there was throughout the village, the same colour scheme. Yellows, whites, pinks, purples and reds. If there was anything, anywhere varying from these colours, orange perhaps, Richard hadn't seen it and wouldn't be surprised if there was a Flower Police checking for such outrages. But he couldn't name a single species and it annoyed him; a flower on its own he might guess at, but a riotous vista like this was too much for his scant knowledge. To him it would be like watching the Albert Finney version of *Murder on the Orient Express* and not being able to name any of the all-star cast.

There was one different colour here though, something finally differing from what seemed to be the official palette. It was a very dramatic single blue and black rose. The petals were a deep liquorice black but the edges were a sultry satin blue and, even surrounded by the flamboyant display framing it, it was sheer drama. A glamorous star stepping out of the chorus. 'I'm surprised that was allowed,' Richard said to Valérie pointing at the rose. 'Someone doesn't want to play by the rules obviously.' Valérie nodded slowly in agreement, her eyes squinting in concentration as she wondered what it all meant.

'You are absolutely correct in what you say, monsieur,' a cool, husky female voice came from behind and they both swung round, startled. 'I am certainly no wallflower.' And before they could say anything, she added without any genuine enthusiasm, 'Hello, Valérie. It has been forever since I saw you last.'

At exactly the same time Richard and Valérie both reacted out loud with 'Oriane Moulin!' and then looked at each other. Valérie was surprised that Richard knew who she was and Richard was surprised that Oriane Moulin knew who Valérie was.

'Aren't you going to introduce me to your companion, Valérie?' She was so composed, so in control. Of course she'd had the element of surprise but even so, there was no expression on her face. These days you could possibly put that down to Botox, but then the famous warm smile softened her features showing wrinkles that were a map of a lifetime's well-lived experience. And if the press were to be believed, she'd certainly had that.

A folk hero and a musician, Oriane Moulin had had a brief marriage to the controversial politician, Bernard Janvier, who came to resent that he was never as liked as she was, and there were rumours of domestic violence. She performed at a televised charity concert sporting a black eye and a cut lip and it caused a sensation, though it did little serious damage to her husband's career. What did harm her husband's career was that, not long after, he was hospitalised having been beaten up. When he publicly pointed out that his wife was responsible, he assumed it would claw back a little of the popularity he had lost. He was wrong and his now estranged ex-wife's new album was a million bestseller. The Frenchest thing about all this for Richard though was that all the gossip magazines – Richard had cast his eye over them at the doctor's surgery only the week before – were full of rumours about a reconciliation and even a political comeback.

Now here she was, one of the most famous faces in France smiling her much-photographed smile and holding out her hand for Richard. 'I'm Oriane Moulin,' she said stepping closer, her voice smoky and deep. With her other hand, she cleared some of her long, dark hair from her face. '*Enchantée.*'

'This is my friend Richard Ainsworth,' Valérie said with a theatrical flourish, stepping between the nascent handshake as she did so. 'We're just visiting.'

It was an odd thing to say and Richard knew it. It was obvious Oriane knew it too as she raised her eyebrows questioningly.

'Valérie,' she said confidently. 'It may have been a long time since we saw each other last, but I still know you well. I suspect a recent tragedy has brought you here, am I right?'

Valérie had recovered her own composure and said simply, 'Richard loves gardening and wanted to see the village in full bloom. Didn't you, Richard?'

Richard was somewhat taken aback by this and wished that Valérie had produced a cover story that he might possibly back up with some sort of knowledge. 'Oh, er, yes. I love flowers.' He turned back to the display behind him. 'That, er, that one in particular. The... white one. What's it called again?' He affected a memory lapse.

A smirking Oriane stepped forward. 'That is *Phlox paniculata*, or summer phlox.' She gently held the flower of a purple plant next to it. 'This is *Dicentra spectabilis*, a bleeding heart. There are also *Salvia dorisiana, Veronica officinalis, Echinacea purpurea…*'

'Ah yes, echinacea. Good for the immune system.' He remembered that Clare took an effervescent echinacea tablet every morning and hoped it was the same thing.

'And the rose…' Oriane continued.

'A "Midnight Blue" from the genus *Rosa*,' Valérie sounded deliberately bored. 'It's very you, Oriane, it likes exposure and plenty of drainage.'

Richard didn't know for sure where Valérie had suddenly acquired this horticultural knowledge, her phone had presumably been working overtime, but he did have the distinct impression that he was now standing between two oncoming trucks who had no intention of swerving out of the way. They may know each other, he realised, but they were not close.

'Valérie! I had no idea you knew about plants! Look, you and Richard must come in.'

'We wouldn't want to inconvenience you,' Valérie replied strongly.

'It's no inconvenience at all. I'm having a little soirée this evening for the village committee, and as you and Richard love gardens so much I'm sure you would love to meet the people behind them.' She smiled at Valérie directly. 'I'm hoping I can help put our recent tragedy behind us.'

She winked at Richard, put her arm through his and led them both up the garden path.

Chapter Seven

If the roadside front of Oriane's property could be described as chocolate-boxy or even twee, apart from the dark cloud of the 'Midnight Blue' rose, then beyond the gate it was very different. From the road all you saw was a winding driveway and what looked like the side of a small cottage. But that small cottage was connected via a very modern, very brand-new conservatory, complete with solar panels, to an old *longère*, a long farmhouse that in previous centuries would have housed not just the family but their most prized livestock as well.

Oriane didn't look like she had livestock, but she was greeted with sullen indifference by a bizarre-looking creature that Richard could only assume was a miniature dog. By the look on Passepartout's face it definitely was a dog, and he'd suddenly adopted a rather leering attitude, a bit like Pepé Le Pew, the cartoon skunk. Richard couldn't see the attraction himself. The beast was slightly taller than Valerie's Chihuahua but her body was almost totally hairless, showing pewter-coloured skin. On her head was a crest of white hair, like a reverse quiff; each paw had the same hair and looked like she was wearing fur ski boots. The tail was short and pointed with a white-haired coiffured ball on the end of it looking like a cheerleader's pompom.

'Zsa Zsa! My darling!' Oriane cooed. And though Richard appreciated the old Hollywood reference to a glamorous actress, he couldn't help thinking that this Zsa Zsa looked more like a dog stripper.

Oriane's toned changed as the two dogs sniffed each other intimately. 'Please stop, Zsa Zsa, you don't know where it's been.'

Valérie took umbrage at the suggestion immediately and pulled Passepartout away, indicating a little too loudly that if dogs were like their owners then Zsa Zsa had probably been about a bit.

'So, how do you two know each other then?' Richard decided to step in before this became a cat fight over dogs. Both women took a moment to calm down and eventually let their two dogs run off together into the garden, yapping away as they did so. 'We were colleagues in the DGSE,' Valérie said, nodding discreetly to Oriane indicating that it was OK to talk freely in front Richard.

'The Direction générale de la Sécurité extérieure,' Oriane explained to Richard, who was already aware thanks to previous explanations from Valérie.

'Yes, I know,' he said, tapping his nose. 'Hush hush stuff, like the *Rainbow Warrior* thing.' The combined look on the faces of the two women could have sunk a ship on its own and it was Valérie who spoke first.

'I did not know you liked your flowers, Oriane, I wouldn't have thought you had the patience,' she said while still managing to give Richard a scowl.

Oriane matched the scowl, even raising the frostiness a touch. 'That was a long time ago, Valérie.' Then she softened. 'I changed after I left the service. The music helped but the gardening more so. I found peace. That's why I'm here in La Chapelle now. A TV production company are starting a new weekly gardening programme and I am the host, working from this garden mainly.'

'Like *Gardener's World* in the UK,' Richard said, hoping to redeem himself.

'Yes, I have watched a few of those.' Oriane smiled. 'So English.'

She didn't add to that and Richard decided not to pursue it.

They wandered through into a magnificent walled garden that covered about an acre, and which again you would never know existed from the road. It was made up of a patchwork of smaller gardening units: there was the obligatory wildflower area, a smart kitchen garden and other areas of exotic abundance. The upkeep and effort needed to maintain a garden like this almost brought Richard out in a cold sweat, and was surely too much work for one person? He could see Valérie was impressed, too.

'And they bought this place for you?' she asked.

'No,' she replied, an edge to her voice. 'This place is mine.' She softened a little. 'Though they have helped with the garden. The producer is a good friend. And what about you two?' she asked, not changing the subject as such but hitting the ball back into Valérie's court.

'Oh, we're just good friends too,' Valérie said quickly, leaving Richard with the impression that the term 'good friends' appeared to carry an awful lot of baggage between these two.

He decided to change the conversation again. 'The village must be very excited that a television series will be filmed here, especially a gardening show.'

Oriane let out a derisive snort, exactly the kind that he thought only Valérie could produce. Perhaps they teach derisive snorts in the French secret service. 'You might think so, but no. Actually it is quite the opposite,' she said, arching a well-groomed eyebrow to an almost dangerous angle. 'They hate the idea.'

'But why?' Valérie's tone partly suggested that she agreed with the villagers, and wasn't a huge fan of cameras herself, but there was also an undertone that Richard recognised: excitement. She had a nose for these things and Richard could see that she was currently putting two and two together and making her usual twenty-two. There had been a tragic accident, OK, maybe murder, and now there was even more potential conflict, it was like catnip to her.

'Because they want to protect their own little kingdom, that is why. The village committee run everything around here. They dictate what people can put in their gardens, right down to the colour schemes. They would tell you what to wear if they could.'

'They mustn't have liked your black rose then?' Richard saw in Oriane the exact same needs as Valérie: complete independence, control and, though they'd never admit it, the need for mischief. The rose was her protest and her eyes sparkled at that knowledge.

'They do not,' she smirked. 'And I have had complaints, official complaints written on La Chapelle-sur-Follet headed paper, but they know they can't do anything to me,' she added mysteriously.

'Not just official complaints I see, Oriane.' Valérie's tone was now serious and she showed Oriane her phone and the changed slate board message on Wikipedia.

'Even the prettiest flower can be poisonous,' she read aloud, then burst out laughing. 'You know what I think? I think I came to La Chapelle just in time, this place needs shaking up!'

'But who posts this?' Valérie asked irritably. It was a show of exasperation, Richard knew, that came from having to deal with someone just as vexing as herself.

'Anyone can,' was the reply. 'It's on Wikipedia. It could literally be anyone.'

'But someone in the village?' Richard confirmed and then both women turned to him and said 'obviously' in unison. 'Is this the first time it has happened?' he asked, ignoring them.

'Oh, I stopped looking at that silly website.'

'So it isn't then?' Richard decided that he was going to have to stand his ground in a three-way conversation involving these two. They clearly weren't keen on showing their hand to the other, but as far as he could see neither of them had much of a hand anyway and they weren't going to get one without some prompting from him.

'No. It isn't,' she said. 'But I am an artist, a public figure and I have a...' she shrugged almost childishly, '...a past. I learnt long ago to ignore what was being thrown at me because I cannot control it.'

Richard knew of her past, everyone did. Oriane Moulin had briefly been one of the most notorious women in France, and even now, a few years down the line, was a byword for shock and non-conformity, though a very French kind of non-conformity. It came well-dressed and was largely accepted because most of society already, ironically, saw themselves as non-conformists. But wherever she went controversy followed, and if it didn't she appeared to do her best to create it. As she said, she was a powerful, independent woman, she was in control, which meant inevitably that she was divisive too and, as far as Richard could tell from his outsider status, the division fell on gender terms; women loathed her, men loved her. Beauty and power can do that, though he would always keep such observations to himself. What was the joke when she married the minister? 'If that's his wife, imagine what his mistress looks like'? It was all very French of course, but it made you enemies.

'Have you had any specific threats made to you?'

'Not specifically, no. Not yet.' She shrugged again, then winked. 'But, Valérie, like you, I can take care of myself. They are just words, and I have had worse.'

The two women exchanged prolonged eye contact. It was obvious to Richard, not that they were hiding it in any way, that they had been through a lot together, and though they were clearly not friends, they had been comrades. Maybe former colleagues of the DGSE were like musketeers and it was all for one, one for all but if Oriane was in trouble, not that she was admitting to such a thing, Valérie felt a duty to get involved because that was their code. He was sure that was how Valérie would justify it anyhow. In Richard's experience she'd never felt the need to justify getting involved in anything before, but she did love a cause.

'You have made a lot of enemies Oriane, you always did.' Valérie said enigmatically. 'But we swore allegiance.' The severity, the gravity of the look on her face might have been that of a soldier on a doomed mission, but it also had a twinkle in the eye and it was matched by a similar glint from Oriane Moulin. It would have been entirely reasonable for Richard at this point to feel left out, a by-stander to a much bigger situation that was beyond his control. To an extent he did feel exactly that, but he also knew though that these women were kindred spirits and they both craved danger and excitement; any excuse beyond that was just gravy.

Oriane looked at her watch and her expression changed. 'Oh my God! My guests will start arriving in twenty minutes and I have no food prepared!'

'Why have you invited them if you think they're threatening you?' Valérie asked, not unreasonably.

'Keep your friends close and your enemies closer.' Richard nodded seriously as he trotted out one of his favourite film quotes.

Oriane giggled and put a hand warmly on his forearm, a gesture that didn't go unnoticed. 'Richard,' she said, the hint of a plea in her smoky voice. 'You know nothing about flowers, do you know anything about food? Can you help a damsel in distress?' She looked up into his eyes, dangerously so in Richard's opinion.

'Richard is quite an expert, aren't you, Richard?' Valérie had a way of making a compliment sound like a criticism and anyway, just because he dished out a few croissants of a morning it didn't qualify him as a domestic goddess. 'Aren't you, Richard?' she repeated icily, and he recognised a cue to leave when he heard one.

'Got any pineapple chunks and cocktail sticks? I have a great hedgehog recipe.' His question was obviously tongue in cheek but delivered to people whose tongues didn't fit in their cheeks and equally hadn't been to a children's party in England in the late seventies. As such the look on the faces of his two companions suggested they were already regretting the proposed division of labour. 'Never mind,' he sighed. 'Just point me in the direction of the kitchen.'

Chapter Eight

The last thing Richard heard as he ventured inside was a concerned Oriane asking Valérie if he was actually up to the task of feeding her guests. 'Oh yes,' was Valérie's confident reply. 'Even though he's English.'

Richard needed no further motivation than that. 'I'll show you two,' he grumbled to himself. 'I may not be highly trained in the dark arts of espionage and covert operations, but I know my way around a *canapé!*' Then he remembered that the French word *canapé* actually means sofa and that they prefer the term *amuse-bouche* to describe drink-accompanying nibbles. It occurred to him that as usual he was losing concentration and the reputation of himself, and perhaps even the country of his birth, depended on this.

He wasn't sure what he had expected walking into Oriane's kitchen but some previous sign of activity would have been the bare minimum. Instead it looked like a show home. A very high-end gleaming with all the latest equipment and gadgets show home, but a show home nonetheless. What on earth did the woman live on? La Chapelle-sur-Follet may only be a few hours from Paris but in effect it was a world away: no late-night *superettes*, no food delivery and no twenty-four-hour takeaways. The woman must be ravenous.

He opened a cupboard and found a neatly arranged shelf of dry goods: cereals, rice and quinoa, expensive pasta, and so on. But nothing he could easily rustle up any tasty tidbits with. He looked in the fridge, which was slightly more promising but hardly an Aladdin's cave for the finger-food gourmet either. There were some cherry tomatoes, a jar of apricot jam, some smoked salmon, some gem lettuce, a packet of cheap pâté and the kind of low-range spreadable cheese that by rights should have a French person's citizenship revoked if they were found in possession of it. Next to the fridge and hidden behind a top-of-the-range metallic food processor were a packet of Pringles, a box of eggs and a box of unchilled white wine, the kind normally reserved for cooking but which wasn't even open.

Things did not look promising.

When he and Clare had first arrived in the Follet Valley and bought their high-end bed and breakfast, they had been very careful to quickly ingratiate themselves in the local community. They held, at Clare's behest, her PR brain kicking in early, a series of 'soirées'. Highly successful evenings that became a weekly event and, in Richard's words, 'a proper old booze-up'. And as these events went on, Richard and Clare's selection of *hors d'oeuvres* became more and more complicated and impressive; they became a centrepiece and the locals loved them for it. French people are always being made to think, sometimes erroneously, that all English people know nothing about food. While the English, equally erroneously, are taught the opposite about French people.

The result being that Richard considered himself a dab hand at the French art of *apéritif* but even he was struggling with these paltry ingredients. He went back outside to find

Oriane; he had the makings of an idea but would need more than twenty minutes. Putting the oven on to warm up, he walked outside and found the two women arranging glasses and champagne bottles on an outside table.

'Do you have a herb garden?' he asked without preamble. That way he could exude a confidence he wasn't totally feeling.

'Yes, of course.' Oriane was busy wiping glasses. 'To the left over there.' She pointed down the garden to where Passepartout and Zsa Zsa were sleeping next to each other in the sun.

'And any edible flowers?' His tone was still that of a military officer out of his depth but pulling rank. 'I'm looking for nasturtium, pansies, dahlias, that kind of thing.'

'Naturally,' was her easy reply, a playful smile on her lips. 'There is a bed next to the herb garden.'

Richard strode off, catching Valérie's eye as he did so. She wasn't used to seeing him so demonstrative and she looked concerned rather than impressed.

Returning to the kitchen with his haul of herbs and delicate flowers he was hit by the smell. It was a 'brand-new oven' smell; the thing had clearly never been used and the kitchen now smelt like an overheating car engine. It was not a good time for Valérie to put her head around the door. 'What *is* that smell?' she asked, her face screwed up like she'd chewed on a lemon.

'A new recipe I'm trying out!' Richard snapped. 'How long have we got before the guests arrive?'

'About ten minutes I think,' was the muffled reply as Valérie had covered her face.

'Well, I won't be ready by then. Keep them plied with drink and I'll serve when they've already had a glass. They won't be on time anyway,' he added. 'They're French.' He was maintaining with some vigour his 'man in control' diffidence, but when Valérie left she had a look on her face that suggested one glass might not be enough to stomach what Richard was about to serve. He was feeling much the same himself and decided to open the box of wine to steady himself. It was vile-tasting, room temperature and just what he needed. He had a second glass.

Some semblance of fortitude restored, Richard got on with his preparation. He beat the eggs, found a rectangular roasting dish, and went about taking the leaves off the gem lettuce. He poured the eggs in the tin and arranged the herbs and flowers on top and placed the tray in the oven. He softened the spreadable cheese even more with a little wine, throwing in a few herbs and using the gem lettuce as 'cups' laid the salmon with the cheese mixture on top. Outside of the kitchen he could hear a number of voices as guests arrived, and on time which was unusual and which to his mind signalled that they didn't like the hostess. Nobody who likes their host arrives on time.

Next he laid out the Pringles, put a square of pâté on each, with a blob of apricot jam and half a cherry tomato. Pleased with his efforts, he waited for his centrepiece to cook. It was unlike Richard to get carried away with himself but emboldened by really quite awful wine he looked again at the dry goods in the cupboard. In his mind was a mix of tomato, quinoa and rice thimbles and he picked out the quinoa packet. It was empty. He got the rice packet instead and that was empty too. In fact, on further inspection all the packets in the cupboard were empty. It was a ghost kitchen, like one of those IKEA set-ups, where everything is a fake or, and this was more pleasing, a film set. *But why? Why make it look like she's living here, when she isn't?*

Valérie appeared at the door again, and fortunately the initial smell had dissipated. 'The guests are here, Richard, a very odd collection too.'

'Look at this,' he said, and opened the cupboard doors.

'Yes?' she looked confused. 'You must know what quinoa is?'

He tutted. 'Of course I know what quinoa is. I also know what an empty box is. And new equipment, and a half-empty fridge and really quite appalling wine.' Valérie still didn't see his point and she shrugged her shoulders. 'It's like she doesn't live here, that it's all a front. I mean, it's possible it's just meant as a TV set, but then why equip it all?' There was a strange look in her eye. 'You don't find that odd?' he asked in exasperation.

She put down her glass and looked at him. 'You are very clever, Richard. That you notice that is very clever. But you see it from the wrong way around. This set-up, if you like, is not someone who doesn't live here now, it is someone who does not want to leave a trace that she ever did. It is habit, I think.'

He nodded slowly. 'You mean training?'

'More than that, instinct. We were good at what we did because we were well chosen. Training only perfected our instincts.' He looked about the kitchen and he saw it more clearly now. 'We were chosen because we were solitary, nomads. And so, we rarely leave a trail, never unpacking, never staying anywhere long enough to leave a footprint.' All of this was said with an air of sadness.

'Are you the same?' he asked. 'Have you unpacked?'

Her hesitant pause seemed to last a lifetime.

The timer beep from the oven interrupted them and though he was not a little unnerved and desperately wanted an answer, he couldn't let his frittata burn either. Valérie left silently while he laid everything out on the table in front of him. His mind was torn. If Valérie was temporary, devastated though he'd be, he could do nothing about it. It was the permanent fixture he needed to concentrate on: Madame Tablier. He downed another glass of wine, feeling very much the wronged man of cinematic cliché. 'Sod it!' he said and stood back to admire his work. It was, even if he said so himself, and partly because he suspected nobody else would, an impressive display. So much so that even he eschewed any further Dutch courage. He may very well be serving food to French people, but the wine tasted like the oven smelled. Instead, he picked up the Pringles and then the salmon trays and ventured forth.

'Bonsoir, *tous les mondes*!' he said with a flourish as he walked outside, his trays held aloft. On each tray he had arranged the 'delicacies' to look like a flower, this being the famous La Chapelle-sur-Follet after all. A central display with the rest circled around it like petals. He placed them down and stood back. Around him were half a dozen people, and even a couple of children running around which he hadn't expected. They murmured their appreciation at the spread and waited for somebody else to start first. One of the children, a small blond boy obliged, taking a Pringle and biting into it before spitting it out with a 'Yuck, that's horrible' whine.

Richard felt like barging him over as he went back for the frittata, but managed to restrain himself. He emerged once again with a flourish, this time tray held more aloft so that people couldn't see it until he placed it on the table. He did so, and there were audible gasps from the gathering.

'Richard!' Valérie and Oriane said in unison. 'Brilliant!

For once he was in agreement, and it seemed to chime with the general consensus. The large rectangular tray was like a work of art. In the centre were sprigs of dill with tiny nasturtium flowers around it, and arranged to look like a bush in bloom. In the top right was a full deep yellow hollyhock, its stamen removed, acting as the sun while other brightly coloured flowers were scattered on the 'ground' giving the whole frittata the look of a meadow in spring.

'Do you want a job, ducks?' Madame Cuistot sidled up to him, a warm smile on her face.

'Ha! Well, you know, it was just something I threw together.'

'What's it supposed to be?' the little boy asked and Richard ignored him.

'My sister was right about you,' Madame Cuistot said. 'You're a good man.'

'Poor Madame Tablier,' he said, his upper lip as stiff as coal. 'Languishing in her prison cell.' The wine had also given him a touch of melodrama.

'Oh, she'll be all right,' the old woman chuckled. 'She's probably given the place a good spring clean by now.' While Richard thought that a strong possibility, he was still a little taken aback by her apparent lack of concern. 'Come on, let me introduce you to the village,' she said, taking him by the arm.

Right, he thought, catching Valérie's determined eye. *Let's get to work.*

Chapter Nine

Valérie had been spot on. They were an eclectic-looking bunch for sure, and as Oriane had also hinted, not a particularly welcoming group either. Specifically, nobody seemed to smile and then it occurred to Richard that their standoffishness was because of their, or rather his, position. They saw him as the caterer, the *traiteur*. His hastily arranged though flamboyant *amuse-bouches* had been greeted with genuine appreciation but despite that, Madame Cuistot aside, these weren't the type of people to mix with 'staff'. He had had a few guests like that in his B&B over the years, people who weren't used to the more informal style of a *chambre d'hôte*. It was even an atmosphere he sometimes cultivated not wanting to get too chatty with any of his paying guests. This felt different though, this wasn't a set of people unaware of the rules, this felt like an old-fashioned class thing.

It didn't help that Madame Cuistot introduced him as Richard 'he made the *amuse-bouches*', and not Richard the... well, what was he exactly anyway? 'My sister's employer'? That didn't sound right either. He was just an interested party here really and to that end, he realised, the anonymity of *traiteur* could really be to his advantage.

He had the impression that the great and good of La Chapelle regarded staff, if they regarded them at all, as practically invisible.

'I enjoyed your efforts very much,' said a tall well-dressed man, though he said it like he had a gun pointed at his back, such was his lack of sincerity. 'I am Christophe de la Cour,' he intoned, leaving a slight gap between the first name and the surname, making it sound like an announcement.

'Ah yes,' Richard replied. 'We passed your *brocante* as we came into the village.'

De la Cour's demeanour changed immediately. 'Your French has a slight accent. Are you…'

'Yes, I'm English,' Richard sighed, waiting for any jokes about the English and their food.

'I am very much an Anglophile,' said the man, now with something approaching warmth, if also still some way off. 'I spent a few years in Oxford working at a fine art auction house.' It was now that Richard saw the 'style' of the man. It was very much of the 'clubbable gentleman' variety: tweeds and an old-style cravat, a rarely seen mode of dressing these days, though Richard had stopped taking much notice about what people wore since going to the cinema wearing football shirts had apparently become socially acceptable. He hadn't noted the style much at first because it played second fiddle to a quite outrageous suntan, so deep he couldn't tell if it was real or fake. 'So what brings you here?' he asked, revealing yellowing teeth through a thin smile – maybe he'd tanned them as well. 'To France, I mean.'

'Oh, you know, work…' Richard replied, trying to make it sound interesting.

'Ah, so we import our caterers now, do we?' The smile vanished. 'I can't say I'm surprised.'

'Are you denigrating France again, Christophe?' A much smaller man joined them and Richard felt there was something familiar about him, not just that he had an air of Arthur Lowe as Captain Mainwaring in *Dad's Army*, but someone else aside from that. 'Lennard Bridille.' He held out his hand, but beyond the name gave nothing away. He had a large moustache which dominated his face and, from Richard's taller angle, completely hid his mouth. It was like talking to someone hiding in the bushes. 'I enjoyed what you did there,' he nodded towards what was left of the appetisers. 'We're always on the lookout for new caterers around here, especially now Madame Cuistot's short-staffed. Do you have a business card?'

Richard patted his pockets, a look of forgetfulness on his face. 'I seem to have left them behind,' he said.

'Never mind, you can always get hold of me at the *mairie*.' The level of importance he attached to this statement seemed to indicate some high office in the local municipality.

'Are you the mayor?' Richard asked innocently, noting the yellow smile returning to Christophe de la Cour's face at the suggestion.

Lennard Bridille blushed. 'Oh no. We have no mayor as such, we run things by committee here, though we're a bit thin on numbers at present.' De la Cour coughed an interruption. 'We are part of a team that keeps things ticking over, for the good of all.' His tone, though idealistic, was pure local politician, a mixture of obsequiousness and pomposity and Richard now realised where he recognised him from. His own local civic facilitator and nemesis back in Saint-Sauver, Noel Mabit. They must churn these people out on a production line, he thought, oily little tykes always popping up with rules, paperwork and bureaucratic obstacles ostensibly 'for the good of all'.

'Richard?' It was Valérie at his elbow. 'Can I introduce you to Madame Agnès Valadon? She has been very complimentary about your *amuse-bouches*.'

'*Enchanté*, Agnès,' he said, briefly forgetting the rules.

'Madame Valadon,' she corrected sternly, which Richard thought harsh even if she was technically and socially in the right. Her manner was that of a woman almost twice her age, which at least suited her rather dowdy appearance.

'*Excusez-moi.*' Richard nodded with forced deference, wishing he'd had more wine to cope with this motley crew.

She looked at him keenly through small round glasses, and after what felt longer than a short while, he was beginning to feel uncomfortable.

'You have been here before,' she said. The certainty in her voice making Richard feel as though, even if he hadn't been there before, he would have agreed that he had.

'Many years ago.' He knew he sounded nervous.

'I rarely forget a face.' It sounded almost like a threat. 'It's my pleasure and duty to look after the church; we share our priest with a wider area, so I never forget an outsider's face.'

'What about insiders' faces?' Richard couldn't remember the last time he'd been surrounded by such an unpleasant bunch of people, and it was also the second time today that he had been recognised and it unnerved him somewhat. Once could be seen as flattering, twice was bordering on surveillance. Valérie spotted his discomfort immediately and whisked him away before he could do any damage.

'Is everything OK, Richard?' she asked, showing some concern.

'My head is in a bit of a whirl, that's all,' he huffed. 'If Cuistot's death was an accident we need to prove it and if it wasn't I'm building up a stack of suspects with this lot, not narrowing them down.'

'Yes,' she agreed. 'They are a peculiar set of people. So very intense. But we need to get to know them for Madame Tablier's sake.'

He smiled wearily. She was right, of course.

'Hey, you there!' The gentle hum of society was shattered by Lennard Bridille shouting at someone further down the garden. 'What do you think you're doing? This is private property. Bloody man's stealing your vegetables, Madame Moulin. Get out of it…' He stopped shouting for a second as he focussed more on the intruder. 'Is that Santos?' His face was turning bright red. 'Felipe Santos?'

Oriane replied, a little sheepishly in Richard's opinion, that it was indeed Felipe Santos. And he threw Valérie a quick glance as if to ask 'who on earth is Felipe Santos?'

'He helps me in the garden sometimes. Have I done something wrong?' The coquettishness in Oriane's voice would have melted most men at that point but Bridille was the archetypal public servant and not easily swayed.

'Has he finished his work? What time does he usually clock off?'

'Five pm.' Agnès Valadon confirmed.

'Thought so,' Bridille clasped his hands in triumph. 'And what time is it now?'

'Four minutes past.' Valérie didn't bother to hide her contempt.

'Ah.' The man seemed punctured by the news. 'Still not keen to be honest.'

'Felipe! Come and join us!' Oriane shouted down the garden to an obviously reluctant Felipe Santos who carried a spade on his shoulder and walked slowly towards the throng. He arrived unsmiling. 'Madame,' he said, addressing Oriane before merely nodding at the rest.

'Do you have permission from the committee to work here freelance?' Lennard Bridille asked, a resurgence of pomp puffing his chest out.

'Do I need it?' was the brooding reply. Felipe Santos was over six foot tall and powerfully built as only those who spend their time working all day outdoors are. Everything was in proportion, his curly black hair neatly trimmed, his olive Portuguese skin making a further mockery of de la Cour's ostentatious fake tan while his large grey eyes showed deep anger.

It was Madame Cuistot who tried to diffuse the situation. 'Felipe is our genius!' she said with delight. 'Most of the village displays are his work, aren't they, Felipe?'

'I do what I can,' was the monotone reply.

'He does as he's told,' Bridille added. 'And you're letting things get out of control, my man.' Richard couldn't help wincing at the 'my man' part. 'Everything's *too early*.'

Felipe Santos took in a deep breath as if it were an ongoing argument and he had had his fill of it. 'I can't change man's stupidity or God's will,' he said quietly, put his spade back on his shoulder and walked slowly back to his work at the far end of the garden. Madame Valadon crossed herself, Bridille looked about to explode and de la Cour was showing his yellow teeth again.

'Such a hard worker!' Madame Cuistot cried. 'I honestly don't know what we'd do without him.' But no one was really listening to her and Richard had the impression that she was acting as a cheerleader to a team that didn't want cheering.

'Now, Richard.' It was Oriane who changed the subject and led him away from the group. 'I'd like to introduce you to some people.'

His initial thought was that he'd had quite enough introductions for one afternoon and his head was seriously starting to swim with it all.

'Oh good,' he said flatly.

'Valérie has told me all about you and I think you could help me out.' It sounded ominous. She led him to a table in the corner where a youngish family were seated. It was clear that they didn't know anyone else there, or certainly not well, and it was also clear that the parents were having trouble controlling their unruly offspring. Particularly the small blond boy from earlier who was banging a brand new toy car on the wooden garden furniture while a slightly younger girl sulked. She kept turning towards her mother, getting her attention and then theatrically turning her back again.

Hard work, Richard thought, *I'll be glad when I can get out of here.* He became aware of Valérie joining them and he hoped that meant their departure was imminent.

'Madame et Monsieur Fournier,' Oriane began. 'This is Monsieur Richard Ainsworth, I think he could help you out.' They both looked at him with a desperation suggesting that whatever their problems were, it was quite probably beyond him. 'They're new here and I'm afraid I've let them down.'

'How can we help?' Valérie's voice was soft and friendly, and the couple relaxed slightly.

'Well…' Monsieur Fournier began.

A slightly more assertive Madame Fournier quickly interrupted him. 'We were supposed to stay at the *auberge*, the Auberge Cuistot, but we arrive and find they have closed the bedrooms for now.'

'I made only a verbal agreement with poor Monsieur Cuistot, you see?'

'And Madame Cuistot says she hasn't the staff to take us in for now.'

'I mean obviously, it's terrible news but…' He lost patience. 'Fabrice, stop banging that car, you'll break it!'

'I don't like cars!' the boy Fabrice snapped back and banged the thing harder.

Richard had a horrible feeling he knew where this was going. 'Well, we can help, can we not, Richard?'

'Well not really.' He thought he may as well put up some token defence. 'We're short-staffed too, remember?' He wanted to put the final nail in the coffin of the offer of help by adding, 'You know, our housekeeper? Currently banged up for murder.' But he didn't.

'That would be fantastic!' Madame Fournier gushed, her change of mood lightning quick. Her husband also looked relieved that his booking error might be rectified.

'They have bought a house in the town,' Oriane explained, 'but their furniture hasn't arrived as yet.'

'It will only be for a few days,' the Monsieur pleaded. 'While we clean the place.'

Richard couldn't take his eyes off the little boy who clearly had a big future in demolition. 'I'm not really...' he began.

'Well, that's settled!' Valérie even seemed pleased by the idea. 'You can follow us back if you like.'

The family stood up to leave, Fabrice throwing what was left of his toy car over the florally decorated fence and into the road.

'Oi,' came an angry voice from the other side. 'Come and pick that up!'

Oriane opened the gate and there stood a street cleaner in a hi-vis jacket, large broom in one hand, furiously rubbing his head with the gloved other.

'I am so sorry, Monsieur Roy,' Oriane apologised. 'We didn't see you there!'

He threw his broom into his hand cart. 'Nobody ever does,' he spat the words. 'Nobody ever does.'

Chapter Ten

In the end Richard drove them both back, but at a much more sedate pace than they had taken to arrive at La Chapelle-sur-Follet. It wasn't just a reversion to his normal self, nor even that he needed time to think. It was just deemed best that the Fourniers following behind would have a better chance of keeping up if Richard drove, rather than Valérie. Though neither she nor Passepartout looked pleased about the situation. In fact the little dog looked positively lovelorn. Richard liked thinking as he drove and he started to go through things. They, though him mainly, had rushed to the village to seek answers to some pressing questions. Among them: why was Duval Cuistot's death now being treated as a murder? And why was Madame Tablier the main, in fact apparently only, suspect?

The upshot of their brief visit, however, was that they were now returning with more questions than they had arrived with and were no nearer to answering the previous two they'd had. Not only that, Richard now had a family of house-moving Parisian refugees to cater for, plus their obnoxious children. Valérie was pensive too, and there was no doubt in Richard's mind that she too was brooding over the afternoon's events, and especially the appearance of her old colleague, Oriane Moulin.

'What do you think of Oriane?' she asked in a way that was meant to sound breezy and inconsequential, two things Richard knew she wasn't capable of. It was unnerving enough that she appeared to read his thoughts, worse that it was this particular issue and so the usual alarm went off in his head. To him it sounded like the Dive! Dive! Dive! alarm of a submarine which was apt as he fancied burying himself deep under something rather than risk the ambush that this question posed.

A number of options ran through his mind. It wasn't difficult to see that the two were rivals as well as former colleagues, but it also wasn't difficult to see that they were both cut exquisitely from the same cloth. Something both of them, he was sure, would vehemently deny and probably rail against, though Valérie had effectively said the same herself.

'She has a very strong personality,' he said, hopefully hedging his bets. A lifetime of avoiding exactly this type of conversation had given him a number of failsafe options and 'she has a strong personality' was one of those descriptions that could be either a positive or a negative. The perfect response to see which way the wind was actually blowing.

'Oh yes!' Valérie's response was a strong one while still not indicating whether it was a good thing or not. 'She likes to shake the tree and to see what falls from it.' From this and the tone in her voice he gathered this was a bad thing. He declined to say who else had that personality trait.

'Isn't that supposed to be a positive in your line of work?' he asked, again going for middle-of-the-road, non-committal.

'Sometimes. But she is no longer in my "line of work". She is a gardener.' She sounded dismissive.

'Shaking a tree might be right up her street then.' Richard knew he shouldn't bother and sometimes offered this kind of humour solely for his own entertainment. For her part, Valérie stayed silent. If she'd got the joke, there was no indication of it.

'And a television gardener too.' Oriane had clearly completely riled her and though his antennae didn't always have a good reception he would lay money that it was something in the past and very little to do with popular gardening programmes. 'She couldn't possibly look after all that garden on her own, it is too big.'

'Well she certainly doesn't spend time cooking,' Richard repeated while he checked that the Fournier family were still following him in their enormous, gleaming SUV. 'She does have help of course, that Felipe fella. Felipe Santos. The town gardener by the sounds of things, moonlighting.'

'Moonlighting?' she asked, seeking clarification.

'*Travail au noir*,' he replied confidently. 'Working two jobs on the quiet.'

'Well,' Valérie huffed in response. 'She knows how to twist men around her little finger.'

Bingo! thought Richard. *That's that mystery solved.*

'Well, she'd already said that people are unhappy about the TV show and that Bridille character wasn't brimming with joy about Felipe working at her place either. It all seemed a bit for show, if you know what I mean. The dreaded committee indeed.' He made the word 'committee' sound as if he was referring to the secret police in a dictatorship; but that's exactly how they came across to him.

'How do you mean?' Valérie seemed distracted.

'I mean, if someone, Oriane specifically, is causing all this trouble in the village, why accept an invitation to her *apéritif*? I understand why *she* invited *them*, but why did they accept, if she's such a troublemaker?' He checked his mirrors again; the Fourniers were too close behind him. *Bloody Parisians*, he thought, *just take your time*.

'That is Oriane Moulin, she is like a honeypot!' Valérie pronounced before taking a deep breath. 'I do see what you mean though. Tell me what you thought of them.'

Richard changed up a gear and took a moment to reflect on how symbolic that mechanical necessity was in conjunction with Valérie asking his opinion on something. Things were changing, the relationship was becoming more balanced, and if he were of a mind to do so he'd give it a little push, but then the nomad in her might not like that. Besides, the truth was that nothing right now was more important than springing Madame Tablier from her jail cell, or at the very least checking up on her background. He still couldn't get over the fact that not only had she not been married, she had also been engaged to her later brother-in-law. Like Valérie had said, *evidence, motive and opportunity*. He became aware out of the corner of his eye that Valérie was still waiting for an answer.

'OK,' he said, trying to sound calm. 'Let's take them in order.'

'Christophe de la Cour,' Valérie said, tapping the name into her phone to make notes.

'How did you know he was first?' Richard asked, taken aback.

'Because I was watching you, Richard.' He gripped the steering wheel tighter. 'Now, Christophe de la Cour,' she repeated. 'What did you think?'

'In a word, aloof,' he said thoughtfully. 'Though that pretty much captures all of them. They all made me feel like a servant, except Madame Cuistot who knew me already but who I think is just a bit dizzy.'

Valérie stopped typing. 'How do you mean dizzy?'

'I'm not sure exactly, a bit scatter-brained, I suppose. And it doesn't seem to bother her that her sister has been charged with murder. It's all just a bit of a mix-up to her. You can see why Madame Tablier thought she needed to look after her. I suspect Madame Cuistot's the kind who could easily be taken advantage of.'

Valérie smiled. 'You are *so* English, Richard.'

He nodded. She was beginning to say this of him more and more and he still wasn't sure if it was meant as a compliment or not. 'Which brings us back to Christophe de la Cour,' he said stiffly. 'He's an avowed Anglophile. Though I'm not entirely sure what that means.'

'It means that he is a snob,' Valérie confidently replied. 'But then he is an antiques dealer, so that much is obvious.'

'He might just like the English…'

'It's not like that. They like the obvious class distinction…'

'You seem to know an awful lot about Englishmen.' It wasn't a question, it was just petulance and he immediately regretted it. He regretted it even more when Valérie replied huffily.

'Well, I was married to an Englishman!'

If Richard's jaw had dropped much further it would have pressed the accelerator. As it was he remained, on the face of it, stoically silent when in fact the truth was that he had so many things he wanted to ask, so many questions, that they were all jammed together in the doorway of his mind, each unable to free itself of the others.

'I didn't know that,' he said stiffly.

'Well, it was not for very long, he wasn't even English, he just pretended to be English. Anyway, he died.'

'Because he pretended to be English?' Richard was on the verge of losing control.

'I think so, yes.'

Not for the first time Richard felt like he'd missed something. Valérie's mind was such a maelstrom of competing winds, with no filter at all, and as usual he was left to sift through the wreckage in the lull, looking for nuggets amid the stream of consciousness. She fed him each new revelation about her past with a quiet air of frustration, as if she had told him already and either he wasn't listening or it had slipped his mind. He was pretty sure he'd have remembered if she had told him this! He was beginning to think it was only him who had led a traditional, down the line, boring existence. Almost everyone else he knew was positively exotic.

'But…' he began, with a hint of trepidation.

'Yes, Richard, you are right. We must concentrate. We have Christophe de la Cour, *brocanteur*, snob.'

'And the colour of the inside of a Jaffa cake.'

Thankfully she ignored him. 'Next, that little man with the big moustache.'

'Lennard Bridille,' he sighed. She tapped the name into her phone.

'Bridille,' she said slowly, as if the name meant something to her. Richard bit his tongue knowing that he was about to ask if she'd been married to him too. He had no idea what the count of ex-husbands was now, but it was seriously endangering his hot meals tally. 'He reminded me of someone, and I cannot put my finger on it.'

'Noel Mabit,' he said. 'He was pure Noel Mabit. Not the moustache obviously, but the same stature and the same petty officiousness.'

'Of course!' He felt her look across at him but he kept his eyes firmly on the road. It really was time he demanded some answers of Valérie d'Orçay rather than fawn like a schoolboy over this glamorous enigma. Again he had to ask himself, what did he really know of her? She drip-fed him little snippets, tiny pieces of a jigsaw that did nothing to clarify the much bigger, and frankly ever expanding, picture. 'This Monsieur Bridille,' she said, 'he told us that they were thin on numbers, presumably that means Duval Cuistot was on this committee too.' She shook her head. 'He does not seem the type to me. We must ask Madame Tablier. Now, Agnès Valadon.'

He let her continue the conversation with herself, while at the same time trying to force himself to concentrate. Whatever he had to ask it could wait for now, though he realised that he was also looking for excuses to put off such a scene. Admittedly he didn't know much about Valérie, but he knew enough of her character to know that she had her teeth sunk into this case already and if they were to clear Madame Tablier he really shouldn't allow himself to be distracted. And besides which, did he even want to know any details? It wasn't just that ignorance is bliss, though Clare would argue that was his habitual approach to reality; it was more that the romantic in him could fill in the gaps in a way that played better to his quixotic nature. Reality could be dull, it could be disappointing, it let you down.

'She said she recognised me,' he said, snapping back to the conversation. 'But I haven't been there in years. Clare and I only went twice. Does she have surveillance cameras set up?' he joked.

Valérie thought about this. 'It's possible. She certainly must know everything that goes on in that place and that is quite a powerful position to be in I think.'

'Like I said, I didn't care for any of them, but they suit the place I suppose. Thing is, they made it sound like it was almost a burden to them. And I didn't like the way they spoke to Felipe Santos, like he was their servant.' He could have added that they had treated him the same way.

'And then there's this Bouchard family, this tragedy.'

'Maybe the father... what was his name?'

'Florian.'

'Maybe this Florian Bouchard was on the committee too? A lifetime of service, Madame Cuistot described it as.' He paused. 'Hardly Nobel Peace Prize stuff though, is it?'

She stayed silent for a moment. 'You really do not like La Chapelle-sur-Follet, do you, Richard?' He could feel her looking at him again. How come she could probe him about his past, yet he felt unable to reciprocate?

She was right, he wasn't keen on the place. The last time he and Clare had visited their marriage was all but over. They were trying things like day trips, meals out, and so on in an attempt re-energise their relationship but it was like blowing up a car tyre that you knew had a slow puncture. The experiment had failed and they were both, if they were honest, a little relieved by that.

'The place just doesn't seem real,' he said eventually, deciding to keep the Clare stuff to himself, to try and be a bit more mysterious. 'It's a façade. Like a film set I suppose. But sinister, eerie, a bit dead. Did you see how many places were empty? It's like a holiday village for weekending Parisians. I tell you one thing, if I were the Fourniers I wouldn't want my kids growing up there.' Just then the immense shadow of the Fourniers' SUV sped past them and the boy, Fabrice, gave them a disdainful look as they overtook, before sticking his tongue out in a gesture of wilful mischief. 'Having said that…' Richard bridled, '…a bit of solitary confinement might do them good. Bloody Parisians!' Then, remembering who he was talking to, 'Sorry, no offence.'

Chapter Eleven

What Valérie was more likely to take offence at was Richard tapping the brakes to slow the car down even further; even the car itself sounded disappointed as its engine whined complainingly at the lower gear. The backlash of her impatience was a risk he was prepared to take, however. 'They can't get in without me anyway,' he muttered, 'and I need to pick up a few bits for breakfast.' But she wasn't paying attention, her mind elsewhere.

He drove the car around the convoluted Saint-Sauver one-way system, a route which even Valérie took slowly. The traffic loop, with islands and pedestrianised squares was designed to slow any traffic to a crawl, not just for safety reasons but so that visitors could also get a proper look at the place and hopefully stop to spend some time and, of course, money in the town. It was a classic small French town, built around an enormous, dominating, largely empty most of the time, church. There were plane trees around a sizeable market square, the market itself bustling into life every Thursday; a gothic house overlooked the square – it looked like the house in the film *Psycho* and was the office of the *notaire*. In recent years life had come back into the town and shops had sprung up in units that had lain empty for years. The small chateau on the bank of the river had been renovated too and Saint-Sauver was thriving once again.

More than that, to Richard it was home. Not just the-place-where-he-lived home, but it *felt* like home. Driving into the town now felt like slowly rising to the surface of a swimming pool: there was a comfort to it and he could breathe again. That's what La Chapelle-sur-Follet lacked entirely. It was a cold working museum, a cynical half-empty money pot and to its apparently few inhabitants it was their empire; nothing existed beyond it, and though visitors were welcome, their stay shouldn't be exceeded beyond strict limits. Where was the community? That was the question that came back to Richard. He drove past Jeanine's bustling *boulangerie*, then René Dupont's Café des Tasses Cassées which was busy with locals and tourists alike. They were both good friends, Jeanine and René, a necessary part of his small, friendly world. A world that welcomed newcomers, unlike Lennard Bridille and his committee; Saint-Sauver was expanding not stagnating. There was even a brand new corner shop, just opposite the *mairie*.

The corner shop had fallen out of fashion in rural France. Unable to compete with the prices the edge of town supermarket behemoths could offer, they had largely disappeared. Two things happened to change that. The advent of self-service tills was an affront to the rural classes for one. Richard had been present when a gang of old women had taken violent objection to one of the machines, leaving it severely damaged and stuck on a prescient vocal loop of 'Please place the item in the bagging area'. The second thing that happened was that a largely Arabic immigrant population left the cities and literally set up shop elsewhere. They still couldn't compete on the price front, but they were smiling, friendly and human and, more importantly, open at non-traditional times for the French like evenings, Sunday afternoons and even Mondays.

The young Sharifi brothers, Taz and Shilal, had bought the old hardware store which had been empty for years, and transformed it into a small supermarket, working hard to establish themselves in the town. Richard, for obvious reasons, was always keen to help newcomers and outsiders and was a regular customer.

'I need some children's cereals, some jam and milk,' he was saying to Valérie as they stood in the shop, but she still wasn't listening.

'Why is she here?' she asked. 'I just do not trust her.' Whatever their history, it was clear that the presence of Oriane Moulin was upsetting her greatly.

'Are we still on that? Well, she said, didn't she? She's fronting this new TV show, this gardening programme.'

Valérie huffed in response. 'And you believe that?'

'She seemed pretty knowledgeable to me. More than either of us are, anyway.'

'Oh, Richard! Anyone can be knowledgeable these days.' She waved her phone at him. 'It's all in here.'

They approached the counter where a harassed Taz Sharifi was trying to work the till, while looking for a plastic bag and holding a sleeping baby in one arm. Richard took the bag from the apologetic young man and did the packing himself.

'Still busy, Taz?' Richard asked jovially.

Taz rolled his eyes. 'Any good at changing nappies?'

'Those days are behind me! Valérie, would you…?' He'd meant it purely as a joke but she gave him a withering look nonetheless. 'You could look up how to do it on your… never mind.'

Richard didn't consider himself a 'lucky' individual; he felt he had to battle too hard to stay afloat to believe that he had much luck as such. But if what he needed was a distraction to extract himself from Valérie's Gorgon-like stare, while Taz visibly backed away behind the till like a Western saloon bartender, fate was at hand.

'Is that Noel Mabit out there?' he asked innocently, knowing full well it was, as he saw the small man through the shop window. 'What's he up to?' For once, he felt well disposed towards Noel Mabit. It was an odd feeling, but Richard was under the spell of the warmth of Saint-Sauver, *his* town, real life. Yes, Noel was officious, pernickety, ubiquitous and not a fan of Richard by any means, but he didn't have the whiff of sinister control that Richard had felt with 'the committee'. And besides, he was part of Richard's circle and right now that meant something. Madame Tablier was in jail, Valérie had practically confessed to itchy feet, the endgame with Clare was finally in view. In a strange way, he needed the likes of Noel Mabit, if only for stability. He shook his head; if he was eulogising about Noel Mabit, La Chapelle must really have got under his skin.

He watched through the window as the man, wearing a set of overalls that were far too big for him, leant a tall ladder against the wall of the town hall.

'Is he trying to break in?' Valérie asked, before adding, as she usually did in any conversation about Noel Mabit, 'the silly little man!'

'He's cleaning out the gutters,' Taz replied. 'He was in here earlier asking if we had any rubber gloves, but we sold out.' The stock issue put a worried look on the young man's face.

'You'd think he would get someone else in to do it,' Richard remarked. 'At his age.' He actually had no idea how old the man was, but his bearing and his oily servility made him seem much older than Richard, though they might even be the same age. *God, that's depressing,* he thought.

'He told me he's always done it and always will. First job every spring, clean the gutters.' It was clear from the way Taz spoke that there was a mixture of the reverential and 'the man's a lunatic' in his view of Noel, but he also knew that you could get nothing done in the town of Saint-Sauver without him being on your side either.

'Silly little man!' Valérie repeated, as they crossed the road towards him.

'*Bonjour*, Noel!' Richard had decided long ago that false bonhomie was the way to go.

Noel looked up from his equipment without warmth. 'Monsieur Ainsworth.' The formality of the man was truly irritating. 'Valérie,' he said, trying to ooze something approaching charm.

'What are you doing, Noel?' Valérie had no time for any of this. 'Going up ladders at your age!'

Noel Mabit pulled himself up to his full five foot six, trying to bat off the perceived insult with the only weapon he knew, pomposity. 'I can give any younger man a run for his money!' He was game that was for sure, though he was only dealing with the gutters on the low town hall extension, not the much taller main building. He turned and picked up his equipment by the handle. 'Besides, this machine I found makes it all a lot easier.' The machine, as he called it, looked like a cross between a leaf blower and a vacuum cleaner with an anteater's nose. He climbed the ladder slowly, betraying no sign of fear.

'Do you have a relative in La Chapelle, Noel?' Richard called up after him. 'Name of Lennard Bridille. I'd say he was the spitting image of you.'

'What are you talking about? Why would you ask that?' Noel Mabit flushed angrily. It was clear Richard had hit a nerve, though he had no idea how. 'I haven't got time for this, as you can see, I'm busy. Valérie, could you plug this machine into that extension, please?'

Valérie caught Richard's eye; she sensed Noel's over-reaction too, but she did as she was asked and plugged in the machine.

'OK, that's in,' she shouted up the ladder.

'Right. Well, if you'll excuse me. I have work to do.' He climbed higher and put the nozzle of his contraption into the gutter, took a deep breath and pressed the trigger. There was a flash on the plug socket and an almost simultaneous shriek from Noel as he started to wobble on the ladder. Richard looked up and saw he was about to fall. Valérie saw it too but her instincts were different and much sharper. Whereas Richard began to shout something not terribly helpful like 'Look out!' Valérie gave an unsuspecting Richard a mighty shove in the back sending him pitching forward and colliding with the tumbling Noel Mabit, breaking his fall.

It was a few moments before a stunned and frankly none too happy Richard was able to gather himself. That he lay under a prostrate Noel was bad enough; that the man was at best unconscious and hopefully not a literal deadweight was worse.

'Brilliant, Richard!' Valérie cried. 'You may have saved his life!'

He was having none of it. 'You bloody pushed me!'

'Oof, maybe a little. But I saw what you were thinking and gave you a little help.'

He thought about this. 'You bloody pushed me!' he repeated, devoid of any spark of something original.

Taz came running over from the shop, the baby still asleep in his arms. 'I saw what happened and I've called the *pompiers*,' he said. 'They're on their way. Are you OK, Richard?'

'He is fine,' Valérie interrupted. 'I think it is Noel that we must be worried about.' She gently rolled Noel over, allowing Richard to get out from under him. Richard checked himself for cuts and bruises and much to his disappointment didn't find any, meaning he had no solid complaining ground to stand on. 'He is alive,' Valérie was checking Noel's pulse. 'But only just.'

A crowd was beginning to gather, the incident having been seen from the café *terrasse*, and Taz went back into the shop as some of the onlookers took the chance to buy viewing refreshment. Valérie took care of Noel Mabit, while Richard sat stunned and leaning against the wall, receiving the congratulations of those who had seen his heroic, life-saving actions.

'You've hopefully saved his life,' the chief *pompier* said to Richard and Valérie later, after Noel had been put on a stretcher and taken away. 'He may have hit his head as he fell, broken his back, who knows? But he's still there just about. Is this what he was using?' The multi-tasking of the French *pompier* system was at work. A cross between an ambulance and fire service, the man was now inspecting the plug that had blown, starting the events that caused Noel to fall.

'He asked me to plug it in for him, and I did so.' Valérie sounded slightly annoyed that she may have been the catalyst for the accident.

'Well, let's be honest. He shouldn't have been up a ladder anyway, not at his age.' The chief snorted, though fortunately Noel wasn't around to hear it. He bent and looked at the plug and extension without touching it. 'It's a dodgy re-wiring job obviously,' he shook his head. 'Amateurs, honestly. I hope he survives, then I can give him a lesson into how to wire a plug properly. They should teach these things in school,' he added, though it would have been a bit late for Noel, whose pride had got to him as usual and he'd done the job himself. 'Are you two OK?'

'Oh we're fine.' Valérie answered for both of them as Richard, still in a state of shock and no little disgruntlement, felt unable to concentrate.

'Have you got my shopping?' he asked weakly.

Chapter Twelve

Valérie drove them both back home. Richard was obviously still in shock and though not always attuned to mood, she was nonetheless aware that he was probably best left to himself for now, rather than rake over what had just happened. He was beginning to recover quite quickly anyway, his faculties given a boost by just how piqued he was at the whole event. As usual, he was seeking solace in rank injustice.

The Fourniers were waiting for them when they arrived at Les Vignes, impatiently standing around their gas-guzzling monstrosity as if Richard wasn't already doing them a massive favour by putting them up in the first place. Of course, technically he wasn't doing them a favour at all, he was in the hospitality industry and they needed a room. It was a simple business arrangement. Even so, Richard sometimes wished he could be more confrontational and actually pick and choose his paying guests. Not many would make their way through the process though, he was well aware of that.

'In a hurry?' he asked, climbing gingerly out of Valérie's sports car, in no mood for the false affability of a meet and greet. Valérie did the same but in a fluid, elegant movement like steam leaving a kettle. A move that wasn't lost on Monsieur Fournier. Unfortunately his reaction wasn't lost on Madame Fournier either who angrily folded her arms and tapped her foot in textbook fashion.

'We have been waiting,' she said coldly.

'Yes, sorry about that,' Richard replied testily. 'Got hit by a falling bureaucrat, might have saved a man's life. You know how it is.'

She ignored him completely. 'We'd like to settle in. We have so much paperwork to go through. Moving house isn't easy, you know?'

'You don't say,' Richard mumbled as he unlocked the gate. Their two children went running through noisily before Richard even had the thing open properly.

'Fabrice! Emilie! Wait for us please!' It was Monsieur Fournier with the futile and possibly far too late attempt at parental control, but if he was embarrassed at being ignored by his children he didn't let it show. Passepartout instead padded through the gate breezily, a model of obedience and sobriety underlining the man's vain strictures.

'I'll deal with her,' Valérie said quietly to Richard and turned to Madame Fournier.

'Let me show you to your room, madame,' she said, Parisian meeting Parisian toe to toe. 'Richard can help your husband with your luggage.'

The two women cat-walked off up the drive leaving the two men behind. Richard hadn't taken to Monsieur Fournier at all but it was clear they had certain things in common and at this point they both stood with a look on their faces that roughly translated as 'the bloody cheek of it', though Richard felt he had far more cause for grievance.

'Richard,' he said, his introduction bordering on the morose, limply hanging out his hand for the other, and still wary of any as yet undiscovered injury from breaking Mabit's fall.

The younger man seemed surprised by the introduction and briefly just stared at Richard's hand in confusion. 'My name is Garland,' he said, offering his hand equally tepidly in return. 'There's not much in the way of luggage, most of our stuff is in storage anyway.'

'Garland? You're not named after Judy are you?' Richard's question had a hint of quiet desperation about it, searching as he was for any sliver of silver lining in the afternoon.

'Who?' The man's head was in the boot of the car and he didn't look up.

'Never mind,' Richard said sullenly, but cheered himself up by remembering one of Judy Garland's most famous quotes. *Behind every cloud is another cloud*, he thought. *Yep, that's about right.* Still though, fancy being called Garland and never having come across that question before? In his current mood that was the world summed up in a nutshell: there was no curiosity anymore, everybody had their own bubbles of existence, there was no… he became aware of a gleaming suitcase sitting in front of him which Garland Fournier was having trouble keeping upright. It was about the size of Richard's old Citroën and it was quite obvious that he was being expected to carry it.

'When are you hoping to move in?' he asked without enthusiasm.

'In a few days.' Fournier's head was back in the boot. 'It's just a matter of signing contracts now.'

'And paying the money.' Richard, with the help of a little conversational diversion, was hoping to grab a smaller case. 'That's always the painful bit.'

Fournier placed two small children's suitcases on the ground at his feet. 'Eh? Oh yes, the money. Of course.' Again the man seemed either distracted or cold and Richard saw his chance and grabbed the smaller cases, one in each hand.

'This way!' he said over his shoulder, giving the necessary faux enthusiasm. 'Let's get you settled in!'

He crunched along the gravel not bothering to hide his satisfaction at what he saw as a small victory in the battle of the suitcases. It wasn't just the cases of course, it was the man's attitude. It went beyond what he considered the usual Parisian detachment, it was downright cold. He left his guest to struggle with his enormous case and opened the door to his kitchen salon. Valérie already had a pot of coffee in progress and the aroma was welcoming. Madame Fournier, however, had a look on her face that suggested all was far from satisfactory.

'Richard.' Valérie rolled her eyes at him, her back to the new guest. 'The room is not ready, there is no bedding at all I'm afraid.'

He had completely forgotten that that would be the case. Obviously with Madame Tablier currently residing in a police cell things had slackened off and Richard had so far failed to fill the breach. If he were honest he would admit to simply putting them off, or hoping that his staunch, irreplaceable housekeeper would be released before he had to step up. He certainly couldn't see Valérie struggling with a king-size duvet cover and matching pillow set, nor could he see her wielding a vacuum cleaner in anger either. He wasn't even sure now that she'd emptied her own case.

He put the luggage down. 'OK, I'll do it now.' And he stomped up the stairs. 'You enjoy your coffee.' His victory over Garland Fournier, who now fell in through the door giving his wife a filthy look, was already a distant memory.

Richard stood in one of the two upstairs family rooms. It was the slightly smaller of the two; Valérie had commandeered the larger one for herself and her 'family' which consisted of just her and Passepartout. Still, this room was easily comfortable enough for four, with a large double bed and two singles under the eaves.

He sighed heavily. He had, for the most part, always managed to avoid this side of his business. An early duvet-related hernia injury had laid him low and made him seriously question his life choices; certainly it had laid waste to his initial enthusiasm as a hands-on host. From then on, Richard had restricted himself to meeting, greeting and breakfasts; Clare had done the accounts and the marketing, and Madame Tablier had taken over pretty much everything else.

He set about dressing the beds but his mind was elsewhere. He went back first to the conversation in the kitchen with Valérie. It unsettled him, and now all he wanted to do was check that she actually had unpacked, that there was some hint of permanence. He also couldn't dismiss the nagging feeling that Valérie could very well have injured him in the process of maybe – and that maybe was definitely worrying him – maybe saving Noel Mabit. She had also plugged the machine in. Was that coincidence? 'Oh don't be ridiculous!' he muttered. 'Noel had buggered up the wiring, the *pompier* had said so.' Still, he often came back to the same issue with Valérie. What did he actually know about her? What was the issue with Oriane exactly? But then again, as had been asked, what did he even know about Madame Tablier? He didn't seem to know much about anyone if he were honest, and that didn't help his current state of mind that everything he relied upon was falling apart. *Why was he so incurious?* 'It's time to delve a little deeper,' he said out loud. 'Let's concentrate on what I do know.'

He was still convinced that Madame Tablier was innocent of the murder of Duval Cuistot, he knew that much. Not that for one second he didn't think she was capable of murdering someone, and he knew full well that she could carry a grudge like an elephant carries around a memory, but he knew somehow that she hadn't done it. He needed proof of course, but deep down he knew.

Which meant either bad luck as far as circumstantial evidence went or she was being framed. Or Cuistot wasn't even murdered and this was just an unfortunate conspiracy of events following an unfortunate accident. The latter of which sounded even more far-fetched than Madame Tablier killing for love. He flapped the large duvet, trying to get it to fill its cover. She'd kill for stains certainly, a coffee mug ring on a polished table, that was feasible. But not a broken heart. He just couldn't see that.

He went downstairs to fetch the hoover and some cleaning products, making his presence as noisy as possible without actually catching anyone's eye.

'Would you like a coffee, Richard?' Valérie asked, assuming that was the reason for his testy behaviour.

'No, thank you,' he replied with false good humour. 'I'm a little busy.' This time he did catch someone's eye and it was the young Fabrice. The boy was giving him a look that suggested Richard was to sulking what Gene Kelly had been to dancing, a standout pro, and that he'd have to up his petulance game if he was to compete. In response Richard flushed and realised that not only was he behaving childishly but that it was a direct result of the situation. He was doing Madame Tablier's job; it was not something he would ordinarily have a problem with having offered to help the woman on countless occasions, knowing of course that she would refuse, but it reminded him that she wasn't there and he was really struggling to work it all out.

'I'll have a coffee when I've finished,' he forced a smile. 'We're a little short-staffed at present,' he said to the Fourniers, 'but just give me five more minutes.'

'There's really no rush, Richard,' Valérie said soothingly. 'We are having a nice chat, are we not?' The look on the faces of Monsieur and Madame Fournier told a quite different story. 'We were talking about Paris. Madame Fournier, Lisette, was just about to tell me where in Paris they have moved from.'

Richard felt an almost solid tension in the room and a definite reluctance to part with any information at all.

'We live in the fifth arrondissement, madame.' It was Garland Fournier who broke the silence.

'We *did* live in the fifth,' his wife corrected.

'Just around the corner from Les Jardins des Plantes. We had an apartment on the rue des Arènes.' The man was now positively loquacious.

'Oh I know it well!' Valérie clapped her hands in delight. 'There is a delightful bistro on the rue des Arènes... oh what is it called, Richard, can you remember?'

He knew she was up to something and bluffed in response. 'I am no good with names I'm afraid, that's your department, Valérie.'

'Oh my memory!' She was the very definition of over-acting, almost embarrassingly so. 'La Petite Pépite that's it! La Petite Pépite. They do a marvellous *filet mignon.*'

The Fourniers exchanged a glance. 'I think you are mistaken, Madame d'Orçay, La Petite Pépite is around the corner, it is on the rue Linné.'

'Oh yes, my mistake.' Valérie smiled winningly.

'And it is vegetarian.' Lisette Fournier did not return the smile but stood a little taller instead.

The tension in the room descended again and Richard decided the best way to diffuse it would be to get the room upstairs finished and put the Fourniers in it as soon as possible. 'Why don't you take a walk around the garden?' he offered, turning for the stairs. 'I'll only be a few minutes.' The Fourniers immediately took up the offer to take their leave of the inquisitive Valérie and went outside. Richard took the stairs two at a time, hoover in one hand and Madame Tablier's homemade scented room spray in the other.

The vacuuming didn't take very long and was completed in a couple of minutes. It was a cursory job, Richard not bothering to hoover under the beds for the Fourniers who, he felt, didn't deserve such attention to anti-dust detail. What took more time, after the events in town, was actually plugging the thing in, fearful as he was of an explosion and no one there to break his fall. After that he sprayed Madame Tablier's concoction liberally around the room and immediately broke into a coughing fit. He didn't know what ingredients the woman used in her spray but the place now smelled like the rear end of a male cat on heat. Looking at the bottle more closely, he realised he'd picked up the wrong spray and instead of filling the room with a welcoming pine-fresh ambiance he had doused the place in limescale dissolver.

'Bugger!' he shouted and opened the windows hoping a spring breeze would disperse the odour. He flapped a towel about hoping to aid the stench removal and leant against the window ledge out of breath with his efforts. 'Why is everything suddenly so bloody hard?' he asked himself, breathing in fresh air and seeing the one constant in his life gently shuffling about in their coop, pecking at the ground. Then, directly below him, in the garden, he heard the Fourniers arguing.

'I don't like it!' Lisette was saying. 'Why is she asking so many questions?'

'She's just nosey that's all,' was Garland's half-hearted reply. 'She's probably bored living out in the middle of nowhere. I know I would be.'

'I don't know,' his wife replied, unconvinced, stubbing a cigarette out underfoot. 'Where are those children now?'

'Well, I left Emilie asleep inside and Fabrice is playing with those hens…'

Richard didn't hear the rest of the sentence as he dashed downstairs in something of a panic. He had seen first-hand the destruction skills of the boy Fabrice and he feared greatly for his beloved ladies. He ran past a startled

Valérie at the foot of the stairs and nearly bumped into the Fourniers as he hurried outside. 'Your room's ready!' he shouted at them and sped off to the chicken coop.

He was too late. Fabrice was sitting cross-legged on the floor of the coop and in his lap, cooing softly as she was wont to do when content, was Olivia de Havilland. Fabrice was stroking her back gently making friendly noises as he did so, a picture of childish serenity and peace. He was like a completely different child.

Chapter Thirteen

Richard watched Fabrice for a few minutes and from a distance. The boy was in a totally different world, almost a dreamlike state that only a close relationship with animals can produce in children. *Lassie Come Home*, 1943, he thought. *Old Yeller*, 1957, *Kes*, 1969. Cinema was littered with the classic child–animal against-the-odds friendships. He'd even seen it with his own daughter Alicia and a short-lived gerbil called Bambi. She had asked for a fawn after seeing the film, but a gerbil had briefly sufficed.

What he couldn't square though was the warmth and care that young Fabrice was showing towards Olivia de Havilland: the complete antithesis to any level of behaviour he had thus far shown.

'Fabrice! Fabrice!' It was his mother shouting from the bedroom window though the boy showed no sign that he had heard her. 'Fabrice!' she repeated in a shrill tone. This time it hit the mark and Fabrice looked up, as if he'd just woken, put Olivia down gently, conscientiously shut the coop gate and ran off.

'Back to work,' he muttered, presumably mimicking one of his parents and reacting like a bored adult finishing their lunch hour. Completely ignoring Richard he ran back into the house.

He was still trying to figure things out when Valérie came and stood by him. 'There is something very peculiar about that family, Richard, something very strange.'

'I agree,' he replied, always grateful when they were on the same wavelength. 'They didn't fall for your trap though, did they?'

'My trap?' Her face was a picture of injured innocence.

'Yes, your trap.' He smiled at her. 'All that stuff about a bistro serving *filet mignon* in Paris.'

'Oh that! It was worth trying, but just because they know something of the fifth arrondissement of Paris does not mean that they're not up to something!' It was hardly an earth-shattering statement and about as far away from proof of wrongdoing as it was possible to get, but she made the statement with such vehemence that it sounded utterly watertight. 'I shall telephone the Commissaire!' she added, seemingly convinced that she'd made a breakthrough.

Richard was more circumspect. 'Really?' His voice was full of doubt. 'We only have a suspicion that they are a bit odd, he's not going to take that seriously.'

'Of course he won't!' she retorted. 'I shall him tell we have new evidence.'

'But we don't have new evidence!'

'I know that, Richard! But I want him to have doubts about the guilt of Madame Tablier. I shall phone him now at his office.' She started playing with the screen on her mobile phone.

Richard seriously doubted it would do any good but he had to admit that at least she was doing something. All

Richard had done was make up a bedroom and had the storming revelation that a child was fonder of animals than small cars. It was hardly the quantum leap they needed.

'*Bonjour*, madame, I would like to talk to Commissaire Lapierre, please…' She paused while listening. 'Yes, I understand he is busy but this is very important…' Again she waited while the person on the other end spoke. 'I appreciate that, but I have new information on the Cuistot murder!' Richard felt his eyebrows shoot up. Valérie d'Orçay certainly did not do things by half. 'He is already following up new evidence, you say? So, he is in La Chapelle now?'

This time it was Valérie throwing her sports car around the tight bends between Saint-Sauver and La Chapelle. Passepartout hid his head under his paws, and Richard held on for dear life not just to the car but to the tailcoats of the mission that Valérie was clearly on. Richard was on the same mission too, but it was fair to say that their methods were markedly different.

'Why are we in such a rush to see Lapierre?' he shouted above the engine roar. 'We don't actually have any new evidence!'

'Not yet!' she countered. 'But it is obvious to me that he has doubts about Madame Tablier's guilt as well. I want to know what they are.'

'But why would he tell us?'

'Oh, Richard!' Her laugh got caught in the headwind. 'I can be very persuasive, you know!'

He knew. He also knew that whatever reason Valérie would give to Commissaire Lapierre, he wouldn't believe a word of it and she wouldn't care. She just wanted the door to the policeman's investigation slightly ajar then she could shoulder barge her way in.

The sun had almost set by the time they parked up which, Valérie whispered unnecessarily, offered them some cover as they made their way to the Auberge Cuistot and the centre of the village, passing the hardworking street cleaner as they did so. Richard said a hearty *'Bonjour, working late, I see!'* but just got stared at for his troubles. Why they needed cover to enter the village again Richard wasn't entirely sure, but he was happy to go along with it for now, knowing of Agnès Valadon and her beady and suspicious eye.

The bright lights of the Auberge Cuistot could be seen from further down the street. It was just about the start of the tourist season and was quite busy, but from their vantage point in the shadows across the street it wasn't just the number of people that struck them but that in the centre of the *terrasse,* on a dominating larger table, were the La Chapelle grandees. Lennard Bridille sat next to a laughing Oriane Moulin; opposite them sat Christophe de la Cour and Agnès Valadon. Madame Cuistot was up and down from her chair at the foot of the table, but at the head, and slightly detached it seemed, at least conversationally, was the young Marcel Bouchard.

'They must have stayed on after the *apéritifs* at Oriane's and decided to make an evening out of it.' For some reason Richard whispered the observation whereas Valérie's response was full volume.

'Oriane, is it?' she said without taking her eyes off the *auberge.* 'Not Madame Moulin then?' Passepartout followed this up by giving him a filthy look as well.

There was a smashing of glass as Marcel Bouchard stood up, kicking his chair backwards as he did so and knocking over his wine. He was obviously quite drunk and Madame Cuistot hurried to his side and put an arm around his waist to steady him. She led the tall young man away from the table and to the edge of the seating area where she talked quietly to him. He walked away from her swaying as he did so and stumbled slightly off the low kerb and into the quiet street. 'Please be careful, Marcel,' she called after him. 'I will see you tomorrow, will I? Give my love to your dear mother!'

He didn't respond, but staggered presumably homewards, while Madame Cuistot looked forlornly in his direction.

Valérie saw her moment and stepped out into the light with a calm Passepartout and a startled Richard both at her heels. If Madame Cuistot was surprised to see them there was absolutely no flicker of it on her concerned face. 'I wish he would go back to his studies in America.' She shook her head sadly. 'There is no future for him here looking after a bedridden mother like this. He must live his own life.' All of a sudden she seemed to realise who they were, as if her gossipy nature had to be fed first before then noticing who she was actually talking to.

'Are we too late for dinner?' Richard asked, hoping to avoid explaining their presence.

'I am afraid so, ducks. You English always eat at the wrong time.' It wasn't an admonishment, more that she was incapable of keeping any thoughts to herself.

'We are not here for food, madame.' Valérie's tone was more serious and also had a hint of mild reproach directed at Richard. 'I'm afraid I forgot…'

'Your little dog's bed,' Madame Cuistot said quickly. 'Of course, now where did I put it? You will stay for a drink though?'

'Oh, I think that would be most pleasant!' Valérie flashed one of her most winning smiles. 'Do we have time, Richard?'

Richard was all out of improvisation and knew that he needn't say anything anyway. Instead he theatrically looked at his watch and puffed out his cheeks.

'Ha!' Madame Cuistot snorted. 'The English eat at the wrong times and drink all the time! Come with me.'

She led them on to the *terrasse* where Oriane immediately spotted them. She was also a little tipsy and jumped up to give them both a warm hug, lingering slightly longer with Richard. 'How delightful that you are here!' she fawned. 'You must join us!'

As more chairs were brought, it was clear that that was the end of the welcoming warmth. Agnès Valadon narrowed her eyes so tightly in a mask of suspicion that she looked on the verge of sneezing. Christophe de la Cour was cold and brusque, presumably not keen on sharing his space again with 'staff', even if one of them was English; and Lennard Bridille had a look on what could be seen of the non-moustache part of his face that suggested someone had trodden in something unpleasant and had brought the stench in with them. Richard not only had the distinct impression they weren't welcome but they had actually interrupted something private. As such, conversation wasn't so much stilted as absolutely non-existent.

After talking to a few other guests Madame Cuistot sat back down. 'Is there any news on my dear sister?' she asked.

The question was delivered as though Madame Tablier had missed a connecting train and was not currently banged up on suspicion of murder.

'Your sister is ill?' Oriane's question was slightly slurred.

'We may have new evidence,' Valérie announced, looking obviously from one person to the next as if overacting in a silent movie. 'Isn't that right, Richard?'

'Yes.' His voice was strong and underlined Valérie's point. 'Possibly,' was the weaker addition.

'Evidence for what?' Christophe de la Cour always managed to sound bored. Richard suspected that if he'd been the one to raise the alarm on the *Titanic* he'd have sounded just slightly put out and not at all urgent.

'My husband's murder.' Madame Cuistot was almost apologetic.

'It wasn't an accident.' Agnès Valadon nodded. She didn't ask the question, she just confirmed her own suspicions.

'Oh no,' Madame Cuistot put a hand to her forehead. 'Sorry, it must have slipped my mind. I've had so much to think about.' She took a sip of wine and avoided eye contact. Richard would be the first to admit to a lack of organisation at times, even forgetfulness, but if his partner had been murdered, he was sure he'd work hard to keep it at the forefront of the day's business.

'Why were we not told of this?' the officious Lennard Bridille huffed and Valérie tutted loudly at his blustering response. He really was the most difficult person to like, which to Richard's mind was pretty solid work considering the competition around the table.

'Ah, your sister...' Madame Valadon was going through her memory hard-drive of village interlopers. 'She was at

108

the funeral, I remember.' She didn't seem impressed by the memory at all.

'Oh yes, she's been here quite a lot in the last year or so,' Madame Cuistot replied, attempting to boost the image of her sister in the eyes of her friends.

'I know that,' Agnès said darkly.

'She was an enormous help while Duval was bedridden.'

'And what is this new evidence, madame?' de la Cour drawled. 'And why should a *traiteur* and his serving team be interested? No offence,' he added, which was the opposite of what he really meant. Richard felt like giving him a mouthful of his beloved Anglo-Saxon but knew that the *traiteur* cover was still a useful one and decided to bide his time. He was saved from answering by Oriane anyway.

'Oh there's more to Valérie than she will let you see, you know?' she said with a smirk.

'And through the years we have all seen almost all of Madame Moulin,' was Valérie's Exocet-like response. It was a side of her that Richard had not seen before, but then he'd known no one who pushed her buttons quite like Oriane Moulin managed to do.

'I still think we should have been informed!' Bridille wasn't letting this go, but his red-faced thunder proved the perfect distraction from a brewing showdown. 'As management committee for La-Chapelle-sur-Follet, we should have been made aware of any developments.'

Nobody felt like arguing, except Passepartout, who growled quietly and therefore spoke for most people at the table.

'Well, I think we should go now, Richard.' Valérie stood up suddenly with the small Chihuahua in her arms. 'We have to cater for a wedding tomorrow lunchtime, do you not remember?'

Of course, it wasn't unusual for Richard to be 'out of the loop' as the saying goes, but it did seem that they might have been finally getting somewhere. Also, and if he were honest, of almost equal importance he was rather enjoying a very fine local white wine and was interested in investigating it further.

'I think they cancelled,' he said, slightly surprised by his own impishness.

'No.' Valérie wasn't the least put off. 'It is back on again. Let's go.'

This time he did as he was told and offering mumbled, surly goodbyes followed a quickly disappearing Valérie back into the shadows across the road.

'What was that all about?' he asked, not unreasonably. 'I'm sure they know more than they're letting on.' He got no response from his distracted partner, who had her eyes on the darkened street. 'We should be pumping them for information,' he said loudly, not entirely sure how you'd pump anyone for information, though that seemed to be the done-thing information-wise.

This time Valérie did reply but with a sharp 'Sshh!' pointing further down the road as she did so. There were only a few street lamps dotted about, ornate lanterns playing up to the carefully cultivated image that La Chapelle projected. Valérie pointed in the direction from where they had walked initially.

'What am I looking at?' This time he whispered, but saw nothing. He kept looking, then he saw it. A figure quite obviously trying and, for the most part failing, to avoid what little light there was. Dashing through the light back into the shadow and then repeating the action, making their way along the main road. Whoever it was stopped in the shadows, not noticing that their silhouette was still visible thanks to a small garden lantern. The silhouette stopped at Oriane Moulin's house, looking about and checking to see if the coast was clear before carefully pushing open the gate and stepping inside.

Valérie produced a torch from somewhere and shone it between hers and Richard's faces. Her eyes looked like they were on fire, only partly from the light, and even Richard smiled. 'After you, madame,' he said gallantly.

Then they heard the scream.

Chapter Fourteen

It wasn't so much a scream of pain or even terror, it was more one of quite monumental outrage. High pitched, though it could have been male or female it was difficult to tell, and lengthy in its drawn out, strangulated high dudgeon. It was like a Tarzan call but with added pique. Valérie led the way with Richard, scooping up a diffident Passepartout, closely behind. It was obvious where the cry had come from, and whoever had been loitering suspiciously at the gate of Oriane Moulin's place had stumbled either on to or into something alarming.

The gate was closed when they got there and all the security lights, if there were any, were dark. The place was silent and pitch black and although Valérie fruitlessly shone her torch around the entrance, there was little sign at all that anyone had been there, let alone discovered something, or worse, been attacked. There were a few coins on the paved driveway; that was all, a few centime pieces. Richard bent down to inspect them as that really was all they had to go on; also, it was ingrained in him by his nan that if you 'see a penny, pick it up and all day long you'll have good luck'. It was now almost a Pavlovian response in him that he should do exactly that.

'Ow!' he whined, standing up suddenly and rubbing the back of his head with his Passepartout-free hand, as he watched a twenty-centime piece roll into place behind the others. Passepartout began his low growl again, adding to Richard's exasperation. 'Don't have a go at me! Things keep falling on me!' he growled back at the animal.

'Ssh, please!' Valérie hissed. 'Both of you.' Richard and Passepartout shot each other a resentful glance. 'Where are you, Henri?' Passepartout growled again; he seemed to have developed his own Pavlovian response to the presence of the Commissaire.

Out of the dark night air came a long, frustrated, heavily soaked in defeat, sigh. It felt like an endless breeze of disenchantment. A muted howl against the injustices of existence.

'I am up here, madame,' came the eventual and formal reply, from a surprisingly stoic and calm Commissaire Lapierre.

The three of them looked up slowly to see a high-level policeman dangling in the moonlight. It was quite a sight. The Commissaire's left ankle was being held in the loop of a heavy rope, while the rest of his body hung limply like a discarded puppet. The hems of his trousers were calf high revealing the tops of his black socks and, even in the moonlight, the whitest calves Richard had ever seen, which from someone growing up in 1970s England was quite some achievement on Lapierre's part. Fortunately his shirt had remained tucked in but his perennially ill-fitting suit jacket had ridden up giving him the air of a failed escapologist. The worst indignity of all from Richard's point of view was the tie. It hung straight down over his reddened, upside-down face and if there was something he could do about it, he'd long since given up. Still, Richard thought, if the tie is as food-stained as it usually is, he could use it like a salt lick if his imprisonment was long term. Remarkably, the Commissaire's porkpie hat was still in place.

Richard's first instinct was to step out from directly underneath the policeman. Being hit by one falling public servant in a day could be considered bad luck; being hit by two falling public servants suggests habit, one he was keen to break. The second was that this was an opportunity too good to miss. So he whipped his phone out and took a picture of the Commissaire, the flash sending the poor man into paroxysms of frustration. 'For my collection,' he said cheerfully.

Valérie turned off her torch clearly deciding that the view was too unpleasant to be continued with.

'Could you help me down, do you suppose?' The Commissaire was trying his best to keep both temper and dignity but both were at breaking point.

'Yes,' Valérie's reply sounded almost distracted. 'Shortly.' She turned to Richard and whispered, 'We should use this Richard, we have our advantage.'

They both heard the Commissaire tut loudly.

'I agree,' Richard whispered back, 'but let's not push it too far, we still need him onside.' Valérie nodded.

'Henri…' Her tone spelt danger for the policeman as it bordered on jaunty and respectful.

'Madame, may I remind you that I am an officer of the law and as such you have a duty, a civic duty, to help me should I require the assistance of…'

'Yes, yes, yes,' was her less than respectful reply. 'There are a few little things you can help us with though, I think.'

'I do not think this is either the time or the place!' Lapierre was finally losing his temper now. 'Cut me down!'

'Why are you here, Henri, what is this new evidence that you have?'

'And does it let Madame Tablier off the hook?' Richard asked. It was an unfortunate turn of phrase given the policeman's equally unfortunate circumstances, but luckily it went over his head. Or under his head, depending on your point of view.

The Commissaire fell silent, mulling over his options which from Richard's vantage point seemed distinctly limited. Just then they heard a commotion approaching from down the street. The Commissaire's cry as he stepped into Oriane's mantrap had clearly carried far through the night air, and it sounded like a posse had been rounded up at the Auberge Cuistot and was heading this way, presumably pitchfork and flame torches at the ready – they seemed the type in Richard's eyes.

'Can I remind you, madame, this is a police investigation and...'

'You don't have time for that, Henri!' Valérie snapped. 'You do not want the whole village to see you like this I presume!'

The Commissaire tried to wriggle free, using his anger as a force but gave up pretty quickly having only succeeded in emptying his pockets further. 'I am not very happy about this, Valérie,' he said meekly while noticing that the noise of the approaching crowd was growing louder. He glanced fearfully in its direction. 'I haven't got the time now!' he pleaded.

Valérie was calmness personified and clearly enjoying herself too. 'Richard,' her voice was steady and clear, 'could you delay them for a little while, do you think? The Commissaire and I have a few things to discuss.'

Without even looking up Richard became aware of a look of pure hostility coming from above, like a really irate bat, but a look that was also tinged with doubt that Richard was up to the task. Richard wasn't sure he was up to the task either frankly, but he saw that they needed time to press home their advantage and Valérie was more likely to achieve that without Richard's presence further damaging the man's ego.

'Right-o,' he said, and disappeared out of Valérie's torchlight, before nipping back quickly, handing over a relieved Passepartout and taking another flash photo of the stricken Lapierre. 'Say cheese!' he said, before scurrying off.

As a rule Richard wasn't the spontaneous, think on your feet, man of action type. Where he did have the advantage though was that, as a former film historian, he had spent a lifetime watching characters who were, and he now had in mind Richard Hannay from *The 39 Steps*, a man chased up and down the country finding himself in scrape after scrape and improvising his way through them with flair and eventually winning out. With that in mind, normally at this point he would spend a moment to decide just exactly which Richard Hannay he was to be: the Robert Donat/Hitchcock version of 1935, Kenneth More of 1959 or Robert Powell of 1978? But then he realised with some disappointment that he really didn't have the time to iron out this particular wrinkle of his upcoming deception, and that he'd better just get on with it.

He staggered out of Oriane's gate and stumbled briskly up the road to meet the throng and head them off as it were. He stopped in front of them, pretending to be out of breath and wiping a handkerchief across his brow, Hannay style. He then dusted off his trousers for added effect. The group watched him silently, but with no apparent concern.

'Madame Moulin,' he breathed heavily, and maybe slightly overdoing it, 'do you always set garden traps for unfortunate passers-by like that?'

A look of horror and embarrassment crossed Oriane's features as she realised what he was talking about. 'Oh, Richard, I am so sorry. That was not intended for you! Are you hurt?' Her concern seemed genuine and Richard decided to milk it for all it was worth even if the others in the party, de la Cour, Madame Cuistot, Bridille and Agnès Valadon looked bored already. Whatever had happened, they conveyed, was obviously not serious enough to tear them abruptly away from their drinks. Resentment hung in the air.

'What's going on here?' Inevitably Lennard Bridille was the one to assume some sort of command and he strode forward like a general assessing the scene, one where the danger had already passed.

'You set traps in your garden?' Agnès Valadon asked. For the first time since Richard had made her acquaintance, the woman seemed impressed by something.

Oriane shrugged sheepishly. 'I don't trust alarms and things like that. Somebody else has to fit them, and so somebody else knows how to remove them.' She pointed her toes inwards towards each other like a child, and put her hands deep in her pockets. 'I have my own methods.'

Richard paused before saying anything else, making a mental note to bear in mind that, in his opinion, she was a very, very dangerous woman.

'And why were you in Madame Moulin's garden in the first place.' As a result of an evening spent in wine,

Christophe de la Cour had turned the 'sneering' dial up to ten. His question showed no kind of regard for Oriane Moulin's safety – presumably he knew she could very well take care of herself – but more a dislike of Richard himself. Whatever brief mollifying effect Richard's English background had had on the man, it had most certainly worn off.

'Sorry?' Richard asked as if slightly affronted, hoping that a visible display of British 'are you talking to me, my good man?' genes might help.

'I asked why you were in Madame Moulin's garden in the first place? Why are you skulking about?'

'Ah,' he said, brushing himself down some more, 'good question.'

He left it there.

'Would you consider answering it?' de la Cour wasn't letting go.

'Well, erm, well, we came back to La Chapelle because…'

'La Chapelle-sur-Follet to you!' snapped the absurd Lennard Bridille.

'Ah, yes, quite right.' Richard was desperately hoping that Valérie had negotiated and released the Commissaire by now, but as she hadn't turned up, he had no choice but to continue. 'Well, we returned to La Chapelle-sur-Follet because…'

'Valérie had forgotten her little dog's bed,' Madame Cuistot intervened helpfully. 'They came back to get it.'

'Yes, that's it.' Richard confirmed.

'It's a long way to come for a dog's bed, isn't it?' Agnès Valadon was joining in on the interrogation now and enjoying herself to boot.

'I think they're very attached.' Madame Cuistot, whether deliberately or not, was helping Richard out enormously.

'Yes, very attached.' Again he backed up her statement.

'And you left it in Madame Moulin's garden, did you?' Richard was taking a very strong dislike to Christophe de la Cour; even in the moonlight his ridiculous tan stood out. He looked like the amber section of a traffic light.

'No!' Madame Cuistot clearly couldn't help herself. 'They left it at my place!'

'And so the question remains.' De la Cour took a menacing step forward, and Richard noticed Oriane tense the same way he'd seen Valérie do so when action might be called for. He hoped it was in his defence.

'It really doesn't matter,' she laughed. 'Richard can visit anytime he likes.'

This time Lennard Bridille stepped forward, though half a pace behind the taller de la Cour. 'I'm afraid it does matter, Madame Moulin, we are charged with looking after La Chapelle...'

'Sur-Follet,' Richard threw in.

'And I don't think our *traiteur* here is interested in flora.' Richard didn't like the way de la Cour said 'traiteur', he made it sound an awful lot like 'peasant', but the word flora triggered something else in him.

'Actually you are wrong.' He stood up to his full height, which was still somewhere below that of the antique dealer. 'I have always had a great interest in flora, ever since I was young.'

His sudden confidence put a slight brake on the committee in front of him.

'Oh yes?' Bridille's suspicions had slightly lost their edge, but clearly he felt obliged to ask for some explanation.

'Near where I grew up, there was an old abandoned church and we used to play there as children.' Richard settled in for a long anecdote. 'My sister fell in love with gardening and created a garden in the church, there was no roof you see.'

'What is your sister's name?' Agnès Valadon was after another name for her database.

'Sorry?'

'What was she called, your sister?'

'What was she called?' he stammered. 'You mean what was her name?' They all took another step closer. 'Clare!' he blurted out suddenly. 'She's called Clare! Anyway, our parents died and a kindly old woman at a gardening group took us in and...'

'Richard, are you OK?' Valérie appeared at his shoulder. 'I found Passepartout eventually, he must have scented your Zsa Zsa, Oriane.' The group visibly relaxed but with some disappointment. 'Did I hear a scream?' Valérie added for good measure.

'That was me,' Richard was pleased to admit. 'I got caught in a rope trap... but luckily I had my gardening knife on me... which I've now lost.' He suddenly ran out of steam. 'Can we go home now?'

'Of course!' Valérie put her arm through his while her other hand held Passepartout's lead. 'Oh, Oriane, old habits die hard, I suppose.'

They turned and walked away slowly, just as Agnès Valadon shouted after them, 'I'll be checking the camera to make sure you've gone!' before she was shushed by Bridille and de la Cour.

They eventually made it back to the car with some relief.

'You were right, Richard, she does have a camera!' Valérie looked back in the direction they'd come and shook her head.

'Well, I hope she enjoys the footage. I'm just glad that's over!' He leant against the bonnet.

'You are very clever though, Richard!' Valérie's smile and her gleaming white teeth lit up in the moonlight as she turned back to him. 'Making up a story like that!'

Richard looked almost hurt. 'Make it up? That's the plot of *Innocent Sinners*, 1958, starring Dame *Flora* Robson.'

'And the little girl in the film was called Clare, the same as your wife?'

'No. That was the first name that came to mind. I'm sure it won't matter.'

Chapter Fifteen

Valérie had been in one of her more pensive moods on the drive back, so Richard had decided to avoid the subject of the upside-down Commissaire for the moment. Breakfast was different though. She had descended full of energy, clearly looking forward to the day, and with an impatience that bordered on rudeness. She even helped serve the Fournier family, though drew a sharp line at any clearing-up. The Fourniers themselves left fairly early as they had a rendezvous in Tours, something about a new kitchen, and the way Valérie practically shooed them out suggested she wanted to get on with her plans for the pair of them also.

'We have an appointment, Richard, this morning, with the Commissaire.' It was a statement of triumph and it was obvious that she felt a breakthrough in Madame Tablier's case was imminent.

Richard was filling the dishwasher and had his back to her. 'Will he be the right way up this time, do you think?'

She didn't laugh and in fact her face as he turned was markedly more serious. 'I do not know.' Her reply left him somewhat confused, but then she had probably not been listening. 'There was no time last evening to get any information out of him, despite your best efforts I must say –

brilliant!' Richard blushed slightly. 'But when I told him that you had taken the pictures of him and that you would use them if you had to, he changed his tune I can tell you.'

He took a moment to deal with this. 'You told the Commissaire of Police that I was prepared to blackmail him if we didn't get our way?'

'Yes!' she exclaimed misreading his sudden very high levels of anxiety as excitement.

'Right-o.' He sat down and whatever flush had briefly appeared on his cheeks had now turned to white, his smile was rictus and he looked like his own death mask. Richard could never have named Commissaire Henri Lapierre as a close friend, not even a friend, but that kind of proxy threat was very much guaranteed to make him an enemy. Needless to say, he wasn't looking forward to the meeting.

'I think we should take my car,' he said finally, standing up.

'We don't want to be late, Richard,' Valérie said gently, without actually saying overtly that not only was the car slow but Richard barely got it out of third gear anyway.

'It's psychology,' he replied, not bothering to address the subtext. 'I think the Commissaire will feel vulnerable after last night, on the back foot as it were...' he added, briefly slipping into English.

'The back foot?'

'It's a cricket reference, it doesn't matter right now. The point is, if we turn up in your car, he'll feel even more put upon, like we're bragging about our position, our status. If we want to get anything out of him, anything of value that is, we have to look like we're on his side, and that we could help him even.'

'We can't just use your pictures?' She looked genuinely put out.

'As a last resort,' Richard sighed. 'What time is the meeting anyway?' He put the last of the breakfast crockery in the dishwasher.

'I said I would be there at eight.' Valérie's chin stuck out as a show of business-like determination.

'And Lapierre said?'

'That he would be there at ten.'

Richard laughed. He suspected that it was done in ignorance but the Commissaire had quoted one of his favourite lines of *Casablanca* and that cheered him up immensely. He may, as usual, not have the faintest idea what was going on, whether Madame Tablier was even guilty of murder or not, but the fact that Audrey Hepburn, Dame Flora Robson and *Casablanca* were obliquely involved was immensely cheering.

'Come on then,' he said, grabbing his keys. 'Hi-ho, hi-ho, it's off to work we go!'

Valérie picked up Passepartout and followed him out of the door suspiciously. 'Are you feeling OK, Richard?'

A couple of hours later and his mood had changed markedly. He had had an idea that Lapierre would try to wrestle back some of the advantage he had lost the previous evening, but he hadn't banked on the man being quite so rude. It was now 11.30 and they were still waiting in the reception area of the local *gendarmerie*. Valérie was verging on the apoplectic and had, on more than one occasion, asked Richard to text his pictures of a suspended Commissaire to give the man a nudge. So far he'd refused on the basis that they may come in handier later and also that Valérie had been texting the man all morning and he hadn't responded. Richard was far more upset that Madame Tablier had actually refused to meet them to discuss what was going on. The young sergeant at the desk had been very apologetic, but the prisoner had rights, she had stressed. Richard couldn't understand her attitude and even felt a little hurt.

'This is intolerable!' Valérie stood up out of her seat for the umpteenth time. 'I pay my taxes and I demand to see the Commissaire. I demand to see him now!'

Richard looked with some sympathy at the young desk sergeant who stared back at him with a look suggesting that Valérie must be Hell to live with.

'Madame,' she tried interrupting Valérie's flow. 'Madame d'Orçay!'

She appealed to Richard for help, who stood and put Passepartout in Valérie's arms to act as a kind of pacifier. 'Here,' he said gently, while slowly the small dog had a calming effect, and the policewoman was able to continue.

'Now. I realise that you want to see Commissaire Lapierre, but he is not here and the appointment that you say you had is not in the Commissaire's diary. There is very little I can do.' She was trying her best and starting to succeed, then she made a fatal error. 'Maybe you could try again after lunch?' she asked, unknowingly lighting the fuse on Valérie's personality Catherine Wheel.

Valérie, while on the one hand being the Frenchest person Richard had ever known, also had a streak of Englishness in her which meant she could skip mealtimes if there was something else going on. As such, she regarded the idea that the Commissaire may have gone straight from breakfast to lunch and bypassed Valérie on the way as the worst possible insult. Richard was waiting for the volcano to blow; even Passepartout looked like he wanted to jump ship.

'Good morning, everyone.' Commissaire Lapierre appeared through the double doors, a cheerful look on his face and not only looking much better than when Richard had last seen him, but better than he had ever seen him. He had forsaken his hat and his hair was parted sharply, hiding whatever was left of the fishing injury. His moustache was neatly trimmed and his tie relatively stain-free. The suit was still at least a size too big, but you couldn't have everything. 'I am so sorry that I am late,' he said, walking straight to his office door. 'Follow me, please.'

An unusually silent Valérie did just that, while Richard caught a glimpse of the equally gobsmacked sergeant as he followed her.

'Are you wearing aftershave, Henri?' a stunned Valérie asked before they had even closed the door.

'I am,' the man puffed in return.

'Hmm,' she said. 'It is stale, I think. Never mind.'

It was clear that he did mind, however, though rather than rise to the bait he asked them both to sit down. 'First of all, I have news of your friend, Monsieur Mabit. He has yet to regain consciousness, but is at least breathing unassisted. If he survives, we have eyewitness accounts, together with yours. It seems, monsieur,' he looked at Richard dubiously, 'that should he live, you will have saved his life.' He looked at Richard as though he were a complete fraud. 'Should he live. Now...'

'I want an explanation, Henri,' Valérie immediately jumped in, 'and I want one now. One minute you are hanging upside down, after lurking around I may add, probably trespassing as you would have had no warrant. It was I who cut you down and Richard brilliantly kept the whole village from seeing you up there like a duck hanging in a butcher's window. Do you thank us? No! You keep us waiting for hours while you look like you have had a breakfast assignation, no doubt with a woman, because that is the only time I have ever known you to wear aftershave or even comb your hair for that matter. You must be very taken with her...' Valérie began to slow down.

'Is it that for which you require an explanation, madame?' Henri asked quietly, and not for the first time Richard felt like he shouldn't be there and that they should sort their past out in private.

'Of course it isn't!' she retorted, and took a deep breath to regather herself. Richard stared down at his shoes. 'I am really genuinely happy for you, Henri...' She sighed and Lapierre looked like he was taking this as a victory, that she still cared about him in some way. A benign smile hovered briefly under his moustache before dropping away, probably forever as she continued. 'But really, I want to know why you were in La Chapelle last night.'

He stiffened. 'Why were *you* in La Chapelle last night?' he countered angrily.

'I can answer that.' Richard stepped in like a boxing referee. 'We left Passepartout's bed at the *auberge* by accident and,' the Commissaire gave him a disparaging look, 'we went back to get it.' Richard gulped.

The Commissaire stood up and walked to his window, standing there with his hands clasped behind his back, balancing on the balls of his feet.

'It is obvious you do not believe us!' Valérie huffed, looking for insult.

'Of course I believe you,' the man said without turning around. 'Why would you invent something so absurd?'

'I would say that you were lucky we were there,' Valérie added, her short sentence brimful of overtone. 'Otherwise…'

This time the Commissaire did turn around and Richard made sure he didn't catch his eye. Lapierre sat down heavily and sighed; finally he seemed to come to a decision.

'I was working late,' he began, and then seemed to change tack. 'I know nothing of gardening or tourism or even small village life so once again I must rely on extra resources, the power as a department, that we can muster when we need it.'

'You looked on Wikipedia too?' Richard couldn't help himself but he thought he should step in before Lapierre choked on his own self-importance. Again, he got an icy look for his troubles.

'Yes, monsieur,' came the tart reply.

'And?' Valérie's impatience was boiling over again.

A look of triumph came into his eyes. There is no substitute for good old-fashioned police work, it said. 'There is an image on the website, it is of a…'

'A slate with a quote written in chalk.' Valerie and Richard spoke in unison and if Lapierre had been a balloon he would at that moment have been flying uncontrollably around the room as he deflated.

'The last time I looked it insinuated something about Oriane Moulin,' Valérie continued. '"Even the prettiest flower can be poisonous," if I remember correctly.' She had. Richard refreshed the Wikipedia page on his phone and it had gone back to the original Audrey Hepburn quote, 'To plant a garden is to believe in tomorrow.' He showed it to the others and they both sat back in their chairs.

'What did it say last night, Henri?'

He pursed his lips. 'It was not a quote that is for sure. It was a taunt, a challenge!'

'What did it say, Henri?' she repeated quietly.

He opened his notebook. 'It said, "You have pruned the wrong flower, Commissaire!"' He snapped the book shut.

'It means of course that you must release Madame Tablier.' Valérie snorted angrily. 'Madame Tablier is the wrong flower!'

'A tip-off is hardly enough evidence to release her!' he fired back.

'It was enough to make you suspect her in the first place.' Richard joined in.

'It is true. This *messenger* gave me the information about Madame Tablier, but that yielded hard evidence.'

'And last night?' Richard felt his own frustration rising to a point of anger.

'Last night!' the Commissaire shouted, then calmed himself down. 'Last night, I was interrupted in the course of my investigation.'

'Of course,' Richard said sulkily. 'We have the pictures.'

There was a moment of silence as everyone regrouped and it was Valérie who spoke first. 'Henri, you have doubts about Madame Tablier's guilt, the evidence is at best circumstantial, as you know. Let her go.'

For the first time since the interview began the Commissaire seemed to regain his composure and, Richard noticed, a rather unpleasant, smug twinkle in the eye. He reached into his jacket pocket and like a magician with a bunch of flowers produced a small blue USB computer stick.

'I cannot do that, Madame d'Orçay,' he announced grandly. The smug look was still there, but it was joined by the cold-eyed swagger of a cobra about to strike. 'I have recorded her confession!' He waved the stick aloft, like a trophy. 'The sergeant and I recorded it last night. It will be typed up today. I will let you have a copy when that is done of course. In the meantime, I demand, *demand*, that you stay out of my way and away from La Chapelle-sur-Follet.' He leant back in his chair and let all of this sink in.

Richard had no idea how to respond. First, his trusted Madame Tablier had refused to see him and now this, an apparent confession to murder. He looked to Valérie for help, but for once she seemed as lost as he was. She stood up, putting an end to the meeting. The Commissaire stood too, followed eventually by Richard.

'OK, Henri,' Valérie said gently. 'You win and your threat is clear. Thank you anyway for at least keeping us informed.' He nodded courteously. Valérie shook her head a little sadly as her ex-husband held out his hand for her. 'I am very pleased for you, Henri,' she said with obvious emotion. 'You look good, whoever she is, I hope that she takes care of you.' It sounded almost as if her voice was breaking and she embraced the Commissaire warmly. 'Goodbye,' she said, as the two of them left, though with Richard wondering what was next.

Chapter Sixteen

It wasn't at all unusual for Richard to feel the weight of responsibility; it was, he had often lamented and without real evidence, his lot. It was a responsibility borne out of confusion. So many things were zipping around in his head, like trapped shooting stars bouncing off the walls of a black hole, that he couldn't distinguish between a man on whose shoulders rested great burden or a man who was simply out of his depth and attempting to give his discombobulation some level of dignity. Not so deep down though, he knew that he simply needed the world to stop still while he took stock and caught up. His stupefaction was debilitating to the extent that he now stood at the warm, pungent counter of Jeanine's *boulangerie* with a look on his face which suggested more that he was being confronted by the blackboard scribblings of a mathematical genius and not a heartening array of breadstuffs.

The growing queue behind him was beginning to grumble at his indecision, something of which he was blissfully unaware and which Valérie couldn't have cared less about. She did have a concerned look on her face, however, as Richard, having placed his order, appeared now to have shut down as though he were a television on standby, a level of inaction that she just couldn't understand. If she could have seen inside Richard's head at that point though it would not have been inaction she saw; instead she would have witnessed a raging battle, one being fought on many fronts.

One skirmish was still his utter, one hundred per cent, rock-solid conviction that Madame Tablier was innocent of the murder, if it was murder, of Duval Cuistot. A personal dogma undermined only slightly by Madame Tablier's apparent confession to said murder. Then there was the tourist village that seemingly hated visitors and was run by a group of squabbling grotesques who were like the cast of an old Hollywood B movie bickering over an inheritance, though that was to their credit as it gave him something to hang on to. The Fournier family worried him too, but he couldn't for the life of him work out why. Aside from the potential murder case, he had an unopened legal letter from his estranged wife. And to top it all, though he would never have admitted this publicly – even internally it made him squirm – Commissaire Lapierre was apparently at the beginning of a romantic relationship, which in basic terms meant that he was getting more action than Richard. It was this inequity that was tipping the balance of Richard's mind. Richard liked to think he knew what women wanted. Hollywood had taught him that it was to be stoic but open, and so he acted like a man who wore his heart on his sleeve without actually doing so, and yet here he was losing out in the romance stakes to a man who not only didn't wear his heart on his sleeve, but wore his breakfast on his lapel.

'It's just not right!' he exclaimed loudly.

'Quite right, monsieur!' claimed a man at the back of the queue.

'It's an injustice!' shouted an old woman, banging her walking stick on the floor aggressively as she did so.

This chorus of approval broke Richard from his internal warfare. Valérie was rolling her eyes apologetically at Jeanine, who despite having a soft spot for Richard, was none too pleased with his new-found revolutionary antics.

'It is hardly my fault!' Jeanine flushed as she addressed the queue. 'The basic cost of flour, of butter…'

'…of bloody everything!' Someone else joined in in support.

'Yes, of everything! It means that I have to raise my prices. I am sorry, but there it is.' The small crowd went back to their grumbling. They knew it wasn't Jeanine's fault that bread was getting more expensive, and they had made their point now anyway. 'So, Richard,' she turned to him, not showing her usual warmth. 'That is one euro twenty centimes, please. I need another twenty centimes from you.'

Richard, in his reverie of investigative self-pity had been operating on auto-pilot and now went back to his trouser pocket searching for the added coinage. He took out his closed hand and opened it out, searching for the right change. Looking down he noticed with a kind of detached resignation that among what his father had called the shrapnel was a blue USB stick. He tilted his head at it like a puppy trying to understand instructions and went back on standby. Valérie took twenty centimes from his palm, gave it to Jeanine, again apologetically, and ushered Richard out of the *boulangerie*.

They walked in silence for a while, until they came to Café des Tasses Cassées and Richard stopped as if suddenly remembering something from the distant past. 'I need a drink,' he said quietly and turned towards the glass doors. Valérie followed silently, almost like a care worker, such was his apparent detachment from reality.

Their way into René's bar and brasserie, a place Richard regarded as his local, was blocked by a brightly dressed couple on their way out who Richard, in his daze, didn't at first recognise.

'Ah, Richard, old man.' Martin Thompson, usually so ebullient to the point of over familiarity looked surprised and a little put out to bump into his friend.

'Oh! Richard, Valérie!' Martin's wife Gennie was caught equally off guard and together they had the air of teenagers who had been caught shoplifting.

It was Valérie who noticed all of this though as Richard, despite previously regarding the Thompsons as a pair of wanton and professional sex maniacs, who constantly and irritatingly sought his company, now regarded them almost as comforts. Never-changing constants in a world of shifting sands. Yes, their 'specialist couples holidays' at their B&B were a blot on the local tourist landscape, in his eyes at least, and Martin's relentless attempts at bawdy innuendo were draining but they were, he'd concluded, good people. Salt of the earth. You knew where you stood.

'Fancy a drink?' he asked pleadingly.

'Ah, well…' spluttered Martin.

'We'd love to but…' Gennie helped.

'We're late as it is, aren't we, old girl?'

'Oh, yes!' Gennie agreed. 'Late.'

'Late.' Martin added after a pause.

'You have an appointment?' Valérie asked, sensing something wasn't quite right.

'Oh yes!' Gennie sounded as if Valérie had guessed it out of the blue.

'And we're late!' Martin was edging away, Gennie at his side, their steps in unison. 'See you… er…'

'Soon!' Gennie finished the sentence as they scuttled away.

Richard shook his head and closed his eyes. It was just one more thing that he hadn't the capacity to deal with for the moment. He slouched towards one of the discreet corner booths that René had recently installed with a view to capitalising on the infidelity market, and slumped down heavily, relieved not to see or be seen.

Valérie sat next to him quietly, waiting for what she expected to be an explosion. Though Richard being Richard, the explosion may occur internally, the only discernible difference to an outside world that a grown man had finally had enough and erupted would be a slight flushing of the cheeks and some form of low-key indigestion. Even René, usually brusque and confident as only men with a history of criminal strong-armery can be, could see Richard was on the edge and delivered their usual drinks in silence, though he winked conspiratorially at Valérie as he departed, indicating he had something to tell her.

Richard began drumming his fingers on the table. 'So let me get this straight.' His calmness was forced and in fact had all the relaxation of a hostage on a kidnapper's video trying to stress everything was fine.

'Yes?' Valérie prompted after what felt like ages.

'You pickpocketed the Commissaire of Police and stole evidence…' She began to interrupt but he held up a finger to his lips like a school teacher and shook his head gently. 'The same Commissaire of Police to whom you have sworn I am prepared to blackmail. You then deposit the stolen evidence into my pocket. Is that about the size of it?'

Valérie had a look of doubt on her face. To her Richard had delivered his statement like an accusation but it was merely the facts as she saw them too. She didn't see his problem at all.

'Yes, Richard,' she said slowly. 'We now have Madame Tablier's so-called confession. We can make our own conclusions! You never know, she may have been tortured!'

'You seem to be missing the point, Madame d'Orçay.' He was trying to stay calm but the stress vein in his forehead looked like a river about to burst its banks. 'If he had noticed the USB key was missing, he would have searched us both and found it on me! Blackmail, stealing evidence… that would have been the icing on the cake to go with his new-found success!'

'What do you mean success, success with what?'

Richard blinked. 'Never mind that. I could have been locked up! He'd have thrown away the key!' He paused, then raised his voice even higher. 'What do you mean torture?' He realised he was speaking far too loudly and lowered his voice, unnecessarily repeating the question. 'What do you mean torture?'

'I do not believe Madame Tablier killed Duval Cuistot any more than you do. So if she has made a confession, it must have been under duress, no?'

Richard fell back into the buttoned leather seating of the booth. The solid determination he had had to bring Valérie to book and to put some order into what was an increasingly messy situation was lost, perhaps only momentarily, but the thought that Madame Tablier might have been tortured into confession took precedence. Not that, for one second, he assumed that to be the case, but that his investigations business partner and friend of uncertain status might actually believe it to be true, that was the worry. *That's it*, he thought sadly, *the woman's gone totally gaga.*

'You don't seriously believe that Lapierre, your ex-husband, would torture Madame Tablier into confessing to a murder she didn't commit, do you? That's insane!'

'Is it?' Her reply was dripping with portent. 'Why does he feel the need to close the case of Duval Cuistot so quickly? It is not like him.' Richard tried to interrupt, but was overridden. 'He is a good policeman, yes. But not a fast one. Who is giving him these clues, this extra information? Why? Why is it now a murder where it was not before? Who is causing trouble in the village of La Chapelle, and who – and I believe this to be important, Richard.' He gulped. 'Who is his girlfriend?'

Richard closed his eyes and went back over what she had said. All good questions obviously, and they needed asking. Except for maybe the girlfriend one which frankly smacked of jealousy. But none of them would explain why she believed Lapierre had tortured Madame Tablier, an idea that became more absurd the more he thought about it.

'Look…' he began.

'Oriane Moulin!' Valérie exclaimed triumphantly.

Richard stared at her for a full minute, trying to work out if, once again, she hadn't blown a fuse. Eventually, and without taking his eyes off her he shouted, 'Two more drinks, René, please!'

'You don't agree?' she pleaded.

'I need far more alcohol before I agree to that kind of theory!' It was only then that he heard the coquettish giggling coming from the booth next door, which had the effect of disgusting him.

René brought the drinks over. 'Are you two all right?' The question was whispered so quietly that they barely heard it, but they duly nodded reluctantly that everything was just about OK. He retreated, looking unconvinced.

'We need to go back, Richard, we need to spend more time there and get under the skin of these people.'

He couldn't argue with that, though it seemed to him increasingly clear that the woman was obsessed with Oriane Moulin, due to some professional, maybe even personal jealousy. A long-held grudge maybe that was clouding her judgement.

'I agree, but Lapierre will arrest us on the spot if he finds us there, you heard his warning and that was before he knew you, we, had stolen his vital evidence! It's too risky.' He sighed which only had the effect of annoying Valérie hugely.

'Oh, Richard!' she exclaimed with some passion. 'You must take risks in life, nothing, nothing can be achieved without risk!' The annoying giggling from next door became louder, interrupting his train of thought.

'They think you are a *traiteur*.' The giggling became almost a guffaw. *Bloody secret lovers*, he thought. 'They also know now that you have an interest in gardening, an interest on behalf of your sister.'

'Oh but that was pretty vague stuff!' he argued.

'It is a start,' she said thoughtfully. 'What did you say your sister was called?'

'Clare,' he replied guiltily. 'I said my sister was called Clare.'

A glass smashed in the booth next door, followed by an angry cry. Then two heads popped up above the partition that divided them. One was of a young man with a smug grin and the second was an attractive blond woman with an angry, very red, very recognisable face. 'Hello, Richard, surprised to see me! I'm your long-lost sister Clare!'

Chapter Seventeen

Richard sat on the bench in the chicken coop while his hens, Olivia de Havilland, Lana Turner and Joan Crawford pecked fussily and warily, unusually for them, at his feet. Under normal circumstances this was Richard's happy place, his oasis, a bubble of tranquillity protecting him against the iniquities of the modern world. The scowl, however, like a dark cloud on his face, strongly suggested that the bubble was under enormous pressure and that the modern world was in danger of bursting it completely.

'Oh do stop sulking, Richard, you're upsetting your hens. I honestly think you care more about them than you ever did about me anyway.' Clare sat on a bench opposite him but on the other side of the coop's chicken wire fence, giving the whole scene a prison visit look but one in which neither knew who was the prisoner or who was the visitor.

'I am not sulking.' Richard's sulky tone was harsher than it would normally be with Clare, or with anyone for that matter, but she had assumed, and was continuing to assume that Richard would be on the defensive. He wasn't, and nobody was more surprised at that than Richard himself. 'Why are you here? Why do you keep popping up like this?' He didn't think either an unreasonable question.

She looked genuinely hurt. 'Why do you not answer any correspondence?' she countered. They both knew she had him there. 'I would hazard a guess you've not even opened the letter that was sent?'

'Well that shows what you know,' he replied a trifle petulantly, beckoning Lana Turner towards him. 'The letter from Forshaw-Banks you mean, solicitors?' He added 'solicitors' as though it were a dirty word, and then went on the attack. 'Who's your boyfriend anyway?'

'His name is Oliver Forshaw-Banks.' She allowed a tactical pause while this sank in. 'And he's not my boyfriend,' again, 1-2-3 and… 'he's my fiancé.'

Bloody hell she's good! Richard acknowledged to himself. *Any boxer would have been proud of that as a jab-jab, uppercut.* What was different though, what was remarkably distinct from how these things usually went, is that Richard was not metaphorically lying on his back on the canvas undergoing the count. This time he was still standing. He had taken her best shots and they had just slid off what was now, perhaps momentarily, his granite jaw. The only element of disquiet he felt was just how little disquiet he actually felt; this was definitely progress. He stressed this nonchalance by picking up Lana Turner and stroking her back, like a cool supervillain.

'I'd say the fiancé thing is a bit premature, darling, wouldn't you?' Inside he felt as coolly nonchalant as Roger Moore. 'What with you being married still?'

She clicked her fingers at him, like a hypnotist waking up a subject under their spell. 'Hello! Richard!' she barked. 'Where were you? Let me guess. It'll be black and white, something David Niven-ish…'

'You're losing your touch, Clare.' He smiled at her, and she smiled back.

'We need to do this, Richard, we need to move on.'

'Yes! I knew it! Yes!' came a sudden and exultant cry from Valérie's bedroom window above and Richard and Clare looked at each other in astonishment. Surely she couldn't be listening? Even if she was, neither could imagine that would be her reaction. 'I knew you were hiding something, Henri!' was Valérie's euphoric follow-up. Richard and Clare smiled at each other again, both a little relieved.

'Shouldn't I vet this Oliver Forshaw-Banks, make sure his intentions are appropriately dishonourable?' Richard put Lana Turner back on the ground and stood up. 'You know what these ambulance chasers are like. Why didn't you both stay here, anyway?'

'Oh, far too awkward, Richard, as well you know!' She stood up too. 'Anyway, Olly certainly thought so. I left him to make a booking nearby and...'

Richard burst out laughing. 'Now I understand why Martin and Gennie were so sheepish! You're staying there, aren't you? Ha! I almost feel sorry for *Olly*. Where is he anyway?'

'I asked him to have a wander around *our* place and to leave us to it,' Clare replied a little too quickly.

'You mean he's pricing things up?' Clare flushed. 'Well, at least you'll get a discount on his bill, smart move.' His level of sarcasm surprised them both.

'Don't be like that, Richard.'

'Clare! Clare!' They both heard the aforementioned Oliver Forshaw-Banks approaching through the garden somewhere.

'I'm here,' she paused, 'darling!' Clare shouted without taking her eyes off Richard. The tall, slim figure of Forshaw-Banks appeared around the corner. He couldn't have looked more like an Englishman if he'd tried. He wore peach-coloured slacks and tan boating shoes, no socks and a dark blue rugby shirt with the white collar turned up. His sunglasses were pushed up through chestnut coloured hair and the whole ensemble had the look of a Next catalogue photoshoot circa 1992 which, Richard noted with some amusement, was probably not far off the year the man had been born.

'Oh, Clare! Honestly! He's about half your age!' He exaggerated for deliberate effect.

Her eyes blinked rapidly and she looked on the verge of a massive eruption, but was interrupted before she could blow.

'This place must be worth a great deal,' Oliver shouted from across the lawn. 'Especially with a successful business attached. I'd knock down that hen coop thing though and add a yurt, they're very popular.' It was then he noticed Richard and added quickly, 'Though the market is depressed obviously.'

'Get together the paperwork, Clare, then we can, as you say, move on.' Richard's tone was pure Western sheriff against gun-toting cattle rustlers. A line had been drawn.

He closed and locked the chicken coop behind him. He had decided to take no chances after discovering the Fournier boy in with his hens. He was just wondering how he could walk away from the situation with Clare and her fiancé when his phone rang. 'Ah,' he said brightly, 'excuse me!'

He walked around the corner where Oliver had come from. 'Hello…'

'Daddy?'

'Alicia! How lovely to hear from you!' One of the sadly many positives of his marriage break-up had been how much closer he and his daughter had become. In his initially beleaguered state he'd considered Alicia a chip off the old maternal block, an unfair comparison which proved how little he actually knew her. He hadn't given her husband, estate agent Sly, much of a chance to impress either, and he had been wrong on that score too. Alicia, it turned out, had made a study of her mother also and had come to many of the same conclusions as he had. That she was something of a social snob and rural France had offered her nothing in that regard. Clare missed the excitement, the travel and the social side of her career in PR and Richard, though she loved him in her own way, was a hindrance to that life. And Richard, feeling bereft at first, realised that she was right and was actually quite relieved.

They made pleasant small talk, moving on to more detail when talking about her and Sly's latest attempts to have children. Obviously Richard zoned out when she started talking about handstands and prime ovulation windows, but he got the gist. Then she fell silent. 'Daddy?' she asked quietly. 'Is Mummy there?'

'She is, yes.' He no longer had to feign enthusiasm. 'Do you want to talk to her?'

'No!' she replied quickly, then fell silent again.

'What's up, love?' Richard asked gently and he heard her sigh on the other end.

'Is she there with that bloke of hers?'

'Young Olly? Yes, she is. She knows how to get a bargain,' he joked. 'She'll get money off his fee I'd have thought.'

'Daddy, it's not funny. Sly thinks he's a crook.'

Richard paused. 'It's not really any of my business.'

'It is if she takes your house off you! Sly thinks there was a bit of scandal a few years ago. He's been married a few times, never for very long, always to a divorcee with property. He's done very well out of it apparently.'

He should have felt aghast at the news but instead felt oddly cheered by it. While he and Valérie had built a business on mystery and crime, he just couldn't consider Clare being involved, albeit innocently, in any criminal plots herself. Besides, seedy, womanising lawyers were a failed film cliché who always got their comeuppance. He was reconciled to losing half of his property, that couldn't be avoided and was only fair. What Clare did with her half was frankly none of his business. He didn't argue with Alicia, just said that he'd keep an eye on things and that she should concentrate on her 'gymnastic stuff'.

They said goodbye and he unwittingly turned back into Clare and her fiancé. That would take some getting used to: Oliver, the fiancé. Safe platitudes about the weather and so on were exchanged and then Richard said he really must get on.

'Do let me know if you need anything.' He smiled.

'That's very good of you, Rich,' Oliver said, as if they'd been rugby club mates for years.

'Richard. Don't mention it.'

'Just act like we're not here.' Clare was oddly nervous.

'Oh, I will,' he replied, not caring that he might be overplaying his hand. 'I really will.'

He left them, even whistling a tune as he did so, but then he was in a jaunty mood, so why not? The marriage had ended long before now and Clare was more than capable of looking after herself. It was very sweet of Alicia to be looking out for him, but she underestimated her mother. If there was a game of legal cat and mouse, brinkwomanship or even downright dark arts, his money would not be on Oliver Forshaw-Banks as a winner, no matter how slippery a customer he was.

He walked into the salon and poured himself a coffee. Then he changed his mind and made himself a cup of chamomile tea instead. He had felt a surge of excitement this morning. He was in control of himself and the situation with Clare and, to an extent, Valérie. He was not being bullied, he had begrudgingly accepted how Valérie had pushed him to *possibly* save Noel Mabit's life, the same with Clare bringing a 'fiancé' with her, he was indifferent about that too. Let them.

But, he was feeling, what? What was he feeling about himself? OK, he decided. He was feeling OK. It might be, finally, the end game in his marriage but news about Noel Mabit was encouraging, sort of, he was breathing on his own anyway. His priority, for now, was still Madame Tablier and none of Clare's or her divorcee collector boyfriend's antics were going to put him off. Hence the chamomile and not caffeine; he didn't want to get carried away with himself. Why on earth would you want to be married so many times anyway? And if it was for the money, as Alicia had suggested, surely there must be easier ways to make a buck than multiple marriages? Richard concluded that he'd prefer to auction off his bodily organs rather than re-marry. Against that of course, property, the right property, could be measured in fortunes, whereas his liver for instance…

'Hang on!' He jumped out of his chair. 'Valérie! Where are you?' He started to run upstairs and bumped into Valérie who was on her way down, laptop in one hand, Passepartout under her other arm. 'Property!' They both exclaimed simultaneously. 'Property!'

Five minutes later they had both calmed down and were sitting at a table. Richard had doubled up on the chamomile while Valérie had poured a glass of wine.

'Henri's USB stick contains more than Madame Tablier's confession, a lot more!' She could barely contain herself.

'But there is a confession?' Richard knew there would be, he had just hoped differently.

'Oh yes, but I do not believe a word of it!'

'No torture?'

'I don't think so. She sounds, I don't know, bored I think. As if she just wants it over with.'

Richard nodded. If it had been an impassioned plea, he wouldn't have believed it. Affected boredom was her default character though. It was like a mess that she wanted tidied up, but he still refused to believe it.

'So what else is there?' he asked, keen to see how they had come to roughly the same conclusion.

'Henri, to give him some credit, has been busy and there are a lot of files he has found about deeds and ownership. Look.' She clicked on a newspaper cutting and there they all were, the committee and a couple of other men, holding up banners protesting against the ruination of the countryside, building new towns, etc. 'There was a new estate built just outside of the village. And also, yes, Oriane Moulin owns her house, but it seems she is one of the few who does.'

'I'm not sure what that means?' he asked, still distracted by the press cutting.

'Maybe nothing. Only that she was always very bad with money. She has been bankrupt more than once, I know...'

Richard thought about this. Firstly, he felt Valérie was still being blinded by Oriane Moulin but more than that, how would that be a motive to kill Duval Cuistot? Quite the opposite, she wasn't reliant on the patronage of the village committee. 'But...' he began slowly.

'All of the other committee members own their property, but a lot of the houses in the village are owned by a trust, and who do you think is head of this trust?'

'The committee?'

'Not quite!' Valérie clapped her hands. 'Guess! No, don't guess, we haven't time, Madame Cuistot! Madame Cuistot is in charge of a trust that owns more than half of the property in La Chapelle-sur-Follet! She is the executor of this trust and the other committee members answer to her.'

'And she inherited this on the death of her husband?' Richard was ahead of her and finding it easier to temper his enthusiasm.

'No! No. It was hers already. It has been for years.' She beamed an enormous smile at him.

'Great!' he replied with lead-density sarcasm. 'And her next of kin is?'

'Oh.'

Richard shook his head sadly. 'Well, aren't we doing well?' he said caustically. 'We've succeeded in taking

Madame Tablier's motive and multiplying it by twelve! Brilliant.'

The door to the salon opened and the heavy cloud that was the Fournier family sloped in, a picture of kinship misery. Sullen greetings were made, even Fabrice seemed to have lost any interest in mischief. They made for their room upstairs, before Madame Fournier turned back to them.

'We shan't need breakfast tomorrow, monsieur, only coffee,' she said this down her nose at Richard. 'We are invited to a party at La Chapelle tomorrow mid-morning. I assume there will be plenty to eat there. It is Madame Bouchard's birthday.'

She turned without waiting for a reply and Richard childishly mocked her attitude behind her back. Then he looked back at Valérie and saw a spark of excitement in her eyes. 'Oh no,' he whined. 'Whatever you have planned, please think about it first. At this rate you'll dig up more evidence against Madame Tablier!'

She gave him an innocent look. 'Who, moi?' it said.

Chapter Eighteen

'It's good of you to give us a lift,' Garland Fournier said without either enthusiasm or any genuine sign of gratitude. Richard was trying to keep up with Valérie who was in front in her own car with Madame Fournier and her daughter. Richard had drawn the gloomier straw with the male side of the Fournier family, though in truth there was little in it.

'Your car smells of hens!' the fickle Fabrice Fournier exclaimed from the back.

'I thought you liked hens.' Richard had no patience for this this morning. He'd had no concrete plans of his own, but acting as taxi driver to guests was certainly not on the list.

'Oh yes. I forgot.' There was a look of puzzlement on the boy's face.

'It's very rare,' the older Fournier clearly felt some conversation was necessary, 'that a brand new car should just give up like that. Very annoying. I wish I knew about cars, but I don't.' He made it sound like one of life's great opportunities had slipped by.

You certainly don't know as much as Valérie anyway, Richard thought. He knew she had done a number on the car in question before she had even told him so. It was an impulsive act that would get them right to the heart of where they needed to be, she'd said. Yes, he'd countered, but without any planning or preparation. 'We're ill-prepared!' he'd told her, and she'd laughed at him, clearly thinking he was joking.

In the car in front, Madame Fournier was expressing equal disappointment in modern car failings, only with a good deal more anger than her husband, and certainly without the misty-eyed soul-searching. 'It really is a disgrace!' she said for about the seventh time. 'You pay good money, you expect a car that works!'

'Well, at least we can get you to La Chapelle ourselves.' Valérie wasn't exactly fishing for gratitude, but the woman was sorely testing her patience. 'Even if we have to take two cars. Neither are built for families I am sorry to say.'

'Good for you!' The woman replied tartly. 'Kids are bloody hard work!'

Valérie looked in the rear-view mirror to see if the little girl Emilie was bothered by this. She wasn't. She was flicking about on her phone. Further back in the car behind, she saw Richard trying his luck.

'You must be very pleased to be invited to a party before you've even moved in?' Richard asked innocently. Having met the big-wig inhabitants of La Chapelle he was frankly shocked at this apparent warmth.

'I suppose,' was Garland Fournier's morose reply. 'I'm not very good at parties, especially with people I don't know.'

Valérie was trying the same tack. 'This is a very good opportunity to meet people. You must feel quite honoured to be invited.'

'Do you think it will go on long?' Madame Fournier answered, looking at her nails.

'What made you decide to move to La Chapelle then?' Richard asked, glad that Valérie was taking it slowly in front.

'Oh, you know…' It wasn't much of an explanation and Garland Fournier continued to stare miserably out of the window.

'Good talk,' Richard muttered under his breath.

Valérie tried a different approach. 'I got tired of Paris in the end,' she said.

'Really?' Suddenly Lisette Fournier was more animated, and in a positive way. 'I love Paris! It has everything I need. I can go out when…' She stopped abruptly. 'It is not ideal for a young family,' she continued, as if reading from a pamphlet. 'We need a change of scenery.'

Richard tried again. 'Does the house need a lot of work doing on it? Plenty of money left over from the sale to do the renovations I suppose?'

'I leave all that to my wife,' Garland Fournier said, shutting down any further discussion.

'It is so expensive to live in Paris, and the property prices!' Valérie was trying her best too. 'You must have done very well from the sale, it is cheaper in La Chapelle, no?'

'My husband takes care of the finances,' Lisette Fournier said with the finality of a bank vault closing.

And from there both cars travelled in silence.

Richard and Valérie gratefully deposited the Fourniers at the gate of the Bouchard residence. It was one of the largest houses in the village and utterly immaculate. Pink roses were trained into a heart shape over a high wrought-iron gate which, though impressive, actually made it look like a funeral home. The gravel driveway beyond had no blemish whatsoever, weeds presumably banned by local edict. There was a marquee on the bowling-green-immaculate lawn and the usual crowd had gathered. The Fourniers walked in nervously, offering greetings and Richard waited until they were out of earshot.

'I don't know about your journey,' Richard said, 'but I had a great chat with Garland. He's a really open individual!'

'Well, that is more than I can say for his wife! She told me nothing!'

'I was being sarcastic, Valérie.'

'How do we get in, Richard?' Valérie hissed, ignoring him, and before he could answer, she started coughing loudly and violently, drawing the attention of the guests. It was Marcel Bouchard, as host, who approached them.

'Are you OK, madame?' The question was delivered in a tone that suggested concern was secondary to the awful row she was making. 'I suppose I should bring you a glass of water?'

'We gave your guests a lift from Saint-Sauver,' Richard interrupted before Valerie gave up on her performance and questioned the man's manners. 'I thought I'd bring this too, to say thank you for mentioning my *chambre d'hôte* to them.' From the boot of his car Richard produced a cool box and opened the lid to show six bottles of Langlois-Chateau Crémant de Loire Brut Réserve. He smiled warmly.

The young man's demeanour changed immediately. 'That is most generous, monsieur, please, both of you, come in.' He opened the gate. 'I am Marcel Bouchard. *Enchanté.*

Though I think we may have met briefly.' His large face broke into a genuine smile as he stood by the open gate. Richard went to close his boot and saw, watching him closely from the other side of the road, the street cleaner. The man's omnipresence was quite unnerving.

'Brilliant, Richard!' Valérie whispered as they were led into the garden. Then she grabbed his arm and pointed at a chalk slate in the garden but visible through the gate from the road. It was the same Audrey Hepburn quote that had been on Oriane Moulin's garden slate, 'To plant a garden is to believe in tomorrow.'

'What does the one on Wikipedia say I wonder?' Richard mused while Valérie attacked her phone like a woodpecker on a tree trunk.

'I don't understand,' she said quietly. '"Nothing is more disgraceful than insincerity." Cicero.'

'Cicero? From Hepburn to Cicero? At least whoever it is is well-read. Or can use Google well…'

'What do you think it means?'

'I think it means that everyone here is faking something, but that could apply equally to us!'

'Ah, I didn't know you two were invited! How lovely! And how's my sister, any news?' Madame Cuistot was her usual gushing self, and emptied whatever was in her head as soon it came into her consciousness. She was like a thought-mulching machine. But quite innocent company too, Richard noted, and certainly not like a rich, powerful woman in charge of a property empire. Or was she an impeccable actress? She certainly scrubbed up well. If she was ten years younger than her sister, she looked more like twenty years. A lifetime of servitude, if Madame Tablier was to be believed, hadn't had any obvious effect on her. But what did he know? The only thing he did know right now was that he needed a glass of chilled Crémant de Loire.

'Here.' A suspicious looking Lennard Bridille handed over a glass flute about three-quarters full, and Richard felt himself salivating. 'I didn't know you'd been invited, did you do the food?' Richard was confused by two things: firstly the reference to food and then he quickly remembered that he was supposed to be a *traiteur*, but also who had spoken. With Bridille standing so close and practically under Richard's chin, his mouth was hidden by his broom of a moustache. Rather than answer the question he took a welcome sip of Crémant de Loire instead, and then immediately wanted to spit the stuff out. It was certainly not the top-drawer wine that he had brought.

'It's absolute muck isn't it?' de la Cour leant in conspiratorially. 'Don't tip it away in any flower beds, you'll devastate the flora.'

'The committee does not have limitless funds, Christophe, as you know!' Richard knew it was Bridille speaking now because he was flushed with anger and his facial hair moved a little.

'Is this a civic event then?' Richard asked innocently. He noticed Valérie move closer to the conversation.

'It is the birthday of Madame Bouchard.' Agnès Valadon had also joined them. Richard had the impression that the committee hunted as a pack. 'Madame Bouchard and her late husband, dear Florian, practically built what we have from scratch. This is their work.' She swept her glass-free hand wide, indicating much further than the borders of the property.

'Florian's work mainly though,' de la Cour said.

'She provided him with tremendous support, Christophe. Florian often said he couldn't have done it without Liliane.'

That seemed to put an end to that line of chat, but they had reckoned without Valérie. 'And Madame Moulin?' she asked as innocently as she could, though Richard heard the slight barb in her tone. 'Is she not coming with the committee?'

'She is not part of the committee…' Bridille again turned red in anger, incapable of hiding his emotions at all despite having what looked like a sloth strapped to his face.

'Yet.' De la Cour, a little drunk, was trying his best to be mischievous, he was also sweating and Richard worried for his tan.

'We'll see.' The moustache brooded.

'Is she not invited then?' Valérie asked.

'She is…'

'Lennard was outvoted on that one.' De la Cour sat down as he spoke.

'It's premature, Christophe, as you know. Florian wouldn't have stood for it, neither would Duval.'

'I agree, Lennard, but until we elect a new chair, there is no casting vote. Those are the rules.'

Richard caught Valérie's eye; they both had the feeling of being present at a family squabble.

'Sorry I'm late, everyone!' Oriane, looking stunning in a bright, wide-flowing trouser suit, her hair in a soft bun, arrived flashing a great smile as she did so. She greeted Valérie with the inevitable air kiss, and shook the hands of everyone else. The tension she created in the members of the committee was palpable.

'You look lovely! Let me get you a drink!' Madame Cuistot was either impervious to the chillier atmosphere, or determined to ride over it. She refilled everyone else's glass too, Richard's included as he was working on the theory that the taste would grow on him given the opportunity. It was the second time he'd found himself in this village of supposedly superior taste drinking very inferior wine.

'*Mesdames et messieurs!*' Marcel Bouchard appeared at the doorway of an ornate orangerie at the edge of the lawn. 'Happy birthday to my mother!'

His mother, Liliane Bouchard, was in his arms. A tiny, frail creature that he carried like a father would carry his small daughter upstairs to bed. She had one very thin arm around his neck, the other hung limply, and she looked as exhausted as Richard had ever seen anyone look. It was plain to see that she didn't want to be there, and that 'there' might include the wider world itself and not just a garden party in her honour. Madame Cuistot helped settle the old woman into a wheelchair and even the Fournier children stopped noisily squabbling at the appearance of Madame Bouchard. There was no denying the fact that the poor woman brought with her a feeling, almost an aura, of death.

It was clear that the stroke she had suffered was a serious one. Half of her face sagged tellingly, while the other half, though showing signs of age and fatigue, was more alert even if both eyes were wet with tears. With her good arm she gave a kind of wave of gratitude, almost like an ageing monarch and tried to force a crooked smile. She emitted courage though and Richard found her very impressive, very dignified.

'Oh, Liliane!' Madame Cuistot gushed. 'You look so much better!'

The stricken old woman rolled her one good eye, indicating to everyone that she knew this was errant nonsense. It also indicated, to Richard at least, that although the body was weak, the spirit was definitely there; trapped maybe, but functioning at least. 'How cruel it is,' he whispered to Valérie, 'to be imprisoned like that. To be incapable of showing emotion. Love or hate.' He found himself quite affected by Madame Bouchard and downed his drink.

'Is it like being English?' Valérie replied. She had also finished her drink and was trying to be playful. Richard concluded that if her attempts at humour were the result of his influence, he had created a monster. He secretly refilled his glass while a chorus of happy birthday began.

There was no getting away from it, the gathering was not a pleasant one. The committee members, in particular Lennard Bridille and Agnès Valadon, tried to make small talk with the prone Madame Bouchard, but as she couldn't talk, or at least not using the speech recognition tool that Richard had noticed on the arm of the wheelchair, it was very one-sided and just represented another trap for the poor woman. On top of which their entire conversation was just a litany of complaints: the weather, the laziness of Felipe Santos, how early all the flowers and roses were, the mess of the 'new estate', and so on. It was no wonder the poor woman looked like she had had enough if this had been the extent of her social life. The Fourniers inevitably kept themselves separate, as did Valérie and Oriane, who, it seemed, had a lot to discuss. Marcel and Madame Cuistot fussed about the place, trying to be cheerful.

There was nothing else for it. Richard knew he'd have to get drunk. Christophe de la Cour had decided the same thing himself and had announced as much to Richard that that was his intention. 'I'm not drinking anymore of this muck,' he'd said a little too loudly. 'I've brought something special of my own.' And he'd disappeared indoors in search of whatever he'd gifted on arrival. Whatever it was must be good stuff, thought Richard, as he could see de la Cour sitting in the orangerie, a sneer frozen on his face as he watched the party.

'Right then,' Richard said to himself. 'I'm having some of that too.'

He walked quietly into the orangerie, and saw the bottle on the table next to the antique dealer. 'Poire William – Eau de Vie', the label said in ornate handwriting. 'De la Cour – Autumn 20—'

That'll be the strong stuff, Richard thought, *not for the faint-hearted.* Also, he realised, probably the only way of numbing the pain of this awful charade of a party.

'Mind if I join you?' he asked warmly, slurring his words slightly as he did so. 'Like you say, this stuff is rotten!' Thanks to the drink his over-familiarity went a little further and he clapped the man on the back in a hearty, and what he hoped, friendly manner. Christophe de la Cour slumped forward, smashing his head on the glass and on the table in front.

'Bloody hell!' Richard said aloud. 'This really is strong stuff!'

Chapter Nineteen

Sobering up is easy when you think you've killed someone.

There were other conclusions Richard might have drawn from the experience but that was certainly his initial and overriding thought, like a cold scientific experiment, almost detached from reality. Christophe de la Cour had fallen forward, smashing the glass on the table as he did so and had lain slumped in that position as Richard had tried to work out what the hell was going on while also trying not to retch at the sight of the dead man's vomit. Christophe's eyes were wide open too, and it felt that even in death the haughty antiques dealer was judging him.

The smashing of the glass and Richard's subsequent expletive-laden reaction had not gone unnoticed, with Lennard Bridille being the first to react as he had been in the kitchen. He had entered the orangerie wiping his hands on a tea towel and had jumped to the same conclusion that Richard had.

'Tch!' he'd tutted. 'Bloody man's drunk again! He's a liability.' He had then wandered back into the kitchen without further investigation.

Valérie had arrived next and had given a more thorough examination. Well, she had checked the man's pulse anyway, in the same manner as she had Mabit's, but this time the subject was dead. She had then disappeared and Richard hadn't seen her since, which bothered him greatly. Through hazy recollection he remembered that the others had arrived en masse, all except Madame Bouchard for obvious reasons, and there had been a variety of reactions. Agnès Valadon crossed herself before fainting into the arms of a startled Garland Fournier, who didn't look much steadier himself, potentially starting a domino effect as he collapsed into his wife. Lisette Fournier didn't look inclined to catch him, however, and stood in the doorway looking frankly furious, as if the inconvenience of de la Cour's death was just one more thing that was putting a crimp on her day. Her children, who she didn't attempt to shield from the sight, rightly looked upset.

Marcel Bouchard had hung around long enough for the confirmation of death and had then rejoined his mother, scooping her up and taking her back upstairs to bed. Eventually he came back down and told everyone that she would be fine and that she was now sleeping, though no one had expressed any interest in that regard, being far too busy dealing with their own shock. Oriane was comforting Madame Cuistot who was distraught. 'What is happening to our village?' she kept asking. 'Why Christophe?' was another. 'He so looked forward to the first eau de vie of the spring, as did my late, dear husband,' she said. And thereafter, what felt like every two minutes she repeated, 'Who would do such a thing?'

These were very pertinent questions obviously, and were being repeated in what can only be described as a slightly more aggressive manner by an angry Commissaire Henri

Lapierre. His anger would have been directed at Valérie but seeing as she wasn't there, Richard was copping it while also trying to still deal with the shock. 'I still don't understand, Monsieur Ainsworth.' Richard had a bad feeling about the man's formality. 'I still don't understand why you are here? Why are you here?'

'I told you,' Richard replied wearily. 'I wanted something to drink. What we were being served was revolting and...'

'That is not my question!' the Commissaire interrupted, standing over a seated Richard, his body blocking the sun coming through the windows. 'Why are you *here*?' He made it sound like a great philosophical question of existence, and he swept his arms wide to illustrate his query.

The thing was, if Richard was honest about the answer it was likely to enrage the policeman even more. Lapierre didn't look in the mood for a 'do you know what? I haven't the foggiest.' Instead Richard shook his head and repeated that they had given the Fourniers a lift because their car wouldn't start.

'Their car wouldn't start?' Lapierre repeated, the words drenched in scepticism. 'A brand-new car, I am told, and it wouldn't start? You expect me to believe that?'

'Well, I didn't check it out myself, but why would they make up something like that?'

'Oh no, monsieur!' Lapierre stretched on the balls of his feet, his deportment of choice when he felt triumph in the air. 'I do not suspect for one minute that they are making it up. And I believe you when you say that their car would not start.'

'Well, that's a relief!'

'But I ask myself *why* it would not start and I think the answer to this question is not here at the moment!' He

163

paused, bent down over Richard and very quietly asked, 'Where is Valérie?'

Richard looked up at him, 'Do you know what?' he said, 'I haven't the foggiest.'

'Pah! That is absurd! You two are inseparable!' The Commissaire was furious and Richard detected a note of jealousy too. 'Yet here we are, her beloved Richard Ainsworth discovers a dead body and she disappears. Why? That is what I ask myself. Why?'

Richard thought it was a damned good question frankly. It's not every day you discover a dead body and he felt that Valérie really could have stuck around a bit longer to keep an eye on him, especially if he really was 'beloved', which he doubted.

'Of course, there is another explanation...' Lapierre continued, a cruel smile flirting visibly with his lips. 'She suspects you of murder, monsieur!'

'What?' Richard stood up quickly.

'She suspects you of the murder of Christophe de la Cour, she is broken-hearted and she flees!'

'Oh, don't be so ridiculous, Henri! You really are a silly man at times.' Valérie's timing, coinciding with her flair for the dramatic, immediately upstaged the policeman's own performance. 'Of course Richard did not kill Christophe de la Cour, why would he?'

'Where have you been, madame? You know it is an offence to leave the scene of a crime yet...'

'I went to take a look at the man's shop. I thought that it might prove interesting.' She said this like it was the most natural thing in the world.

'You know it is also an offence to...'

'Oh, Henri, do stop,' she chided.

Lapierre sighed heavily with defeat. 'And did your visit prove interesting?' he asked quietly.

'Yes. Firstly, it is more than a small village *brocante*, there are a few very valuable antiques. More importantly, there were more bottles of this eau de vie.' She was wearing forensic rubber gloves and picked up the bottle de la Cour had been drinking from. It was only then that it dawned on Richard that Christophe de la Cour was still there.

'Is nobody coming to take him away?' Richard asked, shivering as he did so.

'They are waiting for my orders, monsieur. I wanted to see if the body would disturb any of the guests into a confession. It has not,' he added at the end in disappointment.

Valérie sniffed the bottle and then handed it to the policeman. 'Ammonia,' she said. 'It's faint, but it's there. And it was the same smell in some of the other bottles too. But not all,' she added.

'It is also an offence to tamper with evidence!'

'I didn't *tamper* with evidence. I *found* evidence. There is a big difference! And because...'

'Commandant!' Lapierre had had enough and ignored her. 'Commandant! Oh, there you are. You may have the body moved now and have forensics look at this bottle, fingerprints, and so on.' The sprightly Commandant Delfort did as she was told and a team who had been hanging around in the kitchen poured into the orangerie and began the grim process of logging Christophe de la Cour's death.

Richard, Valérie and the Commissaire went outside into the garden where the remaining guests, Madame Bouchard

165

aside, were still gathered. The atmosphere was muted but from a short distance away they stood and chatted as if nothing had actually happened; it still looked like any other spring party. Though, for good reason, nobody had a drink in their hand. The children were playing again, their parents were seated watching them and the others, Bridille, Marcel Bouchard, Agnès Valadon and Madame Cuistot, were discussing village affairs. Oriane immediately put her arms around Richard and hugged him. 'How terrible for you,' she said, then hugged him again. Richard, now in double shock, didn't like the look on either Valérie's face or the Commissaire's.

'Look here.' Bridille addressed the Commissaire as if he were an underling. 'This is terribly sad obviously, but can we go now? This is a very busy time for the village and I, we, need to get on.'

Agnès Valadon stepped forward. 'We have so much to do and now, without poor Monsieur de la Cour, we are short-handed.'

'What exactly is there to do, madame, monsieur? What is so urgent?' The Commissaire was losing patience very quickly.

'The Spring Fayre,' Madame Cuistot said as if the man were an idiot. 'The new man from the ministry is visiting this year too.'

'What man? What ministry?'

'Our certification,' Bridille said, though he didn't seem to want to expand on that.

'La Chapelle's status as a *Jardin Remarquable* is granted by the Ministry of Tourism and Heritage,' Madame Cuistot explained. 'It's renewed every five years.'

'And it is up for renewal this year?' Lapierre asked, looking from one to the other.

Bridille stroked his moustache. 'It's merely a formality,' he said dismissively.

'We've had the church bell professionally cleaned especially for the fayre!' Madame Cuistot said with some excitement.

The enthusiasm of each member of the committee jarred somewhat with the death of Christophe de la Cour. If he wasn't already forgotten exactly, they certainly weren't entering a period of sombre mourning either. The village, La Chapelle-sur-Follet, was all that mattered to them. Even Madame Cuistot, who had lost her husband and had her sister in prison on suspicion of murder, began chattering away about the all-important Spring Fayre. Richard found it all very unsettling.

'I suppose now that poor Monsieur de la Cour has died,' Oriane Moulin, her arm through Richard's, and making it sound like an inconvenience, 'there is another vacancy on the committee?' Neither Bridille or Madame Valadon seemed keen on answering her question. 'You know I have applied already, and my television show is, as we know, now a criterion of the certification process.'

Commissaire Lapierre finally snapped. 'May I remind you people that this is a murder enquiry! There have been two murders in this village and I think that is of far more importance than church bells, certificates or television shows!'

'Yes, of course. Of course you're right.' Lennard Bridille spoke apologetically though he also looked relieved to avoid answering Oriane's query about her application for the committee. 'I think we're in shock, this is a terrible blow.'

An electronic beep came from somewhere in Marcel's jacket. 'Ah, that will be Maman,' he said, removing a digital device from the breast pocket. 'She must have woken up. I'll need to give her some medicine.'

'That is fine, monsieur,' Lapierre said, 'you may go and attend to your mother. The rest of you will wait here for now.' There was some grumbling which Lapierre rode over. 'I want to talk to each of you in turn.' He turned and went back to the orangerie to supervise.

'Poor Christophe,' Madame Cuistot said, shaking her head. 'This is all too awful. I don't think I can cope with much more.' She sat down and began to cry quietly, while Oriane, finally letting go of Richard, comforted her.

In the meantime Lennard Bridille sidled up to Richard. 'Poor woman, it's a lot to take in,' he said without any real feeling. Then he paused slightly, a shifty look surrounding the moustache. 'Fancy doing the catering for our Spring Fayre?'

Chapter Twenty

The following morning, a weary Commissaire Henri Lapierre helped himself to a coffee while Richard, Valérie and, even it seemed, Passepartout waited for news. As far as Richard could tell he wasn't drawing this out for any dramatic effect, nor even to test Valérie's patience, which needed little testing at the best of times; he seemed actually quite baffled and was running out of the effort needed to hide it.

In the end he couldn't stifle the outburst, and slammed down his coffee, inevitably spilling some on his hand. He winced. 'I keep telling myself, that I have an open and shut case. I have a victim, I have a motive, I have opportunity, I have evidence, I have a confession!' He licked the coffee off his fingers. 'I have therefore a killer and she is under lock and key!' He spread his hands wide on Richard's breakfast bar and leant towards the others, who were all seated. 'Why then do I have another body?'

Richard and Valérie both considered this for a moment and then each responded according to type. '*Strangers on a Train*,' Richard mused. 'Hitchcock. Two strangers agree to kill for each other…' The look on the policeman's face didn't offer any encouragement for Richard to continue and his sentence inevitably tailed off before he added involuntarily, '1951.'

'You have obviously made a mistake, Henri!' Valérie spoke as though this was a regular occurrence and that the man was a simpleton. 'Anybody who knows Madame Tablier knows that she is innocent.' It was a good point except for the fact that learning of Madame Tablier's engagement to the first victim, false marriage to another man and stunt bike ambitions, Richard still wasn't sure that he knew her at all. And he was the one present who should know her best.

'She *confessed*!' The Commissaire slammed his hand down, spilling more coffee. Honestly, the man was messier than a toddler.

'We have listened to that confession and it would not stand up in court!' It was true. Valérie had played them both the so-called confession and it was full of what lawyers would call 'leading questions'. Madame Tablier didn't tell a story as such, more that she was prompted to conveniently fill in the Commissaire's gaps. Madame Tablier had sounded bored throughout but it actually came across as hesitant and any good lawyer would question the duress she was put under.

Richard thought Lapierre was being very good about not pointing out that Valérie had stolen the confession off him in the first place. He imagined that the Commissaire had realised shortly after they had left his office that he had been pickpocketed and had sat down heavily, a look of stoic resignation on his face, like a defeated Japanese general, and decided it was best for his reputation if he just kept quiet about it for now.

Valérie passed him the small USB stick across the bar. He picked it up and put it back in his pocket. 'And the keys to Monsieur de la Cour's *brocante*?' She did the same but with a touch of dignified guilt about her. The Commissaire's remarkable restraint did not last long, in fact he exploded again. 'But the ring, madame, the ring was found at the scene, where Duval Cuistot's contraption had been tampered with.'

'Yes, it was found, once you had been told to go back and look for it! Do you not think that is odd?'

They both took a break from their bout; everyone could see that it was actually getting them nowhere. Richard had had time to think that morning as the Fourniers had once again gone out early. He had come to the conclusion that, while he was still certain of Madame Tablier's innocence there was little he could do about it if the damned woman insisted on being guilty. He began to pace around the room.

'What was the toxicology report on the death of Christophe de la Cour?' he asked without looking at them, though he sensed immediately that they were certainly looking at him and their faces would have bordered on shock at him taking the lead.

'Paraquat dichloride poisoning,' the Commissaire sighed. 'It is a banned pesticide, but it seems that *the committee* of La Chapelle, in their wisdom, had not destroyed their stocks since the European ban in 2007.'

'And who had access to this paraquat?'

'Everyone, madame.' He shook his head. 'Everyone on the committee and Felipe Santos, the gardener, who had a key to the store room.'

'Though presumably not Madame Tablier as she's not a member of the committee and you had her locked up!' Richard thought he'd found a hole in the argument.

'We don't know yet how this paraquat was put into Monsieur de la Cour's eau de vie, it was in all the bottles.' He nodded at Valérie who had suggested it would be. 'We don't know how or, perhaps more importantly, when.'

'Meaning?' Richard asked.

'Meaning that it could have been anytime between the end of last summer when the victim first bottled the mixture and yesterday when he opened it. We do not know yet.'

'Are you saying that Madame Tablier is a suspect in this murder too?' Richard thought this was a bit thick frankly. 'If so, what's the motive? And why are you so sure that Duval Cuistot's death was actually murder and not the accident you originally thought it was?' He felt himself beginning to lose his temper and he couldn't remember the last time that had happened.

As usual Lapierre's index finger shot in the air when he felt a point needed stressing. 'The murder of Christophe de la Cour proves my theory that Duval Cuistot was also murdered! And yes, your Madame Tablier is a suspect in the second murder because she has confessed to the first murder!'

'But, Henri, why would she kill Christophe de la Cour?'

'The motive has yet to be fully established, madame.' It was never going to be good enough. 'We are investigating a few possibilities.'

'That is ridiculous!'

'There are many reasons one might kill, madame! Money, or drugs, or sex!'

Richard felt that none of this applied to the Madame Tablier that he thought he knew and also, seizing on a crumb of comfort for himself, if money, drugs or sex were the reasons one might get murdered, his chances of being so were pretty slim.

'Ridiculous!' Valérie repeated. 'You may as well blame Madame Tablier for the food poisoning that killed Florian Bouchard!' She stared hard at Lapierre, daring him to do just that, which on current form looked a dangerous game and one likely to backfire.

'No, madame. I am ahead of you there. Florian Bouchard died of food poisoning in Miami after arriving on the ship, *Princess Carabaia*. His wife, as you know, survived, though as we saw, barely.'

There was a knock at the door and Clare stepped in. Oliver Forshaw-Banks was there too, dressed like an off-duty Member of Parliament who has been told to 'look normal' – that is, not even close. He walked in sheepishly behind her. 'Morning, Richard, Valérie,' Clare breezed. 'Mind if we have another look around?' Richard didn't verbally reply, just waved his arms in irritation as if the whole thing didn't matter a jot to him. 'Oh, Commissaire, how lovely, have you three got another one of your little mysteries going on?'

Lapierre's English wasn't great but he knew when he was being patronised. He was also French, however, and Clare an attractive woman so he answered with as much charm as he could. 'Yes, madame. *Bonjour*, and this must be your son?'

Richard felt like hugging the man. It was in no way a deliberate attempt to humiliate Clare, he was genuinely trying to be polite and Richard wanted to tell her so, but instead shovelled Clare and Forshaw-Banks out of the door before there was another murder. He returned a few moments later and the atmosphere hadn't changed.

'…that is my theory, madame, and at present it works with the facts.'

Valérie was pursing her lips and it was obvious to Richard that whatever the theory was that Commissaire Lapierre had just outlined, she was struggling to argue against it.

'But…' was her half-hearted response that ran out of steam after one word.

He put his hat back on, turned smartly and left with his chin triumphantly in the air.

Richard made sure that the door was closed behind him and sat down. 'What is this theory then?' he asked quietly.

Valérie turned towards him, and for the first time in their partnership, friendship, acquaintanceship Richard saw doubt creep into her fine features. 'His theory, the impossible man, is that Madame Tablier killed de la Cour and her brother-in-law. Her ultimate goal is to have control of this trust that her sister manages. In order to do that she must eliminate the other committee members.'

'And then ultimately her sister too?'

'So he says.'

'And all for money, all for this trust?'

'Yes, and revenge.'

'And you agree with that?'

She looked defiantly at him. 'I do not. But Madame Tablier apparently does.'

He stood up and went to get a coffee, wishing that it wasn't too early for something stronger. 'We're missing something here,' he said, not because he believed it necessarily but because that's what they always say in the movies at this point. 'Supposing she's being framed?' he asked, another handy cliché.

'By herself?' Even Valérie, not given to scepticism, couldn't avoid that one.

Suddenly Richard went rigid. 'Of course!' he shouted, and then remembering that Clare was snooping, he whispered, 'Of course. She's framing herself. She's protecting someone.'

'Madame Cuistot?'

'It has to be! She thinks her sister killed her own husband, and she's taking the rap for it.' He punched a clenched fist into the opposite palm.

'The rap?' Valérie looked confused.

'Film noir LA District Attorney talk, it means take the blame.'

'Ah.'

'But that means that Madame Cuistot also killed Christophe de la Cour.' Valérie was calm, for once trying to be the more restrained of the two.

'Well, she has the motive, we know that. Property.'

They both remained silent for a moment, each trying to pull apart Richard's theory. But working on the assumption, presumption the policeman would argue, that Madame Tablier was incriminating herself to save her sister then this new approach fitted the facts just as well.

'Something else that has bothered me, Richard, is who Henri's informant is. Who gives him these tip-offs?'

Again they both fell silent.

175

'His new girlfriend perhaps?' Richard asked, arching an eyebrow as he did so.

'Madame Cuistot!' they both said at the same time.

Then doubt crept into Richard's face. 'Really though? Madame Cuistot? And not Oriane Moulin?'

Valérie shrugged and asked, 'Why not?' She asked this not defensively in that their suggestion might be way off beam, but in an 'and why shouldn't women of that age have a relationship?' tone of voice.

Richard recognised thin ice when he saw it. 'No, no reason at all,' he said.

'I would guess that they are of a similar age. They are both around sixty, I think.' When she put it like that it wasn't implausible at all. Richard was guilty of assuming that, as sisters, they would be similar in outlook, that romance wouldn't be Madame Cuistot's thing, in the way that he thought it wasn't Madame Tablier's. But then, he'd already been told that that wasn't the case.

'She's a handsome woman, and Lapierre is… well…' He didn't want to offer anything here really; Lapierre was her ex-husband after all.

'Lonely.' She finished the sentence for him. 'Henri is lonely.'

Something nagged at Richard though. 'But she's just buried her husband, it doesn't seem decent.'

'She may be lonely too, Richard, she may have been lonely for a long time. It is possible in marriage too, you know?'

He knew.

Chapter Twenty-One

With a heavy heart Richard skirted his spoon over the ball of ice cream in his bowl, slicing off a slither that quickly melted. Valérie had rightly declined dessert, but Richard liked to get his money's worth on a set menu. He could of course just not eat it, but René had recently been quite sensitive about his spring menu and Richard, in more ways than one, had enough on his plate without upsetting the former scourge of Parisian bad debtors. He knew it was an overreaction on his part but he had visions of not being able to hold a spoon for the foreseeable future and that would be, at the very least, inconvenient.

'If you don't eat it, it will all melt away,' Valérie huffed like a tired parent with a trying child.

'I don't want it,' Richard moaned through a forced smile, hoping René wouldn't see him hesitating over the bowl.

'Don't eat it then!'

'I don't want to leave it!'

'You can be impossible at times!' she hissed.

'I've just had enough, that's all.' He puffed his cheeks out, like a diver about to hold their breath, and went in. Unfortunately in his effort to get rid of the ice cream as quickly as possible, he took too much. The freeze rush to his brain felt like he'd been tasered, and momentarily he really believed he was about to expire. His eyes rolled back into the top of his head as his brain reacted like it had been forcibly dunked beneath an ice floe. Slowly, very slowly, the feeling passed and he was vaguely aware that Valérie was talking to him. His hearing gradually returned.

'You just cannot trust family,' she was saying for the umpteenth time that day. 'Imagine, framing your own sister like that!'

It was, in Valérie's black and white mind, now an open and shut case. Madame Cuistot, affecting an air of dotty vulnerability, had maybe wheedled her way to the top of the greasy La-Chapelle-sur-Follet pole, taken control of a probably illegally collected property portfolio, was possibly supplying Commissaire Lapierre with misleading information, might even be posing as his girlfriend and, worst of all, had conceivably set up her own sister to take the blame by, as likely as not, planting incriminating evidence.

So why were they wasting time in René's brasserie rather than confronting this monster? 'I still think there's too many ponderables there,' Richard had offered less meekly than usual. 'There's not one thing in that accusation that is certain. Plus, you're forgetting the most damning thing of all. Madame Tablier still insists she's the killer!' He had been trying to dampen slightly her very obvious anger.

'Of Duval Cuistot, yes! She has not admitted to the murder of Christophe de la Cour.' Richard sought a crumb of comfort. 'Yet!' Valérie added threateningly. Then her mood changed immediately. 'Maître Goupille!'

'Another ex-husband?' Richard asked quietly before going in for some more ice cream.

She ignored him. 'Maître Goupille, he is an investigating magistrate, a *juge d'instruction* who specialises in finance in Paris. I will ask him about this trust that Madame Cuistot controls, he will know where to look.' She bustled out of the booth they were sitting in and went outside to ensure her phone call was more private, leaving Richard to stare at his dessert.

'It's a bit much, isn't it?' René, usually such a brooding force, hovered nervously above Richard, who smiled weakly. 'I know, I know. I didn't know what else to do. I have so much of the stuff.'

'I didn't even know asparagus ice cream existed.' Richard tried to sound positive. 'I mean it's nice but…'

'…but coming off the back of a starter of *Asperges Oeuf Mimosa* and a main of Goat's Cheese and Asparagus Quiche, it's just…'

'…a bit much, yes.' Richard nodded in agreement and replaced his spoon.

'You're right.' René picked up the bowl. 'Listen, Richard, do yourself a favour, steer clear of this place for a couple of weeks.'

'Oh, René, please,' Richard was mortified and physically terrified in equal measure. 'I didn't mean to upset you!'

'No, no! Nothing like that. It's just that I've got tonnes of the stuff. It's about all I'll be serving until Ascension weekend.' He tutted as if at the very thought of nature, shaking his head at the bowl as he did so. 'Same every year, you can set your clock by them.'

'Hello, Richard!' Gennie sidled in next to him and Martin did the same on his other side almost squashing Passepartout, who was hiding from any more table tidbits, having also had enough asparagus.

'Hello, old man! I fancy something different to drink, René, what've you got?'

'I'm doing Asparagus Martini as it's Happy Hour.'

'We'll take three!' Martin clapped his hands as a smirking René caught Richard's eye with no hint of apology this time.

'I think Valérie and I are leaving in a minute,' Richard tried to shuffle in a bid to get out.

'Oh I didn't see Val, should've known what with the dog.' Passepartout gave him a filthy look. 'Make it four, René!' Martin shouted across the bar.

'It's two for one!' René shouted back.

'That'll be eight then!'

Richard's heart was still sinking as the drinks arrived at the same time as Valérie returned. 'OK,' she said, very business-like. 'He will call us when he has some information.'

'Hello, Val! Get your mouth around one of these!' Martin had little subtlety at the best of times, but he seemed even more bullish than usual. 'Cheers, everyone!' He lifted his glass.

'Bottoms up!' Gennie did the same.

'You are both very cheery,' Valérie remarked; rightfully, there was a hint of suspicion in her voice.

Martin and Gennie looked at each other and giggled. 'You tell them, love!' Martin said.

'No! Go on, you do it!'

Richard had a sense that whatever was coming was not for the faint-hearted and braced himself, hoping it wasn't ex-wife/new beau related antics, something he definitely was not going to discuss.

'We've been to the zoo!' Martin said, as happy as a child.

'Oh.' Both Valérie and Richard were taken aback by the innocence of their enthusiasm.

'Yes, we go at the same time every year.' Martin had rarely sounded more ribald. 'Every animal…'

'*Every* animal…' Gennie encouraged.

'Just at it constantly. It's spring, isn't it!'

'It's fun,' Gennie offered as though describing a church fete tombola.

'Bloody good entertainment!' Martin was a million miles from a church fete tombola. 'Every year, you can set your clock by it!'

Something changed in Richard and, out of character, he banged the table with some force. 'I've got it!' he shouted, kissed a startled Gennie on the forehead and then turned to Valérie. 'You can set your clock by it!'

Some fifteen minutes later it was Richard, now trying to control his own temper, who skidded Valérie's car to a halt in the gravelled car park in La Chapelle. Valérie had listened to his breathless explanation on the journey, interrupted by Richard talking himself through gear changes.

He pulled the handbrake on and took another deep breath. 'Spring. You can set your clock by it. It's all about habit. Madame Cuistot, and I'm really quite angry about this, knew everyone's habits better than most. Her husband, always the same stunt at the start of spring. Christophe de la Cour, always uncorked his eau de vie *at the start of spring* with her husband. So you see? All of this was planned in the autumn. These traps, no brake fluid, poisoned bottles, they were set up months ago. *You can set your clock by it!*'

'Brilliant, Richard!' Valérie said, though he was already halfway out of the car. 'But shouldn't we call Henri?' she called after him.

Unusually it was Valérie who was trying to inject a note of sobriety into proceedings, but Richard was already off down the street, taking long, purposeful strides. It was a role reversal like no other. Richard, determined and incensed, was off to fight the cause of justice on Madame Tablier's behalf. Something inside him had switched and he wasn't going to hang about on the sidelines of life anymore. Now was the time to act. Valérie, for her part, had an unusually worried look on her face. She had never seen him like this before and wondered whether the stress of Clare, money and the *chambre d'hôte* were finally getting to him or even, and it was a strong possibility, he had overdosed on spring greens.

As a distraction, while Passepartout sniffed the ground, she checked the La Chapelle Wikipedia page and wasn't at all surprised to see that the chalk slate quote panel had changed again. If only there were some way of knowing who was changing these things, she thought, while aware that that could, as Oriane had pointed out, literally be anyone. It's easy to hide on the internet. 'Everything you sow is a seed,' she read aloud. 'Seed bad, harvest bad.' Richard wasn't listening. 'It is so childish!'

Madame Cuistot was on the restaurant terrace when they arrived, wiping down tables. 'Oh hello, you two! You're a bit late for food again, but I can get you some drinks.'

To Richard's mind the woman verged on the sickening. This charade she was playing of the giddy innkeeper, the innocent caught up in a confusing maelstrom of murder and financial chicanery was wearing thin, especially now he knew the truth. He knew it was all an act, the country rube hiding from the pain of the real world was now as see-through as glass and he could barely control himself. Valérie, in her new-found role as Richard's handbrake, might have brought a note of caution but her phone rang and she hung back to take the call, picking up Passepartout in the process.

'I don't want a drink, Madame Cuistot!' he spluttered.

'OK, ducks.' She was completely oblivious to his temper.

'How long has this been going on?' He became aware that it was all very well to go marching into the lion's den as it were, but he was also letting the emotion of the moment get the better of him and he hadn't actually thought through the best way to confront the woman. The situation called for ice-cold calm, whereas Richard was, for once, a hotbed of raging passions and righteous ire, and most certainly, he would guiltily admit, having a high old time.

'How long has what being going on, dear?' The woman was infuriating, rendering Richard even more inarticulate.

'This!' he cried. 'All of… this!'

She looked at him, concern on her face. 'Are you sure you don't want a brandy?'

'No I don't want a bloody brandy, I want the truth.' His head was suddenly a foggy whirl. 'Why?' he asked simply. 'Why did you do it?'

'I don't understand, ducks, do what?'

He shook his head. 'Oh you're good, you're very good. Chiefly your eyes I think, and that throb you get in your voice.' He shook his head sadly as the older woman sat down, her face suddenly awash with guilt. 'When a man's partner is killed, he's supposed to do something about it. It doesn't matter what you thought of him. He was your partner and you're supposed to do something about it.' Richard had no idea why he had decided to forego rigorous interrogation and instead opt for quoting the taut closing scene from *The Maltese Falcon*, it was just an instinctive reaction to a stressful situation and after all, like Mary Astor in the film, she was the murderer.

'It wasn't my fault,' she said quietly. 'I just couldn't think of anything else to do.'

Richard felt a tug at his sleeve as a very concerned Valérie tried to get his attention. 'Richard!' she hissed at him, then shook her head negatively.

'Not now!' he hissed back. 'I'm on the verge of making her talk!'

'No.' She looked adamant about something, that was for sure. In return he screwed up his eyes trying to understand what on earth she was driving at. She shook her head again and nodded once more towards Madame Cuistot. It dawned on him what she meant and he also shook his head and nodded in the same direction. Now she nodded, and Richard closed his eyes, inwardly cursing that he had ever let instinct and emotion be his guide.

'I am just so sorry,' Madame Cuistot pulled miserably at a handkerchief in her lap. 'I tried to make it better and it just got worse. I bought you that new one, but I suppose the little thing knew all along!'

She disappeared briefly inside and re-emerged with a punctured dog bed, handing it guiltily to Richard who took it silently.

Marcel Bouchard appeared from inside, as usual looking like his lunch had been entirely out of a glass. 'Everything all right?' he slurred.

Suddenly Madame Cuistot beamed an enormous smile, 'Oh yes, dear! I feel much better for having got that off my chest.' She turned to Richard. 'I did feel rotten.'

'Yes, well,' he said stiffly. 'Never mind. No harm done and all that. I'm glad we got it sorted.' He sat down at a table, his insides shrivelling like a crisp packet in a microwave. 'I think I will have that brandy,' he said quietly.

Chapter Twenty-Two

'So she's not in charge of this trust then, is that what you're saying?' Richard wasn't going to bother trying to recover his composure or even reputation, but he still kept his voice low as they both sat in the corner watching Madame Cuistot. She was fussing over a visibly upset Marcel Bouchard.

'It is not easy for him, I think. With a bed-ridden mother to care for… the sacrifice he has made.'

'The trust?' Richard pushed; he was all out of patience and sympathy for others.

'No!' She was suddenly very excited and it's fair to say that Valérie wasn't as effective at keeping her own voice quiet, certainly not when she had vital information to impart. 'This trust, it is like an old-fashioned tontine. All serving members of the La Chapelle committee own an equal percentage of this property portfolio. That percentage passes to the surviving members, whose share increases.'

Richard was confused. 'Well, that seems pretty damning to me then! She's in charge, or it's in her name at least, as far as I know she's not even on the committee. She's bumped off two other members, and is probably working on the other two. If,' he added, 'she hasn't arranged to do so already. I don't understand why you stopped me, I could have broken her.'

Valérie gave him a look that bordered on pity, like when an animal needs putting out of its misery. 'But, Richard. Not only is she not in charge of the property trust, the property trust does not even exist.' The look on Richard's face mirrored that of Passepartout who was at that moment sniffing the punctured remains of his travel bed with the air of someone who felt conned by life. Richard made to say something, but nothing came out. 'And anyway,' Valérie continued, with a tone of admonishment. 'Why would Madame Cuistot implicate herself like that? She cannot be Henri's informant and the controller of a trust. It does not make sense. Really, I have never seen you like that, Richard, you must think before you act sometimes, I feel.'

It was the final straw for a man whose dignity and self-confidence was at, even for him, a low point. 'You were the one who said she was the murderer,' he fumed though quietly; his face so rigid he looked like a ventriloquist. 'You were the one who put that idea in my head. If it hadn't been for you suggesting it, I would never have gone off half-cocked like that!'

She looked at him questioningly. 'What does half-cocked mean?'

'Something to do with guns probably. I don't know, best not ask Martin either.' He closed his eyes and took a deep breath. 'So, tell me what this finance bloke said.'

Valérie explained that she had sent a copy of the dossier she had downloaded from Commissaire Lapierre's USB key to her *juge* friend and that it hadn't taken long to recognise it as a fake. 'Maître Goupille told me that although it looks like an official legal document, it is just a mock-up. Fake registration numbers, fake accountancy firm, fake headed paper. None of what it contains, the property portfolio, and so on, is actually real.'

'And so,' Richard was still riddled with the shame of it all, 'neither is Madame Cuistot a murderous real estate magnate, she's been set up.'

'Yes.' For once Valérie sensed his vulnerability and reached a hand out across the table. 'You are allowed to make mistakes, Richard. It was at least for the right reasons.' It didn't completely restore his inner core, but it certainly helped.

Sometime later they were sitting in the garden back at the *chambre d'hôte*. Passepartout was asleep next to Valérie and Richard had let the hens out for a wander around the garden. Clare and her young man weren't there, and neither were the Fourniers. It was a rare moment of calm, but there was work to do. 'So where does all this leave us then?' Richard asked, not for the first time.

Valérie leant forward and stirred her asparagus martini, which they were both becoming quite enamoured of. 'Where does this leave us?' she repeated, as if it were an existential question that only great minds could solve. 'Well... on the face of it, it looks like someone is trying to incriminate Madame Cuistot, but why? She appears so, so *innocent*.'

Richard sighed long and hard. 'You mean who could possibly have a grudge against Madame Cuistot enough to murder her husband and a friend?'

'Yes,' Valérie replied quickly, before catching Richard's tired eyes. 'Oh,' she said softly.

'Maybe we're going about this the wrong way.' Richard bent over to fuss at one of the hens at his feet. 'All the evidence against Madame Tablier, apart from the confession obviously, is circumstantial. So instead of trying to prove her innocence, which typically she doesn't want, let's try and establish, beyond doubt, her guilt.'

Valérie thought about this for a second and shook her head slowly. 'Brilliant!' she said in seeming contradiction to her movements. It was a relief to Richard to have that encouragement, his confidence in his abilities had taken something of a pounding during the day and also, if pushed, he had no idea what he was talking about. It was just one of those clever B-film script paradoxes that he loved so much. 'OK,' Valérie continued, 'if you are right and these murders are not just pre-meditated but planned, even executed, months in advance…'

'…the brake fluid and the insecticide in the eau de vie…'

'…then Madame Tablier could have done it still. The *rapprochement* between the sisters happened last year when Duval Cuistot was in bed, unable to walk.'

'But why Christophe de la Cour?' Richard shook his head again. 'It can't just be the man's absurd tan.'

Valérie either did not hear his flippancy or chose to ignore it. 'Insurance,' she said slowly. 'Remember what Madame Cuistot said? That her husband and de la Cour liked to open the first bottle of spring together.'

'If the brakes don't get you, the poison will?' Richard felt sick. His idea had been to create more doubt around the guilt of Madame Tablier by finding holes in the case, but they were doing an extremely efficient job of condemning the woman even further. 'OK, so she's still in the mix then obviously.' He was hoping blind optimism might be the way forward. 'But she's not the only one. Oriane Moulin must have been house-hunting around that time too, Valadon and Bridille, Felipe the gardener, that street cleaner who just seems to hang about staring at people, the Bouchards...' He was running out of options. 'Though Marcel Bouchard was presumably in the States.'

They sat in silence trying to see through the fog that they had just helped make even more dense. Valérie stroked Passepartout's head, a picture of intense concentration, and Richard did the same with Lana Turner. Madame Fournier interrupted them with a polite but firm knock on a wooden chair.

'Excuse me.' She had a way of being polite that sounded the exact opposite; it was quite a skill thought Richard. 'We shall be leaving tomorrow, we can move in now.' She didn't look exactly thrilled by the prospect. 'Finally, La Bastide du Lavoir will be ours.'

'OK,' Richard's reply was equally cold, 'just make sure you take your kids with you,' he muttered under his breath. Madame Fournier turned smartly away while Valérie, it appeared, hadn't even noticed the brief interruption.

'Why would you need to incriminate Madame Cuistot if Madame Tablier has confessed?' she asked, probably rhetorically, Richard could never tell.

'I can't believe I nearly accused the poor woman of double murder!' It wasn't that Richard was wracked with guilt at the thought, it was a more English response than that; it was complete and utter embarrassment. 'Or even that she might be Commissaire Lapierre's secret girlfriend; that seems even more absurd.'

'No, I think that still might be possible. The informer and the girlfriend might not be one and the same. Why not?'

Why not indeed? Richard thought, suddenly a little jealous of the policeman, not for Madame Cuistot, if indeed that were the case, but for the fact that he at least was trying. Clare was also trying, in more ways than one, but Richard was not, and maybe it was time that he did.

'Well, even if it's not Madame Cuistot, he's certainly getting dressed up for someone. Good on him.'

Valérie almost dropped her glass in a sudden rush of excitement.

'Richard, suppose this is all a red herring!' It looked like she had missed his point. 'You just said it, "if it's not Madame Cuistot"!'

'No. Sorry. I don't get it.'

She picked up her phone and showed him the picture of the Committee Portfolio Trust document. 'This may not be real,' she spoke very slowly, for once trying to control herself. 'But that does not mean that a real version does not exist.' He tried to pick apart the negatives and get to the heart of what she was saying and it made complete sense.

'So what you're saying is that there *is* a valuable property portfolio, there is this tontine thing and there is someone knocking off the La Chapelle committee.'

'Someone is being very clever and they are controlling us, like those very obvious slates in the gardens, or not even in the gardens but online. They change all the time. Someone is playing a game!' Her emotions had gone from excited to angry, like someone had moved her emotional dial quickly across the spectrum.

'Like that one this afternoon, something about bad seeds, bad harvest,' Richard said. The fact that she thought he hadn't noticed had a mollifying effect on her. 'Yes, I noticed,' he underlined. 'It's all very obvious stuff, childish almost.'

'And no way to trace who is responsible, because of so many ways you can hide on the internet. There's always an alias, but it leads nowhere if you are clever. It is like graffiti sprayed in the middle of the night.' Her anger was bubbling over again.

This time it was Richard's turn to get excited. 'No, we can't tell who changes the Wikipedia page, but we can say who hasn't!' He banged his glass down a little too hard, startling Lana Turner into flying off his lap. 'Madame Tablier. Madame Tablier can't access the page, she's in a cell! She doesn't have a computer or a smartphone!' He fell back in the deep outdoor sofa, a mixture of relief and tiredness.

'Richard, brilliant!' was Valérie's welcome response. 'Of course!'

They both reflected on this for a moment. 'So.' Richard sat back up. 'Assuming that there is a property trust, that still leaves us with the remaining members of the committee. Agnès Valadon and Lennard Bridille, but also Madame Cuistot…'

In their excitement and intensity they had failed to notice a shadow fall across their table. Noel Mabit appeared from nowhere, helped by his wife and he didn't look very happy. He coughed. 'I'm sorry to interrupt,' he said, as though about to launch into a state of the union address, 'but I have come to express my gratitude, Monsieur Ainsworth.'

'Noel!' Richard stood up and greeted the smaller man. 'I had no idea you were out! Please sit down.' Noel Mabit declined.

Richard felt a little sorry for the man. Their relationship was a cold one, and it was clear that Richard's greeting had overstepped the mark on that front. But Richard was genuinely delighted to see him alive; their mutual antipathy could now continue for the good of them both. Something he was sure Noel would be keen to re-establish.

Madame Mabit nudged him. 'I am here to offer my sincere, erm, gratitude.' He was nudged again. 'I have been told that it was you who saved my life, though possibly accidentally. I am, erm, grateful.' It looked like this sentence had caused him more pain than the fall.

It was the most wooden expression of gratitude imaginable; if Noel's teeth were gritted any further they'd have been worn down to his gums, but it was as genuine as it could be under the circumstances and Richard did his best to lap it up. Noel wasn't an enemy, he was just a mild irritant and as such, in his opinion, a sometimes helpful and indeed healthy focus for life's frustrations. He didn't wish him harm, far from it, he'd decided he almost needed him and he knew that Noel Mabit felt the same. And he wasn't far from the truth. If indeed he had saved Noel Mabit's life, it had not been deliberate but the result of a well-timed assault by Valérie, whose methods, though brutal, were effective. He was still going to milk it for all it was worth though. It had been a long day, with some very definite lows and now, thanks to the potential hole in Madame Tablier's determination to be seen as a murderer, a very definite high.

'One must be very careful, Noel. Electrics, bad wiring and water – that's a dangerous mix.'

Mabit squirmed visibly. 'It is the first and last time I will use that contraption,' he said.

'That is a good idea, Noel,' Valérie said, surprisingly gentle.

'Yes, bin it! That would be my advice.' Richard was overplaying his hand and couldn't have cared less.

'I have done. It was a waste of money, I know that now. I bought it second-hand and did not check it properly.' He was beginning to regain some of his pomp. 'I have written a strongly worded letter to Monsieur Lennard Bridille of La Chapelle-sur-Follet. I shall expect full compensation.'

Chapter Twenty-Three

Richard put in his card and watched the petrol pump turn cents into euros with alarming, almost comic, speed. A Citroën 2CV is about as economical as a car can be while actually having a working engine, but even so he would have to watch what he spent from now on. They weren't quite in high season yet, so the B&B wasn't full and besides, if he wanted to keep the place as his own he probably needed to buy Clare out anyway. He shuddered at the thought of how much that would cost before allowing himself a half-smile; it didn't matter how much that would cost, he didn't have the money. He barely had the money to put some unleaded in his car.

He'd read somewhere that a car is more fuel efficient if the tank isn't full and he decided to put it to the test, aiming for thirty-five euros exactly. He let go of the trigger. Thirty-five euros and five centimes. He tried again. Thirty-six euros and two centimes. So close!

Valérie leant out of the passenger door window. 'Why is it taking so long?' she asked with marked impatience.

'Nearly there,' Richard replied, not wanting to break his concentration. Thirty-seven euros and six centimes. Dammit!

Eventually he achieved his goal at exactly forty-six euros and couldn't have been happier with himself. It was a win, of sorts, and he badly needed one after yesterday's Madame Cuistot debacle.

'Richard!' An agitated Valérie leant out of the window again to get his attention.

'Yes! OK, I've finished,' he replied irritably, annoyed that his moment of personal victory was being cut short.

'No, Richard, look!'

She pointed across the petrol station forecourt and Richard turned to see what the issue was. He turned back quickly, hoping he hadn't been seen as Valérie adjusted her very un-rural-France headscarf to hide her face, and ducked a curious Passepartout down at the same time. Three pumps down Lennard Bridille was filling up a large flatbed truck hired, according to the name on the door, from a local supermarket. In the cab sat a determined-looking Agnès Valadon.

Of course there was absolutely no reason at all why Lennard Bridille and Agnès Valadon shouldn't hire a large flatbed truck, but coming off the back of Noel Mabit's revelation about his dodgy gutter cleaner and the fact that the two people now driving off were the sole surviving members of a committee that was gradually being bumped off, it did seem an opportunity too good to miss. He collected his receipt and jumped into the driver's seat.

'Follow that cab!' he said in a rush of excitement though after waiting for his receipt, which confused Valérie but she thankfully let it go.

They turned out of the station and sat behind the rented truck at a discreet distance, travelling in the opposite direction to La Chapelle.

'Where do you think they are going?' Valérie's voice was tense.

'I've no idea,' Richard replied, secretly hoping that they wouldn't be going too far and he'd have to put yet more petrol in the tank.

'Maybe you should get closer to them, Richard, we don't want to lose them.'

Richard wasn't going to lose them. Richard was having the time of his life. 'Firstly, Valérie, they're in a bloody great truck and secondly, Lennard Bridille is not driving how a Frenchman would normally drive.' She looked at him quizzically. 'He's using his indicators,' he explained.

After about thirty minutes they approached the outskirts of the town of Romorantin-Lanthenay, where Lennard Bridille and Agnès Valadon turned into the car park of a large garden centre, Jardimarché, its large green signage showing, improbably, an African baobab tree. They parked up as close to the shop entrance as their truck would allow as Richard hid the 2CV behind a much larger car some distance away.

'Do we follow them in?' he asked, hoping the answer was yes.

'Of course,' Valérie answered, while working out a plan. In an effort at disguise, she tightened her headscarf further, tying it under her chin, and put on a pair of large sunglasses. She looked, though Richard wouldn't point this out, exactly like Valérie d'Orçay. As usual, however, he had no disguise for himself; no hats or masks, just his reading glasses which were useless if he actually wanted to see where he was going or, as was the case, follow a suspect. If indeed they were suspects, they might also be potential victims.

He thought about it and eventually said, 'I don't need a disguise, neither of us need a disguise.'

'I prefer a disguise if I am to get close to them,' she pouted, like he was an apprentice.

'OK, well I have one. If they see me I'm here buying catering equipment for my business as a *traiteur*.' The curious thing about modern garden centres he had noticed was that they were far more than just garden centres; they used to just stick to gardening stuff, whereas now everybody and everything felt the urgent need for diversification, which inevitably just meant retail homogeneity. Jardimarché was no different. It was stocked with kitchenware, clothing, hunting and camping equipment, live animals, with usually a well-stocked aquarium besides the more traditional household pets and exotic birds, children's toys and occasionally plants. Richard had no doubt he could purchase a set of disused nuclear warheads and a fan belt for a Fiat Uno if he asked the right staff member.

'Just try to be discreet, Richard,' Valérie cautioned, much to his annoyance.

'I'm not an idiot you know!' he responded acidly as he opened the car door banging it into the next vehicle and getting a filthy look from an old man inside. 'Sorry,' he mouthed.

They approached the entrance cautiously. They had their alibis, as it were, their reasons to be there anyway, but they didn't want to bump into the two La Chapelle dignitaries straight away and possibly spook them.

'They are over there,' Valérie whispered, nodding with her head towards the other end of the large greenhouse where Bridille and Valadon each had an enormous flat trolley which they were filling with plants. Lennard Bridille also had what looked like a lengthy shopping list which he was matching to the labels on the watered display tables.

'Why do they need to buy plants?' Richard wondered aloud. 'Aren't they supposed to grow their own, isn't that a part of the *Jardin Remarquable* licensing? You know, that they're self-sufficient.'

'It is very odd,' Valérie agreed.

'I have an idea,' Richard said. 'This place is like an airport terminal, all paths lead to the tills. If we get past them we can see what they're buying when they have to pass us.'

'Brilliant, Richard!' Valérie said distractedly, before handing Passepartout over to him and moving off.

'If it's so brilliant, where are you going?'

'I want to get closer, I want to hear what they are saying. That is why I have a disguise.'

Richard shook his head knowing it would be pointless to argue, and he made off in the other direction and the heart of the garden centre itself. From experience he knew that to get from the greenhouse and the vast outdoor area of this place, everyone had to go through the same double doors and that's where he headed, to find a spot on the other side that he could watch the doors from. It was the *animalerie* and with Passepartout tucked under one arm, he had the perfect cover. Though Passepartout didn't look too happy about the positioning, or the smell.

The small dog looked nervously in at the sleeping chinchillas as they passed, and tried its best to ignore the rather hungry eyes of a nevertheless bored-looking boa constrictor in a large tank who was, improbably, called 'Aristotle', according to a sign hanging to the side.

Richard eventually found an ideal vantage point where he could watch the double doors without obviously looking like he was doing so and arousing the attention of the staff. Twenty minutes later his quarry came struggling through the doors pushing their unwieldy and well-stocked trollies. Whatever they were buying, they were buying in large quantities and from where Richard stood it looked like they were delivering whole gardens and, interestingly, all the plants matched the La Chapelle colour scheme. He moved slowly along a parallel aisle, following in the same direction. When they stopped briefly to get their breath back, Richard did the same, ducking slightly as he did so.

'Hello, darlin', give us a kiss!'

Richard jumped out of his skin, nearly dropping Passepartout in the process as the rasping voice of what appeared to be a 1950s cockney dockside floozy repeated the earthy question. The very English vernacular was not only unexpected, but it undermined his fragile French-ish confidence.

'Hello, darlin', give us a kiss!'

Then came a chirping mocking laugh which was a bridge too far for Passepartout who responded with a falsetto yapping of his own, and which had the effect of setting off every other animal with a voice in the vicinity and who felt they'd been silenced for too long. It sounded like a riot on Noah's Ark, and what Richard now read was an African grey parrot was also competing to be heard above the din.

'Hello darlin', give us a kiss! Hello darlin', give us a kiss! Hello darlin', give us a kiss!' It repeated with increasing shrillness, Passepartout yapping, equally shrilly in reply.

'Will you be quiet?' Richard begged. 'Please!'

'Hello darlin', give us a kiss!'

'And what is a cockney parrot doing in the Follet Valley anyway?'

He moved quickly down the aisle away from the bird and looking back at the general cacophony, turned sharply into the other aisle, bumping into a low trolley as he did so.

'Monsieur Ainsworth?'

Richard span round quickly to find both Lennard Bridille and Agnès Valadon eyeing him suspiciously.

'Monsieur Bridille, Madame Valadon, *bonjour.*'

'Hello darlin', give us a kiss!'

'Oh do shut up, you silly bird!' he spat angrily. 'Small world,' he added, trying to regain his composure.

'Yes, isn't it?' Lennard Bridille didn't look like he cared for the observation at any price.

'I'm here, er, well, erm...' Then Richard had a brainwave. 'I don't suppose you know anything about clearing gutters, do you?' he asked, the picture of innocence.

'Gutters? Why?' Bridille barked and Valadon leant her head forward, peering narrow-eyed through her glasses, and looking oddly like the parrot, which was thankfully now spent.

'Yes. Gutters. Blocked ones.'

The man made some kind of harrumphing noise as if gutters were the cause of at least ninety per cent of all the world's ills. 'Do it by hand, that's my advice. Always best. I bought some contraption online and I couldn't make it out, but then all the instructions were in English.' He paused and looked like he was about to belch. 'I should have bought that parrot for the job!' He followed up this attempt at levity by suddenly breaking out into the most absurd false laughter. Agnès Valadon joined in with equal ferocity; they had the look of inebriated hyenas. Passepartout wasn't keen on that noise either and started yapping again, and then they all got a 'Hello darlin', give us a kiss!' into the bargain.

'And why are you here?' Richard asked eventually when the ear-piercing noise had died down.

The plastic smiles dropped immediately off their faces and Bridille brushed his moustaches with a plump finger, military style. 'Hmm, well,' he began awkwardly and leant in conspiratorially, 'we have a slight problem.'

'Felipe Santos.' Madame Valadon was obviously not a fan.

'Bloody man keeps banging on about the weather, global warming or somesuch. Doesn't feel bloody warm to me!'

Agnès nodded in furious agreement. 'Climate change, he now calls it,' she added, in case Richard wasn't getting the drift.

'Anyway, some of our displays have been a bit erm…'

'Premature.' The parrot had longer sentences than this peculiar woman.

'Premature, that's right. They're on the wane and they need a bit of erm…'

'Cheering up.'

'Cheering up. Precisely.' He looked a bit sheepish about the whole thing. 'You see we have the visit from the ministry this week about the licence and we can't afford any slip-ups.'

They both looked down at their feet like naughty school-children.

'I'm sure it's for the best,' Richard said positively, and they beamed in gratitude at his tacit support.

'We have the backing of the whole committee,' Bridille informed him, back to his bullish best. This confused Richard somewhat.

'That's just you two though, isn't it? And Madame Cuistot?' He added, fishing for information.

A relieved Bridille opened a wide smile, partly lost under his facial hair but revealing a remarkably good set of teeth. 'Oh no! Madame Cuistot was never interested, too busy. No, we're back to a full complement now though, well almost,' he said. 'We persuaded Marcel Bouchard and Oriane Moulin to join us.'

'Almost a full complement,' Agnès Valadon chirped unnecessarily, sounding short of the full complement herself.

'And we've spoken about you doing the catering. I hope that's still on?' His military stiffness returned.

'Yes, of course.' Richard had not forgotten. 'We need to talk numbers,' he added, trying to sound business-like.

'Oh, about fifty I would say.'

'Yes, fifty.' Bridille had brought his own parrot.

'You're not going to get much for fifty euros!' Richard scoffed, thinking he was playing hardball.

Bridille looked at him askance. 'No, fifty people. Money is, er, no object. Understand?'

'Ah Richard, I have been looking for you.' Valérie was just in time to stop Richard looking really quite far out of his depth. 'Did you find that new barbecue rotisserie motor you came for? *Bonjour*, madame, monsieur.'

He stared at her blankly having no idea what on earth she was talking about.

'He told us it was something about gutters.' Bridille seemed put out.

'Gutters,' Valadon repeated, aping his mood.

'Oh yes, there's that as well,' laughed Valérie, 'but we've decided to do a *méchoui* for the Spring Fayre, haven't we Richard?'

'We have?' he asked, then suddenly turned to Bridille and Valadon. 'We have. A *méchoui*. A barbecue lamb, with all the trimmings,' he added, hoping not to be pressed on trimmings.

'Sounds a bit foreign, but I suppose you know what you're doing. I suppose diversity will impress the minister at least.'

'That's what we thought,' Richard said, doubting if barbecued lamb really did constitute any real level of diversity. 'Anyway,' he said, 'must get on.'

The two couples split and went their separate ways, fifty per cent of the La Chapelle committee chugged with their illicit flora to the tills, while Richard and Valérie backed away pretending to look for the cookery section.

She gave him a wink, knowing that she had just dug him out of a hole, while Richard was lost for words at her ingenious improvisation. 'I don't know what to say,' was his rather lame attempt though he was helped out with an accompanying 'Hello darlin', give us a kiss!'; for once the parrot getting its timing spot on.

Chapter Twenty-Four

Pulling into a lay-by just outside La Chapelle, Clare very slowly, very deliberately turned off the ignition and unclipped her seatbelt. She pulled down the sun visor and looked at herself in the mirror. She was not happy. She was wearing one of Valérie's head scarves to cover her blond hair and a pair of glasses that Richard didn't know she needed. For Clare's part she wasn't sure which upset her more: a disguise designed to hide her attractiveness or that Richard knew she needed glasses. She added to her dullish lipstick anyway, a concession she had negotiated. All of this was done under the watchful gaze of Valérie, who was quite clearly impressed with the woman's flare for the dramatic and her sense of suspenseful timing. Richard had seen it all before of course and whereas he had previously been cowed by the theatre of it all, he now found it vaguely comical. That he found it vaguely comical worried him greatly.

'So let me get this straight,' Clare began, not taking her eyes off herself in the mirror and puckering her lips to smooth her lipstick. 'You want me to pretend to be interested in buying a property here?'

'Yes,' Richard replied simply.

'Why?' Clare shot back immediately.

It was Valérie who answered. 'We think that there is something going on here, it is probably illegal but we need to know more.'

Clare looked from one to the other. 'It's a bit vague!'

'We don't really have much more than that,' Richard admitted. 'Something isn't right here, people have died, and we think it is to do with property and embezzling and... well, something like that anyway.'

'Is it dangerous?' The twinkle left Clare's eyes. 'Because in my experience of helping you two out I tend to be used as bait.' She raised a well-manicured eyebrow above the glasses' frame and Richard rolled his eyes.

'I thought you liked excitement?'

'I like *life*, Richard. I like *life*. And I thought that you *didn't* like excitement anyway?'

'We are wasting time!' Valérie huffed. 'It is not dangerous, Clare, I can promise you that. If it was dangerous I and Richard would go ourselves.'

Clare took a deep breath and then broke out into a laugh. 'You two and your *adventures*! I still don't know why I couldn't bring Oliver though, he knows more about these things than I do.'

'So I heard,' Richard muttered.

'What?'

'Nothing.'

'Well, I'm sure he'll find something to do without me.'

'Probably writing to Father Christmas.'

'Richard!' Valérie and Clare both simultaneously admonished him.

'Clare,' Valérie continued quickly before Richard could do any permanent damage. 'I do not think there is any danger, really. It is only members of the village committee who are being killed we think. But, we must know what the process is. Who gets paid for a sale? Who owns the properties that are for sale? Who gets the commission?'

Clare paused before answering. 'Thank you, Valérie. Now I understand why you asked me to do it. If it's about money, Richard would just bury his head in the sand. Wouldn't you, darling?'

A few minutes later, after being given more instructions, she pulled away, leaving them standing in the lay-by while Passepartout marked some territory.

'We may as well go for a walk,' Richard said. 'There's no point just standing around here waiting for Clare to come back.'

'What did she mean about burying your head in the sand?' It wasn't at all unusual for Valérie to ask a direct question, but she had never before asked about Richard and Clare's current relationship status, certainly not the divorce arrangements, or indeed lack of them. Richard tried to work out why that might be changing and there were a number of possibilities. Valérie might be getting impatient with the status quo. He and Clare were still married and if Richard continued to ignore legal correspondence that wasn't likely to change anytime soon. Valérie was old-fashioned and didn't want to make a move on Richard while he still technically had a wife. That, he decided quickly, was pure wishful thinking. Valérie knew the reality of the situation and was not one for standing on ceremony or waiting, as if in some Victorian melodrama, for when things might be less delicate.

Another possibility was that she was just being nosey, which would be out of character when it came to Richard. Their relationship had never been anything more than partners, co-adventurers really. And although Richard had come to rely on her as a bridge to a different world, a world that he found intoxicating, there had never been a suggestion that she was really all that interested in his marital status. A third option was that she was just making small talk, but then Valérie didn't make small talk.

'I think she's annoyed that I ignore all her solicitor's letters. But now I've met her solicitor, they're probably written in crayon anyway.'

She didn't laugh. 'She wants to move on,' she said, making it sound the most obvious thing in the world, which it probably was. 'And you do not?'

Richard considered the question. 'I do,' he said eventually. 'Of course I do. I just can't afford it. She's entitled to half the value of the house and business. In order to give her that, and don't get me wrong, she more than deserves it, but in order to pay that, I have to sell the house and the business. I can't afford to just buy her out.'

She thought about this for a second. 'It would help if I could sell my apartment in Paris, then you would have the money.'

It wasn't so long ago that Richard, on hearing something like this come from Valérie, would have been doing metaphorical cartwheels and whooping like a rodeo star but he knew better now. It wasn't a proposal of marriage, it was a simple matter of balance. Richard needs money, Valérie has money. It was an obvious transaction to make.

Only Valérie didn't have money either and had been largely taking a sabbatical from the bounty-hunting and assassination game in favour of the bucolic, if less lucrative, delights of the Follet Valley.

'Something will come up,' he said. 'But thank you. And besides, there's no money in heaven.'

'That is a film, yes?'

'*It's a Wonderful Life*, James Stewart, Frank Capra. 1946.'

She said something to him, something which it looked like he might want to hear but whatever it was was drowned out by a succession of very loud passing vehicles. A couple of dustbin lorries, a road-cleaning vehicle and a fourth open-backed truck that contained men with brooms and spades in their hands. It looked like an invasion force, and all the men had a grim look on their face, as if they knew the battle would be bloody.

Valérie bent down to pick up a spooked Passepartout. 'What is going on?' she asked, when she could at last be heard.

'I don't know, let's have a look.' They walked briskly around the corner as the trucks came to a halt in a cloud of dust and the workers jumped off the back. What they saw was the exact opposite of the picture postcard, chocolate box prettiness of the rest of La Chapelle-sur-Follet. It looked like Stalinist Brutalist architecture: a dozen or so drab two-storey grey concrete boxes, obviously poorly built and most of them boarded up.

'This must be the estate that had the committee so angry, Richard. It is so sad.'

It was the right word to use too. If the street had been a person, you would have described it as despondent.

'Come to see how the other half live, have you?' They both turned to see Felipe Santos approaching them; he too had a shovel over his shoulder. 'It's not pretty, is it?' he asked, challenging them to disagree.

'It is no surprise that the village committee protested against it being built.' Valérie talked as if of a bereavement.

'Ha! You think that, do you? This is what they created. Yes, they didn't want the place built, but they lost. So they took the money and kept it for their blessed gardens, and did a cheap job here. You could blow on these houses and they'd fall over.'

'Do you live here?' Richard asked.

'Yes, I do. For now. I get a free place because I work for their precious council, but as soon as I've saved up I'm leaving. The wife and I are going to buy our own place.'

'Away from here?' Valérie sounded a note of optimism.

'A long way from here, somewhere nice for the kids. They've got no one to play with round here, there are no other families.'

Richard shook his head at the sight of it all. He wasn't sentimental about buildings, except for those in films: Manderley in *Rebecca*, Tara in *Gone with the Wind*, but there was something so ineffably tragic about the place. It looked more like a cemetery, each house a gravestone and, apart from the noise of the workmen, eerily quiet.

'Who else lives here?' he asked. 'Anyone?'

'At first, they were all full. But the promised school never happened, nor shops, nor playgrounds. And the houses fell apart as quickly as the promises. Some are even unsafe. The roofs leak, the windows don't stop the wind, the plumbing barely works. It's just me and Rolande live here now.'

'Rolande?' Valérie asked.

'Rolande Roy. He's the street cleaner. His wife left him not long after they came here. My wife and kids live with her mother down south.'

'You must miss them?' Richard asked, seeing the hurt and anger in the man's eyes.

'That I do. Still, not long now.'

'When do you finish, monsieur?'

'My contract runs until the end of this week. They get their licence with the ministry renewed, and I go back to the family.'

'You make it sound like a prison sentence!' Richard joked, but Felipe didn't laugh.

'I reckon there'd be fewer crooks in prison,' he said, his eyes greyer than the houses around them.

Richard decided to change the subject. 'So what are all these men doing today?'

'Isn't it obvious!' Valérie rolled her eyes at him.

'That's right, madame. They're giving the place a polish for the big visit this week.' He smiled coldly. 'Another new minister, and this one that might actually want to see where the money went, and it's got the wind right up them I can tell you. They need it to at least look lived-in.'

The three of them watched as the workers began the process of making the place appear if not presentable then at least inhabited. Boarded-up windows were opened, power hoses were being used on pathways and tiny patches of lawn mowed. Felipe walked away, his shovel over his slumped shoulders, with a sad shake of his head: John Wayne, to Richard, defeated.

'Again, it's like a film,' he said quietly, 'they're creating an illusion.'

Sometime later Clare returned to the lay-by to pick them up. 'Sorry I've been so long,' she said. 'But I got the feeling I was being interviewed.'

'It is quite likely that is exactly what was happening.' Valérie climbed in the front, still angry over the apparent ghost-town side of La Chapelle.

'Who will the property be for? Why do I want to come here? Am I prepared to work for the community? Am I married? That was a tricky one!' She smiled at Richard in the back who just nodded. 'Would I be bringing children too? They advised against that, no infrastructure, they said. I just got the impression they didn't like children!'

'I don't think they like anybody!' Richard scoffed from the back.

'You could be right. The house they showed me was a family home and that's probably why it's on the market.' She speeded the car up. 'It was a bit creepy actually. Nice house though, nice garden as you'd expect. Pricey though, you couldn't afford it, Richard, but look it up it might be online. It was called La Bastide du Lavoir.'

Chapter Twenty-Five

Richard recalled with fondness, and no little embarrassment, the first time he had broken into a place with Valérie. Or, to put it more accurately, the first time Valérie had broken into a place with Richard in tow. He simply couldn't believe what was happening to him. Valérie d'Orçay was the most exotic and quixotic person he had ever met and while ordinarily he would have run a mile from breaking and entering, clashes with mafia assassination teams, brutal murders and certainly poultrycide, he had had the time of his life.

The thought that it might be coming to an end just as they were getting started seemed an unusually cruel trick. Richard felt he was just waking up after a long hibernation. OK, to the outside world he wasn't exactly leaping out of bed, more rolling over and pressing the snooze button, but it was a start and he didn't want it to end.

They had left the car some distance away and come across country to avoid Agnès Valadon's camera, the one they knew about anyway, and now they skirted through the shadows of a sleeping La Chapelle-sur-Follet, dodging street lamps and the few lit windows. The place, devoid of tourists, was deathly quiet.

'It really seems like no one lives here,' he whispered as they gathered their breath under the cover of a fragrant wisteria which fell lazily on to the pavement.

'I do not like this place, Richard,' Valérie agreed. 'It is not natural.'

They moved on silently to the centre of town where they knew La Bastide du Lavoir stood, a stream from the River Follet running through its garden. They huddled once more across the road. The place was shuttered, there were no lights, nor was the Fourniers' car parked in the gravelled driveway.

'They were supposed to move in this morning, I don't get it,' he said. 'They can't have had enough already, surely?'

'And yet it is for sale again.' Valérie looked up at him and the moonlight caught her excited eyes. 'Shall we take a look, Richard?'

He half-smiled. 'After you, Madame d'Orçay.'

'OK. Wait here while I unlock the gate.' She slipped away across the dark street, her shadow barely visible in the gloaming. From where he crouched, he could just hear the click of the lock and he joined her almost as quietly. By the side of the gate was the usual chalk slate message board and Valérie shone her torch on it. 'Families that garden together, grow together,' it read, the usual greeting-card-style sentimental platitude. Like Valérie said, the place was unnatural.

'I wonder what the Wikipedia version is?' he asked.

She hunched over her phone to hide the light from the screen. 'It says, "The cuckoo builds not for himself."'

'But at Oriane's house?'

'I think it's just a way of sending a message, Richard. Maybe the house is not important?'

Richard thought about this. He wasn't keen on being manipulated, he'd had his fill quite frankly but Valérie had a point. Someone was following them, or at least knew what they were up to. He vaguely remembered the quote from school and what seemed like hours poring over Shakespeare word by endless multi-nuanced word. So much so that in the end most of his classmates, including Richard, developed a kind of allergy to William Shakespeare and shrank from his work as though his plays and sonnets were stinging nettles and not great pieces of theatre and literature. The great man would probably be demoralised to see how his work was taught now.

'Well, I suppose it's some reference to spring.'

'Perhaps. But what do cuckoos do, Richard?' She seemed on the verge of a major discovery, but for the life of him he couldn't see it.

'Cuckoos? Well, they go cuckoo, I guess. Cuck-oo,' he added by way of illustration.

Even in the dark he could see that she was wondering if it was one of his jokes, or if he actually was an idiot. 'Yes, but they also lay their eggs in other birds' nests! Someone is trying to tell us that this isn't the Fourniers' nest, I think.'

Richard thought about this. 'That makes sense, but are we now saying that whoever keeps changing this thing on Wikipedia is on our side? Helping us out?'

She shook her head. 'I don't know.'

They moved to the back of the very obviously empty property and Valérie unpicked the lock on a heavy wooden back door. It creaked loudly as she pushed it inwards and they sank down to the ground in case it roused a neighbour, if indeed there were neighbours. After a few moments it was clear that no one was coming and they moved inside, leaving the creaky door open. They found themselves in the kitchen, which was not only pristine but designed as if for a photo essay about classic-style kitchens making a comeback. Richard knew something about the subject and marvelled at how much money had gone into the fixtures and fittings. There were a couple of enormous Belfast sinks with expensive-looking pewter mixing taps, surrounded by gleaming, even in the dark, white brick wall tiles. A large farmhouse-style table dominated the middle of the room with a dried flower centrepiece; the floor was polished red quarry tile and the whole place screamed of an issue of *Country Homes & Interiors*, but also, and equally loudly, it screamed show home, not lived in.

'It's like Oriane's kitchen,' Richard whispered. 'Does no one cook for themselves in this place?'

'It would seem not.'

'No wonder Bridille needs a caterer.'

'What is going on here, Richard? Nothing is real.'

'I agree. This isn't a family home, where are the toys? Where's the mess? And for that matter, where's the family?'

'Clare told us Lennard Bridille made it clear that children are not welcome here. Felipe Santos says that his family moved away because they were lonely, that the children had no one to play with...'

'And yet, there's been a big show of a family moving in. I know.' They were both thinking aloud, safe in the knowledge they were alone. 'It's got to be something to do with the licence, surely?'

They moved through to the hallway and a polished wooden staircase. To their right was an arch that led to the main salon, showing a large fireplace, again unused, or at least not used for some time, and with another dried flower display in the grate. Above the fireplace there was finally some evidence that the place might have occupants. On the mantelpiece was a collection of photographs, in oddly inexpensive frames that didn't match the high-end luxury of the rest of the house. The photographs were of the Fournier family and it didn't look right.

'They look like they were all taken this morning!' Richard felt slightly affronted at how badly this was all being set up. 'It's so obvious!'

'And the way they are posed?' Valérie was equally put out. 'They look like one of those families put together for an insurance advertisement.'

They both looked at each other. 'Why?' they asked at the same time.

Richard sat down on the large leather Chesterfield sofa. 'OK,' he said. 'Let's say it's all a front, the whole place, La Chapelle, everything. But what for?'

'Drugs!' Valérie was so sure of herself that it took Richard by surprise.

'How do you make that out?'

'Because drugs are grown, Richard, and this place is all about growing things!'

Richard was far from convinced. 'Please don't take this the wrong way, but I think that's wishful thinking on your part. You love an international conspiracy.' She looked insulted by that, but also, for once, she recognised his point. 'I don't see Lennard Bridille or Agnès Valadon as international narcotics kingpins, and that's assuming they, or one of them, is the guilty party. The way things are going for the *committee*, they're just as likely to be the next victims.'

'Well, it is clear that there is something going on with money. You saw that place today and how angry Felipe Santos is about it.'

'Yes, yes he was. And he would have reason then to tear the whole place down, starting with the village council.' He paused. 'So where does Oriane Moulin fit into that? He was working for her after all.'

'You always think of her!' was the unexpectedly fierce reply.

'It's a valid question,' he said, springing back to his feet defensively. 'Especially as she and Marcel Bouchard, another who seems miserable at being here by the way, are now on this bloody committee. And why *is* she here anyway? A TV programme, really? And what's your problem with each other? Did you fall out at Crufts?'

'Sshh, Richard!'

'I won't shush! There's nobody here. What is it between you and Oriane Moulin that has you so agitated?' He paused for effect. 'Is it over an ex-husband?'

'Be quiet,' she hissed at him.

And with that he felt like he had gone too far.

'Sorry, I didn't…' he began whispering again.

'Richard, sshh! I think I can hear something.'

They both stayed quiet and stood still.

'I can't hear anything,' he said after a few moments. 'It's probably just mice or something.' He walked back to the hall archway and then turned back to face her. 'There's really no one here, this whole place is a…'

He felt the thwack of wood across the back of his head and he sank to knees. His first thought was outrage, how dare someone attack him. *I own a bed and breakfast,* he thought groggily. His next thought was why on earth was he being hit again, as a large broom this time smacked across his shoulders sending him slumped to the floor. He was vaguely aware of Valérie leaping over him and giving chase through the kitchen and for a brief moment he thought about doing the same, but his knees had other ideas so he remained on the floor. He lay there for a few minutes wrapped up in thoughts of injustice, asking himself questions like: how come it was always him who got hit, and was this really what he wanted in life?

Then the thought occurred to him that yes, yes it is what he wanted in life and in order to do that he ought possibly to see if Valérie needed his assistance. He staggered back to his feet and went to the sink to guzzle some water from under the expensive taps. It was then he noticed an official-looking certificate on the wall. It was written in ornate calligraphy and embossed with the Tricolore flag. It was the official licence, or a copy at least, of the granting of the *Jardin Remarquable* status to La Chapelle-sur-Follet and was signed by all the original members of the town committee: Florian Bouchard, Duval Cuistot, Lennard Bridille, Agnès Valadon and Christophe de la Cour. It was also signed by the then Ministère de la Culture, Bernard Janvier.

'Got you!' he said in triumph and went off into the night in search of Valérie.

Chapter Twenty-Six

A less wary individual, having discovered what they believed to be the key to the case, cracked it even, blown it wide open as they used to say when movies were movies, would have run into the night with only one thing on their mind. Tell their partner. And while Richard had only that one thing on his mind, he also knew from painful experience that running wilfully into the darkness had its downside.

He emerged tentatively from the back door of La Bastide du Lavoir nervously looking both ways, then both ways again the way he was taught to cross a road. It seemed clear enough, as was the gate and he stepped silently into the street. His assailant and Valérie were nowhere to be seen or heard. He decided quickly that the best course of action was to head for the Auberge Cuistot, concluding that that was where most things took place. He still kept to the shadows though just in case.

The lights were now on inside the restaurant, even though it was just past midnight, and from his hidden viewpoint on the darkened terrace he could see Madame Cuistot standing at the bar. She was her usual animated self, a vast array of differing emotions crossing her face in the space of a few seconds and she was talking to someone who was hidden from view, standing or sitting behind a pillar. He changed his viewing angle, still keeping out of the spread of light and then sat down slowly, shocked, as he saw who Madame Cuistot was talking to. It was Valérie. Madame Cuistot lit a large, thick candle at the bar and took it to Valérie's table, sitting down opposite her.

A number of questions, mixed with a certain amount of outrage, ran through his mind. Surely it wasn't Madame Cuistot who had attacked him with a broom? But then if it wasn't, why was Valérie here talking to her? He tapped the table in front of him, then immediately looked around to see if he'd been overheard. Taking a deep breath, he stood up. 'There's only one way to find out, old son!' he told himself and took long, determined strides towards the door, not taking his eyes off the two women inside.

He would remember later that this had been an error. He failed to notice, as he strode like John Wayne into a showdown, a small hairless dog relieving itself against a potted shrub by the doors. The dog, alarmed at having its privacy disturbed, yelped, interrupting Richard's stride pattern and then destroying it completely as he tripped over the animal. He went smashing, stumbling through the doors, crashing into the table where the two startled women were sitting. Reaching out to grab something, he picked up the candle and fell over the table before ending up on the floor. The candle rolled out of his hand disappearing under a table in the corner as he hit the ground.

'Richard!' Valérie cried.

'Monsieur Ainsworth!' Madame Cuistot also cried.

But before he could answer there was an explosion from the corner of the restaurant, partially knocking out the wall and shattering windows.

Once the dust had settled there was a brief lull as the three of them, having been thrown to the ground, stood up and checked themselves for injury. Amazingly, they were all unharmed. Valérie put her arm around an ashen-faced Madame Cuistot, who started to cry quietly with the shock.

'Richard,' Valérie said quietly and with something approaching awe. 'How did you know the candle was an explosive?'

Without answering Richard picked up a fallen chair and sat down. He looked at Valérie and shook his head slowly. 'I didn't,' he said quietly. 'I had no idea.'

'What has happened?' Oriane Moulin came loudly through the open door, the largely hairless Zsa Zsa in her arms with a look of complete innocence on her face. 'Is everyone OK?'

Her concern seemed to be genuine and she flitted from one to the other, checking each shocked victim in turn. Then the commotion started as Lennard Bridille strode in, Agnès Valadon appeared demurely in her pyjamas and Marcel Bouchard, in a silk dressing gown, stood in the doorway, his face a picture of horror at what had obviously occurred. He went straight to Madame Cuistot and put his arms around her.

'Are you hurt?' he asked quietly and a sobbing Madame Cuistot shook her head.

'Someone should call the police.' Richard was surprised that the suggestion should come from Valérie, but it was the right and obvious thing to do under the circumstances, and it was he, wandering outside, slightly dazed, who made the call. He left a message on the Commissaire's mobile and sat down in the fresh air. He felt a gentle hand on his shoulder as Valérie sat down next to him.

'Are you OK, Richard?' she asked quietly. She was as shaken as he had ever seen her.

'I think so,' he sighed. 'You?'

'Yes,' she answered. 'I am angry though. We could have been killed.' She grabbed his hand and held it tightly.

'It's lucky that dog was here. Even I'm not clumsy enough to fall that far without help.' He felt like a fool; yes, he was the hero but just once he wished he could have been a hero in heroic fashion.

'You tripped over Oriane's dog?'

'Zsa Zsa? Yes. She was on the terrace just here...' His voice tailed off and he and Valérie looked at each other.

'Why though?' she asked quietly, before bursting into action. 'Come on, Richard, let us go back in before Henri arrives.'

For himself, Richard understood perfectly well that their time would be better spent indoors trying to gather information from the others, but he'd never survived a bomb explosion before and would have preferred a few moments' rest, an opportunity to gather his thoughts, contemplate mortality, and so on.

'That's not all.' He grabbed her hand, thoughts on the fragility of existence would have to wait. 'Her ex-husband is the minister who signed the licence in the first place.'

She looked at him, trying to work out just what that meant. 'Come inside, Richard' she said eventually. 'We have work to do.'

'But who would do such a thing?' Madame Cuistot was wailing as they re-entered the restaurant area. 'And on such a day!'

'Please, you must sit down.' Marcel led her gently to some bank seating at the side of the room, while the others fussed around. 'I'll get you a brandy.'

'You've always been very good to me, Marcel, thank you. I don't know what I would do without you.' She fumbled with a handkerchief in her lap.

'It is you who has always been there for me.'

'And on such a day!' she repeated. 'My poor mother's birthday. I always light a candle for her on this day.'

Richard and Valérie exchanged a look. 'Who knew about that, madame?' Valérie asked with attempted innocence.

'Everyone.' It was Marcel who answered as he handed over a glass of brandy. 'If you remember we even had a party in memory of your mother last year. It was when you reunited with your sister.'

'And then you went back to your studies the next day, I remember, yes. It was the last time I saw you before your poor parents…' She downed the brandy in one go.

Richard and Valérie looked at each other again. The relationship between the older woman and the young man bordered on the maternal and it felt like a private moment.

'No, I don't think so,' Bridille interjected. 'You came back in the autumn to surprise your father for *his* birthday.'

'Oh yes.' Marcel looked flushed all of a sudden. 'But you all had one of your committee meetings, he barely noticed.'

'Do you mind if I help myself to a brandy also?' It was Oriane who interrupted. 'I'm not sure that joining your village committee is a very safe career move!' She poured herself a drink.

'I'll have one of those if I may?' Agnès Valadon's face looked completely white as she approached the bar. 'Do you really think someone is trying to kill us all?' She directed her question at Lennard Bridille who, rather than showing any fear, blustered noisily instead.

'Of course not!' he thundered. 'And I don't think it wise for you to start drinking either, Madame Valadon. You have church obligations today I believe.' He took the glass that Oriane had filled for Agnès and drank it himself.

There was a lull as everyone took in Madame Valadon's fears.

'I am surprised that no one else came to see what the noise was?' Valérie asked, looking from one to the other, almost challenging for a response. She winked at Richard surreptitiously as she spoke.

'I agree,' he said, picking up the baton. 'Particularly the Fourniers. I'd be worried about the safety of my children if I heard an explosion. I'd want to know what was going on.'

There was an uncomfortable silence that no one seemed eager to fill but eventually it was Agnès Valadon who spoke, having regained some level of composure. 'They went back to Paris I believe. Madame Fournier's cousin has been taken ill.'

'They promised, at least they hope, to be back for the celebrations at the end of the week. The visit of the minister that is.' Lennard Bridille added, though unusually for him he didn't look anyone in the eye as he spoke. He asked Oriane for another brandy and Richard noticed the look on her face as she handed it to him. It was not a friendly look.

'And yet, Monsieur Bridille...' This time it was Valérie who spoke. 'Their property, which apparently they only moved into this morning, is up for sale already.'

If Lennard Bridille felt that he had been unmasked as a fraud, or even as the person who had set upon Richard in the Fournier house, he wasn't giving it away easily. He looked at Richard. 'I think there is some confusion here,' he said calmly. 'I showed *your sister* La Bastide du Lavoir because it is very similar, in layout that is, to La Manoir Saint Sulpice, which is for sale.' He smiled unconvincingly. 'I thought I had made that clear to *your sister*, my apologies.'

Richard didn't at all like the way he stressed the words 'your sister', and thanks to current circumstances, made a mental note to keep Clare away from La Chapelle from now on.

'Why did you not just show her this Manoir Saint Sulpice place instead?' Interestingly it was Oriane who asked the question.

'I don't have the keys, madame. As you know. You lent them to the Commissaire.'

'That is true, monsieur.' Commissaire Henri Lapierre, having arrived much more quickly than expected, walked through the open doors. 'Now, would someone tell me please what has been going on here?'

As he asked the question everyone surrounded him and started talking at once. Valérie, however, tugged at Richard's sleeve and beckoned him closer to the side door that had been blown off its hinges. She leant in close to his ear. 'Richard!' she whispered. 'I want to take a look at that gutter cleaner. I do not trust that little man at all!'

Richard couldn't have agreed more and they both left the *auberge* unseen.

Chapter Twenty-Seven

'You can't come in without permission!' An implacable Rolande Roy leant on his broom blocking the entrance to the La Chapelle refuse tip, or *déchetterie* as it's called in France, which had always pleased Richard immensely as it sounds like de-shittery and therefore exactly what a refuse tip should be. Any word-play happiness was being sorely tested, however, as Roy, clearly aiming for the petty bureaucrat of the year award, was defending his kingdom with some vigour.

'We need to find something and it really is quite urgent!' Valérie had tried charm, cajoling and bribery. Richard had the sense now that she was just a hair trigger away from violence.

'I don't care how urgent it is, you cannot come in.' The man was insufferable. 'You are not from the commune of La Chapelle-sur-Follet and it would therefore be considered trespassing.' He was a strange-looking individual. Thin to the point of being painful to look at, he was wearing a T-shirt and shorts which looked too big for him, his work boots like he'd stolen them from an adult's wardrobe and his large rubberised gloves had an undeniable air of menace. All of this was topped off by a stringy beard, sunglasses and a faded Euro Disney baseball cap. He looked like a child trying, and failing, to look like a grown-up. He was, however, utterly immoveable.

'Is there no way around this?' Richard asked, appealing hopefully to his better side.

'Yes, there is,' Roy said enthusiastically, though Richard didn't like the thin smile that came with it. 'You could buy a house in the commune of La Chapelle-sur-Follet and become a resident!' He chuckled and Richard sensed Valérie bristling with fury. She took just a small step forward and finally Rolande Roy became aware of the simmering danger in front of him, quickly taking a same-sized step backwards and lifting his broom in defence.

'Do you always brandish that broom as a weapon, Monsieur Roy?' Richard asked, rubbing the back of his head for emphasis. 'It looks very new, did your old one need replacing?'

'My other was stolen!' he said smartly, and smiled at his own cleverness. 'And anyway, I had an early night.' He paused. 'Dammit.'

'Why did you assault Richard last night?' Valérie's voice was low, almost a growl.

'I thought you were burglars, someone's got to keep an eye out. We don't like strangers, don't you get it?'

He took another step back and through the gate, snapping it shut and locking it between them.

'Then we'll go to the police, Monsieur Roy!' Valérie's triumph at this statement was short-lived.

'Go on then,' he laughed. 'Like to see you try!'

Valérie stepped right up to the gate and managed to get her hand through the mesh at a very unfortunate height for the now stricken Rolande Roy. She twisted her hand round and he whined in pain. Like any man, Richard did feel a certain level of sympathy, but it was heavily drowned out by the relief that it wasn't him on the end of Valérie's vice-like grip. 'There is another way!' His voice was weak, but he made himself heard.

'And what is that?' Valérie snarled.

'You can get special permission.'

'From whom?'

'Monsieur Bridille!' Valérie let go and he fell back to safety. 'But it's lunchtime now anyway and we're closed, I can't let you in without his say-so.'

'Then we'll be back this afternoon, won't we, Richard?'

'Yes.' Richard was still wincing on the other man's behalf; it was like a phantom pregnancy feeling.

Roy stood with difficulty and took a few paces back for added safety. 'Anyway!' he tried to laugh but just coughed instead. 'It won't help you! We're shut this afternoon. And tomorrow! I have a life too, you know.'

It seemed an unlikely claim in Richard's opinion, but with that ringing in their ears, he didn't see what else could be done for now. They trudged back to the car and sat in silence for a few moments, before Valérie started the ignition and sped angrily away. Just around the corner, she swung the car into a small country lane and stopped abruptly. Richard knew better than to interrupt her at times like these and waited instead for her to speak. He didn't need to though; after a few minutes Rolande Roy's van passed behind them as he went presumably home for lunch and some form of cold compress. Valérie slammed the car in reverse and took them back to the *déchetterie*.

She dug about in the boot of her car, still in a foul mood from the confrontation with Roy's typically bureaucratic French inflexibility. It always amazed Richard that the French were surprised by their own rigidity as regards rules. It seemed everyone else was aware except the French themselves. Eventually finding what she was looking for she emerged with a large pair of chain-cutters.

'Won't it be pretty obvious who broke in though?' Richard asked, feeling a note of caution should at least be considered.

'Yes,' she replied. 'And I do not care.'

'Fair enough,' he muttered.

The padlock chain around the heavy iron gate was no match for Valérie's equipment, which together with her current mood was a formidable combination and they stepped through into Rolande Roy's personal kingdom. Richard remembered going 'to the tip' with his dad when he was younger. At the age of seven or eight, that kind of thing feels like an adventure, as though you're being given a private insight into the world of grown-ups. Of course, all it really was was a mundane chore and an opportunity for his dad to get out of the house on a Sunday.

What he also remembered though were long rows of skips; people would throw things in without any sorting or classification or measure of safety. Just chuck your broken children's toys, paint cans and asbestos in anywhere you can. Not for the first time Richard wondered how they'd all survived the 1970s. This was very different though. This refuse tip, as with all public refuse tips in France, had more order and categorising to it than a library's Dewey Decimal System. They take their recycling even more seriously than rules, he noted, though he kept the observation to himself.

'It shouldn't be that hard to find I wouldn't have thought,' he said, trying to cheer her up as they approached the large containers sunk into the ground. 'A gutter cleaner will be in the electrics section and probably alphabetised between a fridge freezer and a hair dryer.'

'That is if that man is efficient!' she snapped.

'I think you can probably guarantee that,' he replied.

She took a deep breath. 'Yes, sorry, Richard. But people like that… they are so French!' She looked like she might erupt again.

'Never mind, we're in now. And this way we don't have to go through Lennard Bridille.'

'You are right, Richard. Thank you.'

It was an unusually warm reply given the circumstances. Which left him with the feeling that it was actually something else that was bothering her, and that wringing Rolande Roy's bureaucratic neck, and other parts, was possibly just a manifestation of that.

As Richard knew would be the case the *déchetterie* was clean, tidy and well-organised. Everything had its place, something he had found out to his cost when he'd first arrived in France and nearly caused what felt like a major international incident. He had absentmindedly thrown an unflattened cardboard box into the plastics container, which was bad enough, but had then compounded this heinous crime by not removing the lid of an old jam jar when putting it in the bottle bank. At one point he could swear he heard the word 'deportation' in the fuss that followed.

The electrics container was the least full of all of the containers, which on the one hand made their job easier, but also meant climbing down into the thing. 'There's nothing else for it,' he said over his shoulder and, cleverly in his opinion, he pulled a mattress from a neighbouring skip, threw it down and followed it breaking his fall. It still hurt his creaking bones but he felt very resourceful nonetheless, until Valérie placed a ladder next to him and climbed down gracefully, her 'refuse tip jumpsuit outfit' looking too pristine to be in a skip. 'Yes, but where's the fun in that?' he asked cheekily, and she smiled.

They started to rummage in the detritus around them and he continued his 'man of action' playacting. 'I think that's why it's me that gets hit so much,' he said, picking up a leaf blower that looked like it had burst into flames. 'Your criminal type sees me as the more dynamic of the team.'

Valérie, using an extendable litter-picker grabbed an old radio and said, without looking up, 'Or you are just too slow to get out of the way.'

Richard toyed with some curling tongs and nodded. 'Yes,' he agreed without hurt, 'there's probably something in that.' He had on some old-ish jeans and a sweatshirt that had some faded logo on it and his gardening Wellington boots. He figured that the difference in their outfits might also represent a difference in just how dirty each one of them was prepared to get.

'Until I saw Roy's broom, I thought it was Oriane who had hit me last night,' he said, throwing junk around.

'Oh no!' Valérie said quickly and without any semblance of doubt.

'What made you so sure?'

'Because, Richard,' she paused, 'if Oriane Moulin hit you, you would probably be dead. She doesn't take prisoners.'

'I see,' he replied, giving it some thought. 'Funny though, you talking like that. I must be having some effect on you!'

She stopped her arm's length inspection and stood up. 'What does that mean?' Her voice was very serious and he sensed trouble.

'You said, "She doesn't take prisoners." It's an English idiom, not the French *aucune concession*.' He had no idea if he'd offended her by pointing out a trace of Englishness; five minutes ago the woman had been railing against the French. She couldn't have it both ways.

Valérie relaxed. 'I see,' she said quietly. 'No, Richard, I wasn't using an English idiom, I was being very French actually and speaking literally. She takes no prisoners. She is very aggressive, she goes too far. She kills.'

Richard accidentally put his foot into a discarded deep fat fryer. 'I see,' he said, trying to ignore his physical situation. 'Is that the problem between you two?' He lowered his voice, which he felt was the right thing to do. 'Something happened on a mission?'

She helped him to steady as he extricated himself from the filthy cookware. 'Yes,' she said coldly. 'She was too emotional and endangered the life of a colleague because of it.' She went silent.

'And?'

'And I reported her for it, she was a liability. They withdrew her from action and she left the DGSE shortly afterwards.'

Richard shook his head. 'The more I know,' his voice sounded tired, 'the less I understand about all of this. I think she's involved somehow. It's surely no coincidence that it was her ex-husband behind the original, possibly corrupt, decision to give La Chapelle the *Jardin Remarquable* licence?'

Valérie threw down some more broken electrics, this time a desk light. 'I think Oriane is involved too,' she said, kicking at a lampshade. 'But why? It cannot be just to control that silly village committee.'

'Why not?' Richard asked, picking up something that he thought looked like a hand-held food mixer, before blushing and throwing it away.

'Because, as I said, they would be dead and we have had two near-misses as well as two deaths. Her strike rate would be higher than that.'

They continued looking for a while longer, losing hope of finding the gutter cleaner they had come for. 'If someone is doing this to destroy the place, particularly the committee, you wouldn't need to actually *kill* them all, just divide and conquer as it were.'

'I don't understand, Richard, how do you mean?'

'Well, supposing it is Oriane, or even another member of this damned committee? With all this going on, the licence might not get renewed anyway but also you could cover your steps by actually *surviving* an attack. Like Lennard Bridille sells his gutter thing.'

She thought about this. 'But you saved Madame Cuistot, Richard, she didn't save herself.'

'No, but that doesn't mean she didn't have a plan in place to do so. I just stumbled in and did the work for her! And

anyway, she's not on the committee, not officially anyway.'
Valérie nodded. She wasn't entirely convinced and he could
see that, but it was clear she thought the theory had merit.
It was actually Richard who started to break down his own
speculation. 'The thing is, if you are on the village committee,
you've got a pretty cushy number. So why destroy it?'

'Maybe it now symbolises everything our killer hates.
The village, the pettiness…'

'The ex-husband,' Richard added.

'The ex-husband. The injustice.' And he looked at her
confused. 'Felipe Santos,' she explained.

'Or Rolande Roy for that matter.'

'Yes. Or even more than that, a loss of life. I mean a
living life!' She was suddenly very excited.

'I don't get it. What's a living life?'

'Richard!' She grabbed his sleeve. 'Someone who wanted
to get away but in the end had to stay!'

'Marcel Bouchard!' he cried. 'He had no friends growing
up, his parents seem obsessed with the village and ignored
him. Madame Cuistot was more of a mother to him.'

'And we know he came back in the autumn when
everything was set up!' She began to climb up the ladder.

'Where are you going? We haven't found the gutter
cleaner yet.'

Having reached the top, she steadied the ladder for
him as he followed. 'It is not here, Richard.' Deflation
was setting in already. 'Everything here is too old. It is
not here.'

He looked back down, she was right. Then he had a
thought. 'Hang on,' he said. 'Have you got those chain-
cutters?'

She handed them to him and, briefly forgetting himself, he kissed her forehead in triumph and strode over to the little shed office and broke the padlock. He emerged a few seconds later with a boxed-up gutter cleaner.

'Brilliant, Richard!' Valérie clapped. 'How did you know?'

'Like you said, everything here is too old, this is new. That means Rolande Roy can make a bit of extra money by fixing it up and selling it on. Perks of the job.'

Valérie bent down and opened the box. Richard inspected the plug, which had burn marks on it where it had flared, and Valérie produced the instructions.

'Monsieur Bridille was right,' she said, handing the booklet over to Richard. 'The instructions are in English.'

He flicked through. 'Not quite,' he said, a note of victory in his voice. 'These aren't in English, Valérie, they're in American.'

Chapter Twenty-Eight

'Shall we stop for lunch?' Richard asked. 'I feel like celebrating.' He had an ulterior motive too, but he thought it would appeal more to Valérie if he dressed it up as a deserved reward.

'I really think we must hurry, Richard, what if Marcel Bouchard tries to kill again?'

He knew she was right. He knew that that was indeed the more pressing course of action. Lives may be at stake. She could have just phoned Lapierre and told him of course, but Valérie being Valérie she felt a need to be at the centre of things. It was her way. But even so…

'I'm hungry and I need to go to the toilet!' He sounded like an outraged four-year-old. 'Look, over there,' he said as they approached a roundabout. On the left was Patàpain, a chain of *boulangeries* that was branching out into fast food as well. And one which had customer 'facilities'. Valérie tutted as if food or any other human necessity were alien to her and went skidding into the car park. Richard immediately hopped out.

'Wait!' Valérie shouted. 'I can't go in like this.' Clearly what Valérie considered chic enough for trawling through landfill wasn't going to cut it, even in a middling fast food joint, and she handed him one of Passepartout's blankets that she'd been sitting on so as not to dirty the car seat.

'You're not going to change here?' He couldn't believe he was being asked to act as a screen as Valérie was preparing to strip off in a public car park.

'Where else do you suggest?' she asked, with stiletto logic, and turned her back on him.

Richard held the blanket high so that he couldn't see either. In his mind's eye were flashbacks of beach holidays as a child when his mum would hold a towel around him while he removed his sandy trunks. Something he never managed to do without falling over. *It should be an Olympic event*, he thought, *barely less indecent than beach volleyball.*

'What are you doing, Richard?' Valérie pulled the blanket down and was still wearing her overalls, only now she had removed her boots and headscarf, revealing hair let down to its natural shoulder length, elasticated trouser hems, red high-heel shoes, jewellery and a slight floral scent.

'That's the same outfit.' Richard sounded stupefied.

'It is very much *not* the same outfit. It is the same jumpsuit, I have changed the ensemble that is all. And you?'

'I've only got this,' he said miserably. 'And an old T-shirt underneath.' She sprayed him aggressively with perfume, as if he were an attacker and it was Mace. And with him now coughing and struggling to control his bladder as a result, they went through the automatic doors. She looked like a model and he looked like he'd come to unblock her drains and heaven only knows what Martin would make out of that.

He immediately made for the toilets while Valérie joined the lunch queue with a look on her face that suggested she needn't have bothered smartening herself up, and to be fair to her, Richard was thinking, it just didn't suit her to be holding a tray and plastic cutlery.

Her face hadn't changed a great deal by the time Richard rejoined her at the till, though he himself felt a relieved man.

'I chose a couple of pain au chocolats, that is all.' She managed to purse her lips as she spoke. 'We can eat proper food later on.' If the cashier felt any level of affront at Valérie's dismissive opinion of the menu she didn't show it, handing her the receipt even though it was Richard who paid. Valérie left Richard to carry the tray to a table in the far corner, presumably not wanting to be seen, though by whom Richard couldn't fathom, *Vogue* magazine possibly. Then Richard recognised someone else who seemed to be hiding from sight and who saw him and Valérie at the same time.

The colour drained from Commissaire Lapierre's face as they approached. He looked awkwardly downcast at their sudden appearance and Richard felt a little sorry for him. He was all spruced up again and the look in his eye suggested that they were intruding on his personal space. Not that that would matter as he would also know from experience that Valérie, like an invading force, didn't recognise those boundaries. For her part Valérie looked equally embarrassed, which Richard put down to the fact that they were effectively in a roadside café, far from her natural habitat.

'Ah, Henri, glad you are here.' It was said with the certainty of someone who had arranged a meeting, not someone who had just got lucky. 'We want to talk to you.'

He sighed in defeat as Valérie slid into the seating opposite. 'And I want to talk to you two as well,' he said, looking fed up. 'You both left the scene of a crime last night, before I could take a statement. This is becoming a habit, madame, not a good one.' He looked from one to another and as expected saw no remorse. 'Do either of you have experience of IEDs? Actually, madame, do not answer that, I know your answer. And you?' He looked wearily at Richard.

'What's an IED?'

'Only a fool would answer like that and be believed. And yet, I believe you.' Richard frowned in confusion. 'An IED is an improvised explosive device. It does not, sadly, need much skill to make one. Any competent mechanic, for instance.'

'Oh right. We had a neighbour who used to buy them to kill the moles. The moles ruined his lawn… Anyway, that's really what we wanted to talk to you about. Mechanical stuff and the people, well, mechanics.' Richard was hoping that his sudden burst of enthusiasm might rub off on the policeman. The look the Commissaire gave him suggested strongly that it had not.

'What is that smell?' Valérie asked screwing up her nose.

'Now look,' Richard slammed down his paper cup. 'You can't have me digging around a *déchetterie* all bloody morning and expect me to come up smelling of roses!'

'It is roses, Richard!'

'Why did you leave so quickly last night?' Lapierre interrupted.

'It is you, Henri, it is a very feminine scent.'

His shoulders slumped. 'It was a present. It is called Bleu de Nuit. Now…' He looked from one to the other. 'Talk to me, please.' His voice was drowned out by the sound of squealing tyres, piercingly invading the room and getting everyone's attention in the process. It was a motorbike and it was being handled expertly as it skidded around the car park before disappearing back on to the road. It reminded Richard, somewhat belatedly, that their discoveries about Marcel Bouchard cleared Madame Tablier. She could now be released.

'You have to release Madame Tablier!' he blurted. 'She's innocent and we can prove it.'

The Commissaire, with an air of sadness, watched the motorbike race off, not looking at Richard as he spoke. 'Monsieur Ainsworth, much as I admire your loyalty to your *femme de ménage*, in many ways it is most er… admirable but…' Then Richard did catch his eye, and he recognised what he saw, it was defeat.

'Oh, stop being so pompous, Henri!' Valérie hadn't seen it. 'Richard is exactly right. She did not do any of these things, these murders.' She could spot an interruption a mile off, so she raised her voice and continued. 'That is despite what she says. It is perfectly obvious that she has been covering for someone else.'

The Commissaire sighed and took one more quick look at the car park before wiping his moustache, a sign that he had something important to say. 'Valérie, it does not really matter what I think, or what you think and certainly not what he thinks.' He pointed at Richard without taking his eyes off his ex-wife.

'Bloody cheek.' Richard couldn't help himself.

'It is out of my hands,' the Commissaire continued. 'The *juge d'instruction* has a case, so my work is largely done.'

'You mean she's going to court already?' Richard was alarmed at the speed of injustice.

The Commissaire sighed, clearly marking Richard down as a bit thick. 'No, monsieur. In France we have a different system to you English. The *juge d'instruction*, a magistrate, is in charge of the investigation. He is effectively my superior officer...'

'Who isn't?' Valérie interjected tartly.

Lapierre closed his eyes, trying to stay patient. 'I create an investigation dossier for him, he then decides to act on it. In this dossier, I have provided evidence that Madame Tablier had motive, that there is evidence to tie Madame Tablier to the scene of the first murder and that Madame Tablier, and this really is inconvenient for any *theory* that you may have, Madame Tablier has confessed! It would be a very odd investigating magistrate indeed to ignore a dossier like that.'

He leant back in his plastic chair which made a rather embarrassing sound, pricking his pomp entirely.

'But...' Richard tried again.

'She also has the necessary skills to have engineered these traps, these murders in advance.'

'But...' This time it was Valérie's turn.

'With all of this in mind, who do you think she is covering for, the murder fairy?' He chuckled diabolically at his own joke and for a moment Richard thought Valérie was going to perform some kind of martial arts manoeuvre that would leave the Commissaire inextricably, and permanently, a part of the Patàpain furniture.

'Marcel Bouchard,' he and Valérie said at the same time.

'She is covering for Marcel Bouchard?' he repeated the name as if they'd suggested a non-French wine to go with dinner.

'Yes.' Valérie, unsurprisingly, hadn't entirely picked up on the derision.

'Well, sort of.' Richard realised that there was a certain amount of cross-purposes going on.

The Commissaire leant forward. 'But, madame, monsieur. We can at least agree that the preparation was done in the autumn of last year, can we not?' He didn't wait for a response. 'Marcel Bouchard was in the United States, at a university in Miami.' He produced a small note book that was on a chain for good measure. 'To be precise the Florida State University. He did not miss any of his lectures on biomedical engineering.'

'Henri.' Valérie was as calm as an assassin, which was perfect considering Richard suspected that was part of her day job. She wasn't wielding a weapon, however, she just had knowledge that clearly Commissaire Henri Lapierre did not. 'Marcel Bouchard came back to surprise his father for his birthday. It was October the seventh. He arrived late on the sixth and left very late on the eighth. Maybe he did not have any lectures to miss over a weekend.'

It wasn't Valérie's style to sit back, the way the Commissaire had, and gloat. So Richard did it for her and as he did so watched the extraordinary performance that Lapierre's eyelids performed, like he was trying to communicate with them via Morse code; it was almost creating a draught.

'If you hadn't broken the law last night by *leaving a crime scene…*' It was all he had left it seemed. 'Then I would have been in possession of this information, assuming you might have told me.' He looked crushed by the knowledge and stared down at his dry *jambon beurre* baguette as if that were

244

responsible for all the world's ills. The chain on his notebook slowly wound the book in and under the table, as if the object itself was embarrassed. Even Valérie showed surprising diplomacy by not saying anything else. 'Motive?' he asked eventually, without taking his eyes off the half-eaten baguette.

'We think the village was a lonely place growing up and he came to hate it. When he came back for his father's birthday, he barely saw him because his father was in committee meetings.' Valérie said all of this slowly and to Richard's mind it all sounded a bit thin.

'We think that tipped him over the edge,' he added hopefully.

The Commissaire looked at him dolefully. 'Evidence?'

'We have a gutter cleaner in the car.' Richard felt embarrassed for the man.

'Richard found it in the *déchetterie* this morning,' Valérie added with pride.

'And this is why you are dressed like this.' It wasn't a question from the Commissaire, it was a statement of fact, but it was directed solely at Richard and not at Valérie who had only added some high heels and a pair of earrings. 'And what does this gutter cleaner prove?' He looked back at Valérie.

'It was bought by Marcel Bouchard in America for Lennard Bridille. He rewired it for the French electrical system.'

'But Monsieur Bridille has said nothing about this, and trust me,' he snorted, 'he most certainly would.'

'He prefers the old-fashioned, by hand method,' Richard said. 'He sold it on. It is the gutter cleaner that nearly killed Noel Mabit.'

'And you, Richard. It nearly killed you too.' He was delighted to see how offended she was by this.

'Anyone can rewire a plug, madame!' the Commissaire exclaimed.

'Yes, they can,' Richard replied. 'But a biomedical engineer would know how to do it really, *really* badly.'

The Commissaire looked back at his baguette mournfully, then at the car park with an equal sense of loss. 'Come,' he said. 'Let us go and get some real food.'

Chapter Twenty-Nine

Richard demurred and decided to go home instead to shower, leaving the former married couple to discuss whatever former married couples discuss – he was yet to properly find out about that, the distance not officially achieved. He had arranged to meet them both at the *gendarmerie* later, but aside from cleaning himself up, he wanted to clean the *chambre d'hôte* as well. He was certain that one of the first things Madame Tablier would want to do would be to check that standards hadn't slipped in her absence, convinced as he was that she would be released later that day.

He spruced himself up properly too. Since he had realised that the Commissaire was making something of an effort these days, and since also determining to do the same, he had done nothing about it. In fact, Richard had the distinct impression that he and Valérie had interrupted an assignation earlier that day at Patàpain, though it seemed a place singularly lacking in romantic ambience. Either way, Richard himself was not making much of an effort, or hadn't been until now, and it was time to change all that. Valérie was a highly attractive woman, desirable you might say and with a healthy average of ex-husbands testament to her reluctance for hanging around and waiting. Also, if Clare was fine with moving on to another relationship, though he knew Oliver Forshaw-Banks was not the first, it was time Richard took more control of his own affairs, quite literally of his own affairs. He put on a pair of smart chinos, that were, like so many of his clothes, a little tighter than the last time he'd worn them, and under a green tweed sports jacket wore the kind of roll-neck jumper, in this instance black, that was considered an integral part of a chic male Parisian's wardrobe. He had bought it recently and not yet had the nerve to unveil it publicly. He looked at himself in the mirror hoping to feel a surge of confidence, but he felt silly instead. It just wasn't his thing and he knew it and perhaps it was too late to try to be someone else anyway. Still, if anyone asked he could say he had dressed up for the release of Madame Tablier.

That prospect looked unlikely, however, as an almighty hullabaloo was taking place at the police station when he arrived, with Madame Tablier at the centre of it.

'I have my rights.' She wasn't shouting, just confirming things as they stood and they apparently stood on a bedrock of granite. 'And if I say I killed someone, you should bloody well believe me.'

'She is really quite adamant that she is the killer, Richard.' Even Valérie seemed reluctant to step in to the eye of the storm as the old woman, built like a rugby-playing grizzly bear, looked every inch a potential killer and perfectly ready to take on anyone who doubted it.

The Commissaire saw Richard arrive and a brief wash of hope crossed his face, presumably under the mistaken impression that Richard held sway over the woman. 'Monsieur Ainsworth, Richard,' he pleaded. He had never called Richard by his name before and it was slightly unnerving.

'Madame Tablier.' Richard used as calm a voice as was possible and still be heard. 'We know that you are not guilty.'

'What do you mean?' she asked, screwing up her eyes in suspicion. 'And why are you dressed like a Frenchman?'

'Never mind that,' he said testily, slightly piqued that she had been the only one to notice he had scrubbed up. 'I know you are covering up for your sister, for Madame Cuistot, because you think she killed her husband. She didn't kill her husband.'

'Of course she didn't!' was the dyspeptic reply, giving Richard hope that they were getting somewhere. 'I bloody did!' They were getting nowhere.

'And Christophe de la Cour?' Valérie asked with disbelief. 'Yes.'

'And you attempted to murder Lennard Bridille also?' The Commissaire jumped on the bandwagon.

'Why not?'

If Lapierre was regretting his involvement he wasn't showing it; instead, he was more like a prosecuting counsel who has his witness on the ropes. Though this witness had thrown herself on the ropes. 'And you almost ended up killing Noel Mabit by mistake?'

'Even better!'

'And why would you want to kill Noel Mabit, even in error?' Valérie's innate sense of reason and logic was feeling offended at what was becoming an increasingly absurd merry-go-round.

'You've met him!' Madame Tablier was not weakening in any way.

Richard approached her, he had no fear of anything other than her vicious tongue, but he also had a secret weapon and from a carrier bag he produced her favourite dustpan and brush. He didn't do it with a flourish but more as for a child who had briefly been separated from their favourite toy. 'And why,' he asked softly, 'would someone try to kill Madame Cuistot, your sister?'

The change was immediate, if unexpected. Richard, the cinematic romantic that he was, had expected Madame Tablier to be becalmed, to be overcome with a quiet determination to seek justice. Instead, the upshot of his words wasn't dissimilar to the result of loud clapping under a perilously angled mountainous sheet of snow. It began slowly enough, a low rumble seemed to emanate from somewhere in the woman's oesophageal area, exactly like distant thunder. Then her enormous hands tensed and snapped the handle of the brush she was now holding. Richard feared for the dustpan handle as well, but before she could break that too she made a sound like iron girders being rent by an earthquake and somewhere within that noise was a question.

'Who has tried to kill my sister?' Each word dripped with a kind of promised vengeance and nobody was quite brave enough to be the one to tell her.

'Madame,' Valérie said eventually, giving Lapierre a disappointed look, shrinking him like a salted snail. 'We are waiting for some more evidence. The Commissaire finally did his job and this evidence, which will prove your sister and yourself to be innocent, will be with us shortly.' It was quite a declaration and Richard hoped that she hadn't overreached herself, promising something they couldn't deliver.

It certainly had the effect of soothing Madame Tablier though, who shrugged, looked down at her broken brush in some surprise and asked to be taken back to her cell until there was confirmation.

An officer led her away while Lapierre, Valérie and Richard went into the Commissaire's office to await the news. With his new attitude of male grooming Henri Lapierre smoothed his hair in a small round mirror on the window sill, checked his moustache for crumbs and regained his usual air of practised, if fragile, authority. He beckoned for Richard and Valérie to be seated while he remained standing.

'I hope you know what you are doing, you two,' he began pompously. 'I have spoken to the *juge d'instruction*, he is aware of developments.' He preened himself some more.

'Are you all right, Richard?' Valérie straight up ignored the Commissaire. 'You look… you look, different.'

Richard was taken aback by the question, having in the end expected his efforts not to be noticed. 'I'm fine, I just thought I'd be taking Madame Tablier home, thought I'd, you know, make the effort.'

'I see.' She didn't sound like she did. 'Madame Tablier was correct, you don't suit looking like a Frenchman.' Richard caught the eye of the Commissaire and a surprising thing happened; a bond was struck up, a connection, a shared experience perhaps. Richard saw something in Lapierre's eyes which he was grateful for. He might have mocked him, but he didn't. What Richard saw was empathy and, if he wasn't horribly mistaken, a warning too. 'I prefer you as an Englishman,' she added as if writing out a recipe. It was just a little too late though.

Richard decided to change the subject. He was getting tired of being put upon, tired of being the one that was inevitably being ill-informed and somewhat behind the 'news' of the case. It was time to be more assertive. 'I take it we're waiting for the US reports on the death of Marcel's father?' he asked. It worked, and he put it down to the roll-neck.

'Florian Bouchard. That is right,' the Commissaire also seemed grateful for a change of subject.

'Well,' Richard tapped the desk in thought. 'Does this mean that this property fraud, if there even has been property fraud, is all a ruse then? Because it certainly does feel like something's going on. The Fourniers for instance, I mean, what's happened to them?'

The Commissaire stayed silent for a moment, weighing things up. 'I have it on good authority that there is a fraud in La Chapelle,' he said. 'And that it goes all the way to the top.'

'To Lennard Bridille?' Richard asked naively.

'The top of government, monsieur!' Lapierre slammed his fist down like it was the sword of justice, then realised he was being quite indiscreet and repeated in a whisper, 'The top of government.'

'Your informant, Henri,' Valérie asked, leaning forward. 'The one who left in a hurry this morning on the motorbike, the one who gives you this nice perfume, the former wife of the minister at the heart of this alleged scandal. She told you this?'

The poor man – and it was Richard's turn to feel some sympathy – looked horrified, embarrassed and strangely proud at the same time. Horrified that Valérie appeared to have worked it out, embarrassed that he'd been publicly stood up and proud to have it known that he may or may not be in a relationship with the famous and alluring Oriane Moulin.

'I am not at liberty to say, madame,' he said stiffly, though with a twinkle in his eye.

'Of course.' Valérie now had the air of a cat toying with a mouse and Richard thought he knew what was coming. 'She could be making it up. There might be no fraud, no deceit. It might just be a complicated revenge on her former husband who, I believe, wishes to stage a return to politics.'

'And you think that she would commit murder for that?' the Commissaire scoffed.

Valérie paused. 'She is more than capable of doing so, Henri. I have seen it.'

Richard interrupted, 'Sorry, are you saying that she has installed the Fourniers, wheedled her way on to the committee, is killing off the people who were on the committee when Bernard Janvier was the minister for dishing stuff out and all because she wants revenge on him?'

'Neither of you know her as well as I do, remember that. I have seen her at her worst and I think she is capable of anything, and yes even that.' The look on her face was as hard as a marble bust.

'Then what is all of this about Marcel Bouchard?' Lapierre threw his hands up in frustration.

'Is she your girlfriend, Henri, your Mata Hari in the village? Was it she who approached you first?'

253

Lapierre sat back, doubt riddling his face. 'Again, I am not at liberty to say.'

'I'm not at liberty at all!' Madame Tablier flounced into the room with a couple of carrier bags of clothes and an embarrassed Commandant Delfort behind her.

'Sorry, sir,' she said, with a *what can I do?* shrug.

'Do we not lock cell doors anymore?' Lapierre looked ready to take his frustration out on someone, anyone.

Another officer appeared behind the Commandant. 'Sir, that file has just arrived from the States.'

'Finally!' Madame Tablier huffed and took the printed notes off the startled policeman, handing it to Valérie, the person she considered most likely to be in charge. Valérie, however, for once recognising that politics is a useful game to be played, handed the papers over to the Commissaire.

'Thank you,' he said and gestured for Madame Tablier to sit down and for the Commandant to close the door behind them. They all sat in silence while the Commissaire flicked through the notes; occasionally he sighed, or looked irritated or looked downright angry and would throw the odd glance Valérie's way as if it were her fault. Eventually he slammed the papers on the desk.

'Well?' Madame Tablier spoke for all of them.

The Commissaire stood. 'Monsieur Florian and Madame Liliane Bouchard left by ship for Florida on December the fifth last year to visit Marcel Bouchard at his university in Miami. It is where Florian and Liliane had met, and they knew it well. They arrived safely and stayed with their son for a few days before he left to go on a field trip. They both began to feel unwell a few hours after they arrived and he was reluctant to go.'

'But he went anyway?' Valérie asked with a disbelieving tone.

'Madame Bouchard explained that they had eaten a lot of seafood on board, something they rarely did. Four days after arriving, Florian Bouchard died of haemolytic uraemic syndrome of E. coli O157. Liliane Bouchard almost died as well, but instead suffered a stroke. She was found by Marcel on his return from the field trip, she had been too ill to raise the alarm. Later she returned home with her son and her husband's ashes. The conclusion of the US authorities was death by food poisoning.'

'Did they trace it to any particular food?' Richard asked.

'That investigation is still ongoing, but...' He raised his finger. 'There is no evidence to suggest that Marcel Bouchard poisoned his parents.'

'But the rewiring of the plug, Henri?'

'Anyone can make a mistake.'

'The candle then?'

'There is no proof that he made an IED, or tampered with eau de vie, or food, or plugs!'

'And my brother-in-law?' Madame Tablier snarled.

'Perhaps it *was* an accident?' he replied quickly. 'Or really you did do it.'

'I didn't do it.'

'Your ring?'

'I put it there.'

'Why, madame?'

'I told you, I thought my sister might have done it.'

'Again, I ask why?'

'Because she hated him. She wanted kids, and he said no. La Chapelle wasn't good for kids was his excuse.'

'And de la Cour?' interrupted Valérie.

'Suicide,' he said unconvincingly and again they fell silent. 'All of the evidence we have is circumstantial. From that you have concocted the theory that Marcel Bouchard is our killer because he wanted to destroy La Chapelle-sur-Follet. Or it is Oriane Moulin out to destroy her ex-husband. Why not Agnès Valadon or Lennard Bridille, why not Madame Cuistot even? People who have survived and been attacked.'

'Back to the property-owning angle you mean?' Valérie asked.

'Yes, perhaps there is this real portfolio that we do not know about? You could ask your *friend* the *juge*. The one you told me about.' Valérie didn't reply.

'My sister guilty?' Madame Tablier stood. 'In that case, that statement I withdrew, I withdraw my withdrawal.'

'Sit down, madame, please,' the Commissaire placated, and he did the same. 'For what it is worth, I do not believe it is your sister. She is not on this committee either, which seems to be the target.'

'In that case I withdraw the withdrawal of my withdrawal.'

Richard had sat quietly trying to follow all of this. 'Why is Madame Cuistot a target then?' he asked quietly. Everyone looked at him. 'Well, look, all the others you can see why, but not Madame Cuistot.' He looked nervously at Madame Tablier. 'Sorry, but to me she seems a bit of an innocent. She seems to genuinely love the place, unlike the others who would profess to, but don't. It's their kingdom, to be defended. Madame Cuistot seems happy, and she loves Marcel Bouchard like a son, the child she never had maybe?'

Valérie looked at him. 'Brilliant, Richard!' It was her turn to stand. 'It is the destruction of everything the village represents, the fake family ties, the same things every year at the same time. The *raison d'être* of the village itself. Look at the deaths. Duval Cuistot, dead-headed. The Bouchards and Christophe de la Cour, weed-killed, if that is a word. And, as Richard said, it could be planned months in advance and executed from a distance. Madame Cuistot lights a candle at the same time every year. Madame Cuistot, the very symbol of the Bouchard's ignorance of their son.'

They had all listened attentively, even the Commissaire, and he was the first to speak. 'Madame, evidence! I need actual evidence! The plug is not enough. The candle is not enough!'

Richard had a brainwave. 'Well, if Marcel has failed in some of his attempts, he will surely try again, won't he? But this time, we can be there and we can catch him red-handed.'

The Commissaire nodded encouragingly. 'We set a trap, you mean?'

'Yes, and don't arrest him yet, make him think he's getting away with it. Which means…'

They all turned to Madame Tablier who had stood up noisily and picked up her carrier bags. 'Which means I go back to my cell,' she said with disdain. She looked directly at Richard. 'Just make sure my sister doesn't get hurt.' It was a plea and a warning at the same time. 'And another thing,' she added angrily. 'Bring me some ironing to do, this place is so boring.'

Chapter Thirty

Once again Clare was at Les Vignes that evening, just 'making some last-minute notes' as she put it, 'because we're driving back overnight.' He didn't like the sound of 'last-minute notes' but what he liked even less, however, was the man-child Oliver Forshaw-Banks, dressed as ever for an impromptu game of rugger, wandering around the place with one of those laser measuring devices. They were sitting on the *terrasse* and occasionally in the twilight you'd see an arrow-straight red beam, like the sight of an assassin's gun, which in a way it was. With Richard feeling he was the intended victim.

Richard sat down next to Clare, with Passepartout and Valérie opposite. Clare sipped at her gin and tonic, something approaching a frown on her face, which annoyed Richard even more as he'd have liked to have seen signs of Botox vanity, some vulnerability akin to what he felt, but there was none. She looked fantastic. 'So this Lennard Bridille fella,' she said slowly, using an olive on a stick as some kind of pointer, 'he showed me a property that wasn't for sale but that was similar to one that was, why? I mean I know about the keys and all that, but the property wouldn't really have been the same would it? It's not like it's an estate.'

A red beam rather unnervingly centred on her forehead. 'Sorry, darling,' Forshaw-Banks said as he passed, his accent pure public school. 'To my mind it was a gauge to see just how interested you are, how serious a buyer you might be.' He moved off measuring whatever else he could find.

'Did he get that toy for Christmas?' Richard asked innocently while Clare pretended to yawn.

'It is a sort of test then, but of what?' Valérie mused, apparently asking the question of a disinterested Passe-partout, who was now curling up on to her lap.

'Whether you really have the finances, I suppose,' Richard answered, taking a large glug of his own drink, a local rosé.

Forshaw-Banks strode back into the action. 'Not just finances,' he said, taking a long and not altogether confident view of the roof tiles. 'Suitability. Like for a gated community or a shared apartment block, they want to know if you're the *right type*. That you'll fit in. Almost like a job interview.'

'You said as much, Clare,' Valérie's tone was complimentary.

Clare put her drink down. 'Well, yes, that's how it felt. Would it be a second home? Did I have children? No jokes, Richard, please, it's becoming most tiresome. Would I be renting it out? You know, that kind of thing.'

Richard leant back. 'The kind of thing that's really none of their business once a sale has been made.'

'Yes, that's right I suppose.'

'You see,' Richard tilted his head back and spoke to the stars. 'We have Marcel Bouchard, we think, determined to destroy the place and its so-called committee, but I can't help thinking there's more to it than that.'

'You mean with the property sales and ownership?' It was Valérie, and not so much a question as an agreeing statement. 'But what? The portfolio we thought we had found was fake and if there is another, where is it? Who controls it?'

'It's all very complicated,' Clare said with an air of boredom.

'Oliver!' Richard shouted into the darkness and it wasn't very long before the younger man arrived.

'Yes, Rich.'

Richard took a deep breath trying to quell his irritation. 'We're trying to work this out. We think there's some scam going on in La Chapelle, with property sales, and so on, but we just can't see how. You're the expert in these things, what are they up to?'

Very slowly, very deliberately, Oliver Forshaw-Banks sat down next to Valérie and Passepartout.

'So that's it, is it?' The public school shine had left his complexion and his eyes hardened. 'What have you heard, mate?' His middle-class enunciation had vanished too, as estuary English poured in. 'Whatever it is, it's bollocks! What have you been telling them?' He directed this aggressively towards Clare who just looked amused by the sudden transformation.

'What is there to tell, darling? Do go on.' She was ice cool.

Forshaw-Banks slammed his hand on the low table in front of him and Richard noticed Valérie just move Passepartout to her side, the opposite side of the angry solicitor.

'Some poxy detective agency, how did you find out? I thought it was just you two. How did you find out?' he repeated.

Nobody knew quite how to answer that as they really hadn't found out anything at all. It was Richard who spoke first.

'You can't cover up things like that,' he said, an edge to his voice that, if asked, he had had no idea he possessed. 'There's always a paper trail.' It was vague enough to sound like he knew something without giving away that he didn't and he caught Valérie's eye as she winked at him.

'Well, you listen to me,' Forshaw-Banks leant over the table menacingly and picked up the knife Richard had used for slicing the lemons. 'You better not repeat it anywhere, you hear me?' Richard could have told him just how difficult that would have been, considering he didn't actually know anything. 'And if I hear you have,' his face was now inches away from Richard's, 'I'll kill those precious hens of yours!'

It was becoming quite wearisome how any potential violence towards Richard must first be directed at his avian flock. *I mean*, he thought, *what had they ever done?* The threat, however, was short-lived as the man spasmed as though electrocuted, dropping the knife in the process. Whatever Valérie had done to the back of the man's neck had been quick, silent and painfully accurate and he now doubled up in pain but with a look of shock on his face, directed at Valérie. For her part, she looked serene in the moonlight as if it was nothing to do with her. Passepartout had barely moved.

261

It was a few moments before Forshaw-Banks was able to move and speak again. 'A lucky punch!' he said through gritted teeth, though evidently still in pain.

'Perhaps you would like another?' Valérie asked the question as though she were offering a cocktail top-up.

The man shrank again.

'Perhaps, darling,' Clare leant forward and put her hand on his, 'you'd better wait in the car. I'll say my goodbyes and be with you in a few minutes.' She always had that vague air of amusement about her that Richard found so very trying, even more so now. Her solicitor/boyfriend had practically admitted to being a crook and had threatened her soon-to-be ex-husband with a paring knife covered in lemon juice; Clare was treating it like all the man had done was broken wind at the dining table.

Without another word, however, Oliver Forshaw-Banks, with as much dignity as he could muster, stumbled off down the driveway.

'Is he overtired?' Richard couldn't help himself and even Clare managed a smile at that one.

'Will you be all right, Clare?' Valérie's concern was genuine. 'Do you think it is safe to travel with him?'

Just then they heard the engine start as the car accelerated down the road. 'Well, he's rather taken that out of the equation now!' Again she smiled as if it were the tiniest inconvenience. 'I'll make my own way back, it'll give him time to cool off.'

'You're not going back to him, surely?' Richard asked. 'He's dangerous and a crook!'

'Oh, he's harmless, really. What has he done by the way, what do you two sleuths know?'

Valérie and Richard swapped glances. 'Nothing,' Valérie shrugged. 'I think Richard really was looking for legal advice, nothing more.'

'She's right. Oh, there are some unsubstantiated rumours that our network have uncovered,' he bluffed, in his head building up Alicia's part considerably. 'Though come to think of it, he's just substantiated them. All I wanted was an expert legal view, I'd obviously have taken an expert property swindler's view as well but I didn't know for sure that was the case.' The confidence in this rather overblown statement was helped enormously with a look of pride from Valérie directed at Richard.

Clare laughed loudly. 'How funny!' she said eventually. 'Well, that should knock his price down.'

Richard couldn't believe his ears. 'You're still going to use him?'

'Of course I am. It saves us both money, Richard.'

Richard shook his head and sighed. 'I'll get some more drinks,' he said, getting up stiffly. 'Same again?'

'Just a *tisane* for me, Richard.' Valérie yawned. 'You know what I like.'

It was a perfectly innocent thing to say, but Richard saw Clare's face freeze over, her look of permanent gaiety now locked in acrimony. He hurried off into the kitchen.

Inside the now dark salon, the one inadequate light over the sink was casting dull shadows so he made his way to the bottom of the stairs to turn on his film camera arc light, the one Clare had hated so much and which meant so much to him. It shone brightly, lighting the scene perfectly. What an odd evening, he muttered to himself with the usual understatement, making his way to the fridge in the far corner.

He never made it.

Tripping over something, Richard tumbled on to the ground without even the time to curse as he did so. Coming swiftly to a halt he remembered some of Valérie's lessons in self-defence and got quickly on to one knee, ready for his attacker. His attacker, however, looked in worse shape than he did. Lying with her back to the wall was Oriane Moulin, her face scratched and bruised, dried blood had dripped from the corner of her mouth and one eye was closed.

The arc light was blinding her and she weakly lifted an arm to cover eyes, she was pure Norma Desmond. She spoke with difficulty. 'Forgive me, I didn't know where else to go.' Then she fainted.

Richard went to her immediately and tried to pick her up, but she was like a deadweight and, unfortunately for his brave leading man status at this point, he'd put his back out in the fall. He half-straddled her across one leg and tried to clear the hair from her face. Her eyes fluttered as he did so and with surprising force she threw an arm around his neck and kissed him so tenderly, yet at the same passionately, that he thought his back might give in altogether.

'Richard, you really are incorrigible these days!' Clare stood above them, the look of amusement having returned and once again playing on her features. Valérie was next to her and her face looked like sheer grey cliffs in a battering storm. 'He was never remotely like this when he was with me.' Clare twisted the knife for good measure.

'I – I just found her here,' he stuttered. His cheeks smeared with lipstick, mascara and blood. 'Honestly!' he added pointlessly.

'We believe you, darling,' Clare said jauntily. 'Who is it anyway, do you know?'

'Oriane Moulin,' Valérie answered coldly. 'Is she hurt?'

'I haven't had the chance to properly find out,' Richard said, attempting to lay the once again comatose Oriane carefully on the floor.

'You had time to get to know each other a little better though.' Valérie's voice was arch as she spoke.

'It's really not like that.' He couldn't hide his anger. 'I just found her here!'

'It must be lovely to have women literally falling at your feet, Richard, it's what you always dreamt of.' There was no doubting the tinge of jealousy in Clare's voice either.

Richard ignored her and looked at Valérie instead, though she looked even less supportive. Clare was right though. All of his life he had dreamt of being the down-at-heel gumshoe, the private eye, the shamus, surrounded by danger and dangerous women; and he'd lived that life through movies, Bogart, Powell, Mitchum – now it really was him and he was entirely lost. It appeared on the face of it that he had one femme fatale, beaten up and who had made a serious, albeit probably concussed, pass at him. An ex-wife who may or may not be feigning jealousy and a business partner who was also exhibiting slight signs of jealousy despite never having laid any previous proprietary claim on him.

He stood up sharply, dropping the prone Oriane to the floor where she hit her head with a thud. 'Oh, this is too much. You think I'm carrying on an affair with Oriane Moulin, that we get our kicks out of bloodied kisses on a kitchen floor? Well I don't, and we aren't. I barely even know the woman. I mean why is she here? And you?' He pointed at Clare. 'Why are you here?' Then he looked at Valérie. 'I know why you're here, but I don't know *why* you're here! I watch films, I make breakfasts, I talk to hens, I'm as boring as hell, everybody says so and people agree I look like a fool when I wear a bloody stupid French roll-neck. Don't you see?' He was now pleading. 'This shouldn't be happening to me, I'm English for God's sake!'

He sat down heavily on a chair and Valérie put her hand gently on his shoulder, smiling sympathetically at him.

Oriane began to move. 'Hang on,' Clare said, 'I think she's trying to say something.' She bent down gracefully and leant in very closely, her ear to Oriane's mouth, then she looked back at Richard and Valérie. 'Who's Marcel Bouchard?' she asked innocently.

Chapter Thirty-One

The sun pierced through a crack in Richard's shutters, as piercing as Forshaw-Banks' measuring laser. Another warm, sunny spring day was in the offing, so Richard covered his head with his pillow, shutting it out. There had been times in his life when he had been unjustly accused of hiding; there had been other times when he had hidden. The current situation was a strong combination of the two and he was determined, if cowardice and responsibility-shirking can be done in a determined manner, to stay literally barricaded in his cinema room cum bedroom. He needed to work out a survival plan.

Clare, having cleaned Oriane up and deciding that she wasn't too badly hurt at all, insisted on sharing a room with her. She had obviously sought Valérie's advice on the subject, and Valérie had concluded that they were safe. Richard also suspected that Clare wanted to keep Oriane away from him, seeing as she now had him down as some rural France Casanova type. It was clear Valérie also harboured similar suspicions about Oriane and so the two women were put in the room opposite hers. Richard, railing against the injustice of it all, had muttered something about gaining a reputation based on nothing to which Clare had replied, 'Try being a woman, darling.' He had then skulked off to bed to seek solace in classic cinema, and had there again made a poor choice. *Operation Petticoat*, the Cary Grant, Tony Curtis classic where, and this was now Richard's jaundiced description of it, the American war in the Pacific was going swimmingly until 'a load of women' had got involved.

He now sat upright in bed hiding from his own 'load of women'. His phone beeped and he viewed it with caution as it was inevitably from Clare. 'Will you be joining us for breakfast, darling, or have you found another straggler from your harem?' Damn the woman, he cursed as he showered and dressed, this time eschewing the roll-neck for a dark shirt. He was now in the position of not just having a sex-less existence but having to prove it too.

All three of them, Valérie, Clare and Oriane turned towards him as he opened the door to the salon and he nearly buckled. It was like a modern take on Shakespeare, something he loathed even more than classic versions, and he was confronted by the three witches of Macbeth. Not three harridans on a remote Scottish glen, however; these witches were kitted out by Versace and had hair by Vidal Sassoon, which made them even more terrifying in his book.

'Can I get you anything?' Clare asked, without standing up.

'Eye of newt, toe of frog?' Richard muttered.

'What was that?'

'Nothing. I'll just grab a coffee.'

It was Valérie who watched him closely as he sat at the table and she smiled at him nervously, which unnerved him greatly. Something was up, he was sure of that.

'Thank you for helping me last night, Richard.' Oriane Moulin put a warm hand on his and looked gratefully into his eyes.

'Oh, you know,' was his inadequate response which brought a snort of derision out of Clare. 'You don't look too bad this morning.'

'Constantly working aren't you, darling!' Clare was becoming very arch.

'Oriane has explained to us what happened, Richard.' The look on Valérie's face suggested, in fact insisted, that the explanation was at best inadequate and at worst total codswallop.

She was still chewing it over fifteen minutes later in the car while Richard was trying his best to mollify the situation while simultaneously defending his position. It was a tightrope walk.

'I get why you don't trust her, she let you down on a mission way back. But that doesn't mean she isn't telling the truth now, does it?' He was trying to look nonchalant as Valérie's driving took them regularly to the brink of death. 'The thing is, the attack on her fits all the facts.'

'I knew you would take her side,' Valérie said petulantly.

'I'm not taking anyone's side.' Richard laughed, once again quite unable to fathom women. 'If Marcel Bouchard is killing the committee members, why *wouldn't* he attack Oriane now that she is a committee member? It makes sense! Well, it makes sense if you're a psychopath anyway.'

She stewed on this for a moment and threw them into a tight bend, sliding to a stop in a lay-by.

'I do wish you'd stop doing that!' Richard couldn't help himself.

'Now, Richard, we need to go through this again. You know my training and my skills, yes?' She didn't wait for an answer. 'So, tell me, if you were to attack me, what do you think would happen?'

He didn't have to think about that for very long, but he let the dust settle first. 'Well, at a guess I think you would break every bone in my body, mash me to a pulp and feed me to your enemies through a straw as some kind of smoothie.'

She didn't smile, just nodded, which was worrying. 'And if Marcel Bouchard attacked me, what then?'

'Much the same, only with more hair and that might clog up the straw.'

This time there was a faint glimmer that she was getting the joke, but she suppressed it. 'Oriane Moulin and I did the same training, Richard. If someone had assaulted her last night, especially Marcel Bouchard, they would be in serious trouble, *if* they were still alive.'

Richard brooded on this and it made sense. 'Also,' he added, 'Marcel has only killed, or tried to kill, remotely, from a distance. This doesn't seem his style at all.' She nodded in agreement. 'Hang on though,' Richard sat up suddenly knocking Passepartout off his lap. 'What if you're more right than you think? What if he did try and attack her, and she did actually kill him?'

Valérie's phone rang, interrupting them. 'It's the Commissaire,' she said, 'I'll put him on speaker phone.'

'Valérie? It's Henri. Marcel Bouchard has disappeared, pfft! Vanished. His phone is off and he cannot be located. This is serious. I knew that I should not have listened to you!'

'He's got a nerve!' Richard whispered away from the phone. Valérie was stony-faced.

'I will meet you in La Chapelle,' the Commissaire continued. 'I shall also bring Madame Tablier with me, there is no point in keeping her here and anyway, she has run out of ironing.'

That Madame Tablier had ironed her way out of jail was no surprise; that she was sweeping up around the Auberge Cuistot when they arrived, chastening builders who were making urgent repairs was no great surprise either, but her apparent warmth at seeing Richard, nearly knocked him off his feet.

'Oh, it's you,' she said, then nodded while looking him straight in the eye, there may even have been a faint lip wobble and certainly a pause. 'That's good. Now, mind that pile of dust I've swept up there with your bloody great feet.' And with that she went back to her task. Not many people would have seen what passed between them; it was brief, but it was there and for Madame Tablier it was practically gushing. And Richard knew that if he ever mentioned it again, she would put that broom where further attempts at a sitting position would prove impossible.

He went over to the opposite corner where Valérie and the Commissaire were in heated conference near the bar. Every so often Madame Cuistot would appear like a puppet from beneath the bar, complaining about sciatica.

'Can I help?' Richard asked.

'No, you're all right, ducks,' she said, holding her back. 'That's very nice of you, but these glass washer heating elements are very tricky if you don't know what you're doing.'

She bobbed down again to carry on working and Richard turned his attention to Valérie and Lapierre.

'She has given me no reason not to trust her.' The Commissaire was trying to control his temper. 'Quite the opposite in fact.' He led both Richard and Valérie away from the bar, out of Madame Cuistot's earshot.

'What are you talking about, Henri?'

He looked about just to make sure that they weren't overheard. 'I have been given to understand that Madame Moulin is here on official business.'

Valérie laughed coldly. 'Oh, Henri!' she began.

'Official. Business.' Lapierre repeated, putting an end to that conversation and Richard could see that Valérie was fuming at the idea, true or false.

'Have you been to see Madame Bouchard?' Richard asked, thinking an interruption was called for. 'Does she know where her son might have gone?'

The Commissaire sighed but also nodded at Richard, grateful for the intrusion. 'She does not and I did not tell her why we are looking for him either. Poor woman. It is no life, lying there all day surrounded by screens and monitors. She can do almost nothing for herself.'

'Did she not ask why you were there even?' Valérie had calmed down a little.

'I told her there had been some burglaries in the area.' The Commissaire was becoming irritated again.

'Well, I'm sure that really put the poor woman's mind at rest!' Richard was becoming ever more proud that in contrast to everything Valérie had taught him – a modicum of self-defence, breaking and entering, Chihuahua husbandry, and so on – in return he had seriously advanced the cause of sarcasm.

They were interrupted by a loud drilling starting up in the corner causing Madame Cuistot to drop the glass she was now cleaning. 'Oh, I swear they'll be the death of me!' She clutched her chest and went to sit on the terrasse where the others, except Madame Tablier, joined her at a far table.

'This is all getting too much!' she wailed, for once the mask of coping and being everyone's gossipy friend dropping. 'First my poor Duval, Christophe…'

'You.' Madame Tablier joined them and reminded her sister that she had barely survived an attack herself.

'I don't understand what is going on!' She looked around the table for answers, but no one wanted to upset her further with the news that her beloved Marcel was now chief suspect and apparently on the run.

'Sorry to interrupt, love.' One of the builders emerged from inside, covered in dust and with an unlit roll-up cigarette stuck to his bottom lip. 'We're going to knock off early if that's OK, we need to price another job.'

Madame Cuistot's demeanour changed immediately. Whether it was the stress of the situation and she'd just had enough or that they were now seeing a different side to her, no one could tell, but it felt like a different person.

'You're going nowhere until that hole is filled in,' she growled.

'But I…' The builder clearly didn't fancy her tone either and backed away slightly.

'I paid you a lot of money up front to get this done.' Her eyes were cold, hard as diamonds.

'Yes…'

'So I suggest you get it done.' The builder decided that further argument would be futile and went back to work while Richard couldn't help noticing a worried look cross Madame Tablier's face.

'Are you OK, madame?' Valérie asked and once again Madame Cuistot's entire personality changed in an instant. She stood up and started fussing with glasses on the table.

'Oh yes, dear. Duval used to deal with all of this, so I'm still learning. Money's the only thing these people understand and he left me a tonne of that! He was very clever with money, I just signed whatever he put in front of me.' She paused, and her eyes glistened over. 'Silly old sod.'

Her phone rang and she plucked it from her apron pocket. 'Yes,' she answered, holding the phone away from her ear. 'That's me, yes. Do I know a Marcel Bouchard? Of course I do, why?' If she had been aware of these things she might have noticed everyone else seated at the table lean towards her as a group. 'He's done what?' She chuckled. 'Back to those old tricks is he?' She put her hand over the phone as if it were a landline. 'Marcel is on a train back from Lyon. He had no ticket and he's lost his phone.' She rolled her eyes as though Marcel was a sweet eight-year-old who had muddied his trousers. 'Yes, I'll come and pick him up. The train will be there in half an hour. Thank you. Bye.' She chuckled again as she put her phone back in her apron.

Commissaire Lapierre stood up, adopting an official stance. 'Madame, you have so many other things to think about, please allow me to give you a lift.'

Chapter Thirty-Two

The drive to the train station took about twenty minutes. La Chapelle-sur-Follet didn't have a station of its own, or hadn't done for years and the slow, seven-hour train to Lyon, stopping almost everywhere on the way, went through the nearby station of Saint-Aignan Noyers. There were a number of people waiting for the train when they arrived at the station, which didn't stop the Commissaire letting it be known that he wasn't happy with the convoy, as Valérie, Richard and Madame Tablier had followed him and Madame Cuistot in a separate car.

'This is police business!' he fumed on more than one occasion, to which Valérie just responded with a shrug of the shoulders, Madame Tablier with a glare and Richard as if he hadn't heard. Eventually the policeman gave up and as the information screen in the station indicated a further thirty-minute delay, they all made their way to the brasserie across the street.

'Do you want food?' the owner asked brightly, as the five of them came in through the door. Valérie looked around, distinctly unimpressed, and answered with a very definite 'no'. Richard was hungry though, as was the Commissaire, and they both ordered an omelette while the sisters ordered andouillette, a French sausage 'delicacy' that Richard knew from bitter experience tasted like a combination of bicycle inner tube and beached flip-flop. He had never seen anyone actually finish an andouillette sausage; foreigners ordered it with a sense of bravado and were immediately put off by the burnt rubber smell and the French people he'd seen order it did so out of a sense of culinary duty and would quietly slip most of it under the table to their dogs and even some of their dogs balked at the stuff.

'I'm so worried, it's not possible to eat.' Madame Cuistot put her cutlery down on her cleared plate. 'I'm going to the toilet.'

'Well, I've only had prison food for nearly a week!' It was clear Madame Tablier was holding the Commissaire responsible for her incarceration. 'And that was just slurry.'

Richard had stayed briefly in the same jail and had found the food to be actually far better than most station cafés, but he wasn't going to argue.

'Madame,' the weary Commissaire wiped his plate with a crouton of bread, 'if you will go around confessing to murders you did not commit, what am I supposed to do?'

'Well, I thought it was my sister, I was looking after her.'

'And now you do not?' If Lapierre was joking, he was playing a dangerous game.

'Why did you really think it would be your sister though?' Valérie asked, saving Lapierre from a probable butter knife in the thigh.

'I would have, if I were her.' Her gruff response wasn't helping the situation and Lapierre shook his head sadly.

'We are here at this station to arrest Marcel Bouchard for the murders of Duval Cuistot and Christophe de la

Cour. Also, the attempted murders of Lennard Bridille and Madame Cuistot, and too the attack on Oriane Moulin. Only, according to you, it is Madame Cuistot who could be our culprit, Madame Tablier, and if she isn't, you could be. This is madness. I wish people would just be honest with me.'

'Poor Henri,' Valérie said with mock concern. 'Crime is so full of dishonest people these days.'

'She didn't do it!' Madame Tablier said forcefully. 'I'm just saying, he would have deserved it and she had the skills. But she didn't do it.'

'It's none of my business,' Richard began carefully, 'but why would Duval Cuistot have deserved it?'

Madame Tablier nodded slowly. 'Like I said, children,' she said quietly. 'All my sister ever wanted was children and then as soon as they married he changed his mind. Only with her though; he's got children dotted about. Not that he cared, she was only supposed to look after him, that was his idea, not have any distractions. It broke her heart.' She put the last of the andouillette in her mouth and added, 'Plus, she's just as good with engines as I am. But she didn't do it.'

She seemed to have inadvertently made a very good case for the prosecution, and Richard toyed worriedly with his cutlery as Madame Cuistot returned to the table.

'How long do we have to wait now?' she asked anxiously.

'A few minutes, madame, not long.' The Commissaire paused, wiped his moustache as seemed to be his habit now and added a question. 'You worry a great deal for Monsieur Bouchard, am I right?'

'Marcel?' There was a surprise in her voice as though the Commissaire's question was too obvious to contemplate, then she added sadly. 'I've always been there for him, he had no one else.'

'But his parents?' Valérie interrupted and got a glare from Lapierre for doing so.

'Oh they were always too busy, and there were no other children in the village to play with.' She sighed. 'I used to pick him up from here a lot. He would run away from home, then get frightened and ring the *auberge* asking for me. It was our secret.'

'His parents did not know?' Again it was Valérie asking the question.

'They did not notice. Their lives were all about the village, nothing else mattered. I remember, oh a long time ago, none of us had been here very long, Florian and Liliane having a great row because she was pregnant with Marcel. She screamed at him once in their garden, we all heard it, we were there. "I gave up my career, I'm not giving up my baby!" Well,' she shrugged, 'it was obvious what he had asked her to do.'

'That's very sad,' Richard said quietly.

'But even though she had him, she wasn't really that interested. Such a clever lady too she was, so clever. She had no time for a child, a child couldn't keep up with her.' She tapped the side of her head, indicating brains. 'So he was a lonely little boy and I was his friend. And then he got the chance to go to America and he could get away.' She wiped a tear from her eye. 'Oh, now she noticed him, his mother, he was going where she had gone as a student and on a scholarship too, paid for by that minister, Bernard Janvier. Oh yes, now she noticed him. That's why they went there to see him. It was their first holiday in twenty years.'

Outside they heard the bells ringing on the crossing barriers and Valérie gave Richard cash to pay the bill for everyone. 'Business expenses,' she winked, 'be sure to get a receipt.' There was a sadness over the group though as he watched them cross the road to the station, he sensed that. Yes, they were there to arrest a murderer but they all felt a certain sympathy for him too and that was a difficult thing to reconcile. Richard waited for the receipt from the owner who was pre-occupied with another customer and as he did so he looked up at the television, bolted to the wall in the corner. On it a football match was coming up to half-time and it went straight into the adverts; he looked away and saw himself and the television reflected in the mirror behind the bar. Suddenly he recognised a face. On the screen was a family packing for a holiday; the music was happy, the smiles were wild and the colours vivid but it was the young boy in the TV family that he recognised. It was Fabrice Fournier, smiling like Richard hadn't seen and with a family that wasn't his own, just as Valérie had thought when they broke into the Fourniers' place. Then the penny dropped; he made a note of the company being advertised, grabbed the proffered receipt and ran across the road to join the others.

He was just in time. Marcel was being hugged breathless by Madame Cuistot, who was in tears again. 'Oh, Marcel, my boy,' she wept. 'Why did you run away?'

The Commissaire balanced on the balls of his feet, trying to make himself as tall as his quarry. 'I was about to ask the same thing, monsieur, why did you run away?'

A rather dazed Marcel Bouchard sat down heavily on one of the metal chairs that stand for comfort in rural train stations. 'But I didn't,' he said quietly, rubbing the back of his head. 'I didn't run away.'

'So you went to Lyon for a *repose*, a break?' The Commissaire was enjoying his moment of triumph but overdoing it somewhat and it was Valérie who interrupted while Madame Cuistot sat next to Marcel and fussed over him like a mother.

'Why not let Monsieur Bouchard just tell his story, Henri? It would be much easier, no?'

'At the station, yes!' Lapierre was adamant.

'We are in a station,' Richard joked involuntarily, getting an official skunk eye from the policeman.

'That is right, Richard!' It was Valérie's turn to be triumphant. 'Go ahead, Marcel, what happened?' The Commissaire threw his arms up in the air and looked around for any support, which wasn't forthcoming.

'Well, I'm not sure what happened,' the young man said, looking up at Valérie with big sad eyes. The Commissaire huffed in response. 'I was walking home last night and I was hit from behind…'

'Excuse me,' Valérie interrupted, and put her hand gently behind Marcel's right ear. 'Does it hurt there?'

He winced and nodded his confirmation.

'Who hit you?' Madame Cuistot was outraged at the very idea.

'I have a good idea,' Valérie muttered, looking from the Commissaire to Richard. 'It takes skill to deliver an accurate mastoid punch.'

'Then what happened?' Lapierre chose to ignore Valérie's obvious inference.

Marcel looked up and shrugged. 'I woke up lying in the garden and I panicked. I was frightened. I just wanted to get away from the place, from everything. I cycled to the station and bought a ticket to Lyon. I used to do that when I was young, when I wanted to get away.'

'The ticket can be verified.'

'Be quiet, Henri!' Valérie hissed. 'Continue, monsieur.'

'I knew I had to go home, to Maman, to Tata.' He held Madame Cuistot's hand. 'But I had no phone or wallet, I must have been robbed when I was asleep. So I hid in the toilet on the return journey, until the ticket inspector became suspicious. He had handed me a fine.' He produced a written ticket from his pocket and gave it to Lapierre. 'Then he allowed me to call the *auberge*. I think he felt sorry for me.'

The Commissaire stared hard at the written fine that Marcel Bouchard had been given, deciding what to do. 'It seems likely that you have an alibi for the attack on Oriane Moulin, though we shall check that thoroughly.' Marcel looked more confused than relieved at the suggestion. 'But, Marcel Bouchard, you are under arrest…' Madame Cuistot began wailing as though at a funeral. 'You are under arrest for the murders of Duval Cuistot and Christophe de la Cour!'

'No!' Marcel Bouchard stood up quickly, crying, almost laughing at the accusation.

'Also for the attempted murder of Lennard Bridille and Madame Cuistot here.'

This time Marcel did start laughing, a maniacal, frightened laugh. The reaction of someone who either completely misunderstands the situation or is good at pretending that is the case.

'Why would I try and kill her?' He pointed at Madame Cuistot, who looked equally stunned.

'Maybe you were just trying to make it look like you were, to throw us off the scent.'

'This is all utterly ridiculous!' He sat back down, a total lack of comprehension on his young face as he put his arm around the weeping Madame Cuistot. Something, Richard noticed, Madame Tablier had not done.

Valérie had remained silent throughout this, and now she spoke quietly but firmly. 'I'm afraid we have evidence, monsieur.' The tone of her voice meant the smile on Marcel's face quickly became an ugly fixed grin, like a frightened chimpanzee. 'You brought a piece of equipment from the United States, a gutter cleaner for Lennard Bridille?'

'Yes?' He looked from one face to the other. He now looked hunted.

'You offered to rewire it for the French system, but it was designed to kill him.'

The change in Bouchard wasn't immediate but slowly the colour drained from his face completely. His eyes darted in fear until after a few seconds he put his head in his hands and wept.

'Marcel Bouchard, I arrest you for the murder of Duval Cuistot and…'

'Yes, yes, Henri. You have said that already.'

Chapter Thirty-Three

Lennard Bridille had made it clear to Richard that as far as he was concerned, the food and the table set-up were entirely his business. 'I,' he said, with the solemnity of a great monarch, 'am far too busy dealing with government officials and other dignitaries. This is entirely in your hands and I trust you will do a good job.' Richard had been right not to believe a word of it, Bridille couldn't have been more hands on if he'd worked in airport security.

Richard had assembled a team to help him, which in effect meant delegating to people with far more, or at least any expertise. The brothers Taz and Shilal Sharifi had joined forces with René to handle the food preparation side of things, after first getting permission from their wives to do so as they would have to look after the shop. René was more than happy to step back from his own brasserie for the day and away from asparagus, which was not on the Spring Fayre menu at his insistence. Martin and Gennie were to help with serving the drinks from a makeshift bar area, though René had said that for this they could use the two hundred litres or so of asparagus martini cocktail that he had already prepped. Jeanine would supply the bread and pop over when her *boulangerie* shut at one.

It was Richard with this team, minus René and Jeanine, who had been given a run-down on events by Bridille in full Colonel Blimp mode, while Agnès Valadon hovered nearby fussing over the admittedly magnificent floral arrangements; one in particular looked like a static firework display shooting up from an ancient, enormous half-barrel.

'We'll have two rows of tables, I think,' Bridille said, as if it were open to negotiation. 'Twenty-five on each, try and keep the children separate, maybe even on another table, they make a mess in my experience.'

Is he bussing a crowd in? thought Richard.

'You have children?' Gennie asked, with a touch of surprise.

'Good God, no!' he replied, as if it were a direct question about personal hygiene. 'Now, this *méchoui*, what is that again?' It was an absurd question to ask, a *méchoui* being a long tradition in France.

'It's a whole barbecued lamb, innit?' Shilal, Taz's younger brother stepped forward enthusiastically, his diamond earring glinting in the morning sun.

Bridille didn't look happy. 'It won't be too spicy, will it?' he asked, raising his voice as though Shilal was deaf.

'No mate,' Shilal giggled. 'I'll leave all the flavour out for you.' For some reason this seemed to satisfy Bridille, and Shilal leant in close to Richard. 'Where d'you find him, man, in a museum?'

'Kind of like a spit roast?' Martin asked inevitably and this cheered the small town official enormously.

'Ah yes, I like those.'

'That's interesting…' Martin began.

'Not now, Martin,' Richard and Gennie said simultaneously.

'Do you want us to dig a barbecue pit or use the barrel method?' Taz asked, writing notes as he spoke.

'Dig?' Bridille went bright red. 'Nobody's digging! Nobody's digging anywhere!'

Taz smiled. 'Just thought I'd ask. It's better anyway, we can cook the veg under the meat.'

At that point Felipe Santos appeared, inevitably a large shovel held menacingly in one hand. 'Did you hear that, Santos?' Bridille tried to make it sound like a joke, but he didn't have the skills. 'They want to dig a hole, right here!'

'They can do what the hell they want,' Felipe said darkly, before turning to Agnès Valadon. 'Step aside please, madame.'

She flushed in embarrassment. 'I can do this kind of thing, you know.'

'I'm asking you to step aside please, madame,' he repeated without a change of tone. She did so and with a sudden surge of violence he wielded his shovel like a Claymore and attacked the flower display with frenzied savagery. Agnès Valadon screamed, while the others were just dumbfounded. There was such anger in Felipe Santos's actions, such frustration and pent-up resentment. He swung wildly at every flower and stem, leaving nothing unbroken, at times using his tool like a bludgeon and at others like a guillotine. Nobody dared step in or even say anything, such was the sheer barbarity of the assault, which continued long after the display had been wrecked. He ground the last white gardenia under his heavy boots and looked down at it. Richard could see the muscles in his jaw tightening and loosening, tightening and loosening. Felipe sniffed, put the shovel on his shoulder and said, without looking up from the crushed flower, 'Garden centre's still open, you'd best get over there.'

Richard was recounting this extraordinary episode to an open-mouthed Valérie and Clare, as they sat waiting for an early evening dinner at a smart restaurant in Tours. Clare was heading for a few days' pampering in Paris before taking the Eurostar home. He finished his Felipe Santos story with, 'and that was it, he slung his shovel over his shoulder and he strode down the road into the sunset, well, obviously it wasn't sunset…'

'…Like John Wayne at the end of *The Searchers*, I knew that was coming. Is he imbalanced do you think?' Clare asked, the table candle flickering in front of her as she sat opposite the other two.

'I couldn't say,' Richard replied, a little put out. 'I think he's just had enough of the place; he sees it as a sham and he's glad to be getting out.'

Valérie shook her head, trying to make sense of it all. She had spent most of the day 'in conference' as she put it with Lapierre and had told Richard and Clare all about it. Marcel Bouchard had confessed to everything but had steadfastly refused to explain any details. Apparently sneering at the Commissaire with, 'it took a great scientific and engineering mind to plan all this months in advance, so you should have to work it out yourself!'

'This leaves me only with more circumstantial evidence, that's not enough for the *juge*!' the Commissaire had whined and so eventually Valérie had persuaded him to release Marcel for the Spring Fayre.

'It may tip him over the edge to act,' she'd suggested strongly.

'It may cost me my job,' he'd replied, but feeling he had little option.

'Everything is a sham in this thing!' Valérie animatedly picked up on Richard's earlier point. 'I googled your Fournier boy, Richard. The one you saw in the advertisement. Yes, a child actor called Jordan – Jordan! I ask you! – Jordan Forin. All of the other Fourniers are actors with the same agent, but the agent would not tell me who had booked them for their current job. Client confidentiality or some other rubbish.' She paused for breath. 'And who will help out poor Oriane in her garden now that Felipe Santos is leaving?' she added acidly.

'How is she by the way, anybody know?' Clare unusually hadn't yet fully picked up on Valérie's antipathy towards her former colleague.

It was Richard who answered. 'The Commissaire seems to think she's on official business…'

'Pah! Official business! That does not mean, even if it is true, which I doubt, along with this gardening television show as well, that she can go about framing people for assault. Marcel did not attack her, she attacked him!'

'But why would she do that?' Clare asked. Richard was grateful that she did because if he'd asked, he'd have been accused of defending the infernal woman.

'I do not know for sure.' Valérie shook her head.

'There's obviously a long history between the two of you, what's to tell?' Clare continued, while Richard squirmed at the directness of the question.

287

'Oh, it's all in the past,' Valérie said, which may have been the truth but it was certainly also very much in the present. 'It's been a long day, maybe I am in a bad mood. I thought my apartment was to be sold today, but no. Still it sits there.'

Richard relaxed a little at Valérie's crunching gear change of a non sequitur.

'Dear Valérie,' Clare ran an immaculately manicured finger around the rim of her wine glass, 'I do believe you're avoiding the question. Isn't she, Richard?'

Inside, Richard screamed like a man falling off a cliff. 'Well, er, you know. Possibly.' Clare glared at him and he took a deep breath. 'I do think it's relevant to all this, Valérie. You seem to think she's involved, maybe it would help to get it off your chest. You know, only if you want to that is.'

'So forceful,' Clare muttered into her wine glass.

The waiter arrived with their meals and that put an end to that. For a while they ate in silence, and not just because the food was good. For different reasons, they all felt this was an important step. How much did Valérie trust Richard? How far was he prepared to push her for that trust in return? And for Clare, she'd quite happily admit that she would like to see her estranged husband happy.

'I've never seen you choose fish before, Richard, you really are branching out, good for you.' Clare wiped her chin delicately with a white napkin.

'I'm trying to lose a bit of weight,' he said sheepishly. 'I thought less meat might help.'

'Good for you!' Clare repeated, smiling at him with genuine affection.

'It was a long time ago,' Valérie said quietly, not catching anyone's eye. 'An undercover mission in Libya in 1998. Three of us, we were the advance team to negotiate or at the very least, gain the release of a French hostage of a jihadi group.' She put down her cutlery, still not catching anyone's eye. 'Oriane wanted the glory, it was not about the hostage or her safety, it was about Oriane's career. And if it was just her that came away from it all, then so be it. That would satisfy her.' Both Richard and Clare held their breath. 'She was not prepared to negotiate, she wanted a show of force, her force, and she chose the wrong moment to do that. The hostage was killed before we could get to her. Oriane was injured too, though not seriously. I saved her and called for back-up and we were rescued, but it was a mess and hushed up.'

Richard had never seen Valérie this emotional, and he put his hand on hers and saw Clare smile at him for doing so.

'And the third colleague?' Clare asked.

'Captured and, we found out later, executed.'

'Poor soul,' Clare said quietly. 'What were they called?'

'His name was Edmond Masson.' She looked up firstly at Clare and then at Richard. 'And he was my husband.'

'Is everything OK with your meals?' The returning waiter asked, his timing perfect or appalling depending on your point of view. They all replied that it was, Richard and Clare doing that very English thing of doing so over-enthusiastically, before they returned to silence.

'So, will you go back to this Oliver Forshaw-Banks?' Valérie's mood shifted back to where she liked it, directing conversational traffic.

'Oh, yes.' Clare nodded enthusiastically. 'Even more now I know he's bent. I can get him for cheap, that's good for both of us.' She nodded at Richard, whose mind was elsewhere. His phone rang and shook him from his thoughts and he saw that it was Alicia.

'I have to take this,' he said, without letting Clare know who it was.

He wandered outside into the warm air and dodged the smokers by the door, crossing the street for privacy.

'Daddy?'

'Yes, sorry, love. I'm in a restaurant, actually with your mum. I thought I'd come outside.' In actual fact, he was now standing outside another restaurant but it was still quieter. Alicia was filling him in on her day at work and he glanced through the window at this quieter, more intimate place. By the wall, on his own, and looking unhappily at his watch was Commissaire Lapierre, a sagging bunch of paper-wrapped flowers flopped on the table in front of him. There are some appearances so obvious to the rest of the world that they cannot be mistaken, the dance people do when they miss a bus for instance, pretending they were never going for it in the first place, the gritted teeth of congratulating a rival and this, the hollowed-out pain of a man on his own in a restaurant, already on dessert and still clutching a bunch of roses. Richard felt for him, and he wanted to tell him so but knew that the man would be mortified if Richard, ostensibly a rival, knew.

'And so, Daddy, the big news, wait for it! I'm pregnant!' He looked at his phone in disbelief. 'But don't tell Mummy, I'll tell her when she gets back. I didn't even tell her we were trying, you know what she's like.' Richard was ecstatic and sad at the same time, and while they chatted for a few minutes, he was trying to take in everything that had happened in the last half-hour or so. He didn't feel emotionally equipped to do so, and briefly considered what film could neatly package this for him later. Two different worlds had collided, two extreme emotions and both required a level of empathy that was tearing Richard in two. He came to a conclusion; it would have to be *Casablanca*.

'Don't forget, don't tell Mummy!'

He took a last look at a forlorn Lapierre asking for the bill. 'It'll be our secret,' he said solemnly.

Chapter Thirty-Four

There was so much going on in Richard's head it was difficult to know what to deal with first. There was, of course, the hope that Marcel Bouchard would not only stick to his confession, but also reveal the details and evidence of how he had killed two people, and attempted to do the same to a number of others. And all of which without actually killing someone else in the process. That was ostensibly his, Valérie's and Lapierre's priority for the day, and in his opinion the sooner the better. He had had quite enough of La Chapelle-sur-Follet and its self-importance, its lack of real community and its odd, vacuum-like silence. It was like the child-hating country of Vulgaria in *Chitty Chitty Bang Bang*, a film reference that would normally cheer him, but which he dismissed quickly from his mind, unable to afford the distraction.

There was also the not inconsiderable task of catering for fifty people at the Spring Fayre. He was not a *traiteur*, he got nervous serving croissants to a few guests at the B&B, never mind a large crowd. A crowd which was due to include the new Minister of State and may, or may not, play a significant part in the renewal of La Chapelle's precious *Jardin Remarquable* status. It was an invidious position to be in. Personally, he'd rather the licence wasn't renewed. He didn't want Lennard Bridille and Agnès Valadon's cold elitism to be rewarded, but then he didn't want Marcel Bouchard's motives, the destruction of the place, to be vindicated either. *Do I do a good job, or do I sabotage?* he kept asking himself, making him feel like Alec Guinness in *The Bridge on the River Kwai*.

Again, he told himself to concentrate.

There was also the guilt. Richard generally felt guilty about something, rarely about anything specific, just a general 'I must have done *something* wrong' attitude to life. This time he knew what it was though. He was going to become a grandad, and yes that made him happy. And he was delighted for Alicia and Sly. But the guilt came from the fact that that was not the main concern that had come from the night before. Valérie's explanation of Oriane's and her history and the death of her husband had come out of the blue. In some way he might have seen it coming, there always seemed to be a former husband of Valérie's yet to be revealed, but this felt different and it quite clearly still hurt. In truth, he hadn't yet worked out what to think of either revelation.

Everyone was quietly getting on with their jobs. Richard and René, with the help of the Sharifi brothers, had put the tables out, while Martin and Gennie had set up the bar area. Taz and Shilal were now prepping the lamb and the vegetables, Jeanine had delivered the bread and René was now laying places.

Again, he reflected on how different Saint-Sauver was to La Chapelle. He watched Bridille and Valadon who were standing by the display that Felipe Santos had destroyed the day before. They were both dressed as if for a royal visit, but a royal visit in a 1950s English village rather than twenty-first-century Republican France. She wore a very old-fashioned hat with a kind of fishnet veil over her face and Bridille was in a very un-horticultural grey suit. He also sported a medal on his chest, but Richard couldn't make out what it was. The flower display itself was still looking in a pretty poor state, even if it had been cleaned up a little and Agnès Valadon was placing a chalk slate in front of the barrel base. 'This display was prepared by Madame Agnès Valadon,' it read. 'It is a metaphor for what we are doing to our beautiful planet.'

That's a bit rich! Richard thought. *And Felipe Santos doesn't even get credit!* He had noticed Santos hovering about, thankfully shovel-less though Rolande Roy was about too with his broom at the ready.

'I wonder what the Wikipedia version is saying?' Valérie asked, as usual appearing silently at his shoulder. 'It is bound to be more honest than that.'

'Would it have changed if Marcel is in Madame Tablier's pristine prison cell?' This place was making him more cynical than ever, and Valérie sensed it.

'A rotten house cannot be repaired. It must be torn down in order to build a better one,' she read. 'I think I agree with that.'

'And who said that?' Richard asked.

'Godwin of Wessex.'

'Never heard of him, but I like his style.'

She tapped her phone some more. 'He was an English earl.'

'Oh, *that* Godwin of Wessex.'

She smiled at him. 'Let us hope this is all over quickly,' she said. 'I do not like this place.'

He was about to agree when their peace was destroyed by the arrival of an enormous coach. A smart double-decker coach, not as tall as a London Routemaster, but much sleeker and with tinted windows. With a hiss of its brakes it came to a stop at the 'ROUTE BARÉE' sign at the end of the road and out stepped a portly driver in a short-sleeved shirt and tie.

'Where do you want this lot?' he asked Richard, who pointed him in the direction of Lennard Bridille.

'They can get out here,' Bridille barked, and with a cautious look at Richard added, 'then you should make yourself scarce. I'll call you when we need you.'

The driver tipped his forehead, 'Right you are, guv. And you can keep them as long as you want as far as I'm concerned.' He stepped back into the bus. 'Right, you lot!' he shouted out of sight. 'Off you get and take your rubbish with you!'

What happened next was like one of those scenes from old British documentaries about works outings in the 1960s. The sleek, aerodynamic coach, presumably the last word in modern bus travel, was now just an old-fashioned charabanc as fifty or so people of all ages, shapes, sizes and genders disgorged themselves, stretched, shielded their eyes, vaped or lit cigarettes.

'Unbelievable,' Richard said quietly. 'He really has bussed them in. This will be the population of La Chapelle then.' Valérie shook her head too, for once speechless.

Lennard Bridille was the opposite of speechless, he was totally shameless and he produced a loud-hailer from a carrier bag. 'Now then,' he shouted as the reverb made him wince. 'You all know why you're here, you've been given a brief. When you are invited to sit at the table for lunch just plonk yourselves wherever there isn't a name card and that's it, just act normally.' There was some murmuring from the crowd.

'Where are the toilets?' A lady at the back shouted, getting support from plenty of others.

'There are porta-loos on the other side of the church,' Bridille replied. 'Now, before you move off. It's very important, unless you have been specified a speaking role that you do not talk to anyone official. That's very important. Any questions from someone you don't know, direct them to me or Madame Valadon here. Understood?' More grumbling. 'Now, where is Fabrice?'

A young boy nervously stepped forward and Bridille looked down at him. 'Young man, how do you like…' The small boy nearly fell over backwards as Bridille forgot to remove the loud-hailer from his mouth. 'Sorry,' he said, again through the loud-hailer.

'Take it away from your mouth!' Some wag in the group shouted, as everyone laughed.

'Young man,' Bridille started again, this time without unnecessary amplification. 'How do you like living in La Chapelle-sur-Follet?' The boy's face contorted with nerves. 'Well?' asked an impatient Bridille.

'I don't know, monsieur, I've never been here before.'

Again, the large group laughed.

'Honestly!' Bridille was outraged, before the original Fabrice Fournier stepped forward.

'I love it here, I have lots of friends and it's important to be surrounded by nature.' He may have been a pro but he trotted out the words as if he was sick of hearing them and Richard wanted to shout 'once more with feeling', but stopped himself, realising that that would be offering this blatant charade support it didn't deserve.

'Good,' Bridille said. 'Now, I'll be taking the minister to your house before food, so put some effort into it, young man.' He put the loud-hailer back to his mouth. 'OK, you may go to the toilet and then make your way into the church. You will be told when to start singing.'

Richard and Valérie just looked at each other as the bus beeped its reverse and made off, presumably Richard thought, to be then covered in camouflage netting in a copse somewhere. 'Aren't we just helping to perpetrate fraud here?' Richard asked, a touch of anger in his voice.

'We are here to catch a murderer, Richard. That is our only concern.'

'Well, can't you just beat the evidence out of him? I really want to wash my hands of this place.'

'Richard!' she cried, though there was a touch of play-fulness to it.

Bridille and Agnès Valadon approached them as if nothing had taken place. 'You can start the cooking now I think, Monsieur Ainsworth. I like it overdone anyway.' Valadon, with her absurd hat, nodded in agreement as they started to walk off. 'Oh, and by the way,' Bridille half-turned back, 'you can tell your sister that the Manoir de Saint-Sulpice was sold last night, a cash buyer too.' They strode off to take full control of their pantomime.

'I don't think Clare will be too disappointed,' he said to their backs. Then he turned to Valérie. 'Are we absolutely sure it's Marcel? Because if I could, I'd happily arrange for it to be one of them two, or both. I mean, I know someone has tried to kill him, but why not try again? And why has she got away without injury?'

Valérie had a sardonic smile but before she could make comment Madame Cuistot arrived with Oriane Moulin, who was sporting a plaster on her forehead. 'Did you see them all arrive?' The older woman was either excited or agitated, it was difficult to tell. 'That's why I can't do the catering, not on my own.' She was wringing her hands nervously as if she actually was doing the catering.

'Don't worry,' Richard said calmly, 'everything's under control.' He hoped that was actually the case and the smell coming from the Sharifi brothers' set up certainly suggested it was. Martin and Gennie, however, seemed not to be at their bar. Then they both popped up at the same time, looking flustered and as shameless as Bridille and Valadon had been though, Richard could guess, for very different reasons.

'And how are you, Oriane?' Valérie's voice was tense. 'Have you been attacked today?'

The reply was a cold stare, although there was something else behind it rather than just enmity, something more private. 'He is better off in custody,' was all she said, before throwing an enormous smile at Richard, leading him by the arm and leaving Valérie deep in thought.

Marcel Bouchard wasn't in custody, however, and he was approaching from the opposite direction, pushing his mother in a highly equipped wheelchair, with a vigilant Commissaire Lapierre in tow.

'I hope you know what you are doing?' he whispered to Valérie when they had reached the others.

'What is he doing here?' Oriane made a poor show of being afraid; she looked more affronted by his presence, knowing that he wasn't really a threat, but that it put her honesty under question. Madame Cuistot weepily gave him a hug, still yet to be convinced of his guilt.

Surprisingly it was Madame Bouchard who spoke, though she spoke through a voice box attached to a screen on the wheelchair. 'He is here for me, madame, one last time.' The voice was metallic and rasping and looked disconnected from the old woman who was deathly white and clearly so very, very tired.

The group separated around the laid tables, with René policing the area in case he saw any cutlery being moved without his approval. Martin came to offer everyone a cocktail, an offer which only Richard and Oriane took advantage of. Valérie was watching Marcel, who was attending to his mother, talking to her softly and wiping her chin. Lapierre looked tense and Madame Cuistot was quizzing Taz and Shilal about their underuse of spices.

They waited for about an hour and in that time the noise from inside the church steadily grew louder, but they weren't the sounds you would normally hear from inside a church, there was no hymn, no prayer incantation, no organ music. What there was sounded like a riot. A French church, like all churches, is built to impose, to put fear into those who see it and especially those who live under its shadow. The acoustics are meant to cow the penitent too, but this sounded like a particularly ill-tempered football crowd and was far more fear-inducing.

The crowd had turned ugly and as Richard opened the small door set in the larger double doors at the entrance, he was amazed to see what was going on inside. But, firstly, he couldn't get inside because two enormous men in bulging dark suits, dark glasses and earpieces were blocking his way. They were bigger even than ordinary nightclub bouncers; the impression they gave was that they were bigger than the coach that had dropped off the rented crowd.

'Name?' one of them asked.

'He's with me,' Lennard Bridille intervened, which didn't seem to make any difference at all, so Richard took a long detour around the two giants.

'What's going on?' Richard asked, his voice carrying further than he'd imagined.

'Going on?' Bridille replied, affecting surprise.

'Going on?' Agnès Valadon appeared at his shoulder.

'Yes,' Richard sighed. 'What is going on?'

'We're waiting for the minister.'

'Minister.'

Richard shook his head and turned to leave, unfortunately walking straight into one of the terrifying, presumably government, goons. It felt like walking into a granite wall. The man didn't look down but, holding his earpiece, spoke over his head to Bridille and Valadon. 'The minister is five minutes away,' he intoned, sounding not unlike Madame Bouchard's speech-generating device.

'How exciting!' Madame Valadon cried, for once speaking first.

Bridille lifted his loud-hailer again, an unnecessary ego-driven manoeuvre that almost succeeded in deafening everyone in the church as he asked, 'Where's the priest?'

A small man down the front ran up the few pulpit steps, adjusting his collar as he went. 'Here!' he shouted urgently, before repeating in a much more unctuous tone, 'I am here.'

'Then get on with it,' Bridille ordered.

'If the congregation will please rise,' he started, though most were already risen. 'We will begin with "L'Hymne au Printemps".' It took a few minutes of the most monstrous caterwauling before eventually the majority seemed to have settled on some kind of unity. Richard wanted to get out of there before his eardrums suffered permanent damage but this time he walked straight into Valérie who looked like she might scream.

'What is going on?' she shouted.

'That's what I keep asking!' he replied, his voice also necessarily raised. 'This is all quite desperate. If the minister sees any of this, there's no way that they'd be taken in.'

'I think they are quite insane, how do they think this will work?' Valérie was becoming quite frantic herself; this was not the controlled event that she had in mind at all and chaos upset her greatly.

Now the fake congregation was finding its voice and the hymn reverberated around the church, drowning out anything else, making it feel like the walls were caving in.

'Can I play the bells now?' Agnès Valadon practically screamed the request at Lennard Bridille, who appeared lost in what he saw as the inevitable success of his grand deception. He nodded, however, and Madame Valadon scurried through the nave and the chancel with Valérie instinctively following her. Lennard Bridille watched her with a proud look on his face and leant towards Richard.

'She's been looking forward to this,' he shouted, his face in rapture. 'The bell has been out of use for a year being cleaned. This is her first chance to ring it since last spring.'

Richard offered a false smile at the man's obvious lunacy. *Really?* he thought. *Is that what this is all about, bloody bell-ringing. So what if it's the…*

He didn't even finish his own thought as he sprinted after the two women, dodging children on the floor and almost knocking over the cross in the chancel, briefly stopping to apologise to the man on the cross, who looked like he'd had enough of these apostate shenanigans. Reaching the door of the bell tower he pushed hard and forced it open. Both women were at a bell pull.

'Now, Madame d'Orçay,' Agnès Valadon cried, pulling heavily on her rope. 'Now, with me!'

Richard leapt at the two women, bowling them over to the back of the stone room as the bell smashed heavily into the ground, spreading dust and devastation all around. Agnès Valadon screamed.

Chapter Thirty-Five

It took a couple of hours for the dust to settle. The ancient dust that had been violently disturbed in the church bell tower and the metaphorical dust from another devastating episode in La Chapelle's recent history. The one positive that Lennard Bridille could take from the events was that the minister had been immediately informed and had driven on, bypassing the centre of town and any stain of controversy.

'Maybe it won't matter,' he'd said to a distraught Agnès Valadon, who was being propped up with hefty quantities of asparagus martinis and who looked like she might finally buckle and throttle the man. The crowd, some of whom were singing so boisterously that they failed to notice the bell falling from its perch, were given a packed lunch, plenty of cocktails and shoved unceremoniously back on to the coach, but only after the driver had been placated by being given one of the minister's goons as on-bus guard. The man barely fitted through the door and it was fortunate that the 'Fournier family' were asked to stay behind, as one seat would never have been enough.

Now, with most of the tables and chairs stacked and with René and the Sharifi brothers having gone, the post-mortem could begin in earnest despite the fact that it was only Valérie and Richard who wanted to do that. Everybody else was spent and wanted the whole thing over with.

'I'm sorry about the bell,' a diffident Marcel Bouchard said, to no one in particular. He didn't look sorry at all and nobody replied. The young man stood up and placed himself at the rear of his mother's wheelchair; the frail old woman was either barely awake or, Richard suspected, barely alive. 'Can we go now, Commissaire?' he asked gently. 'I would like to spend some time alone with my mother before I go back to the cells.'

Madame Cuistot began to sob at the thought of this and it was Oriane who comforted her, before a shadow fell over them both as Madame Tablier appeared from nowhere with Passepartout in his expensive carrier bag. 'I thought you might need this,' she said, handing the small dog to Valérie, who took him gratefully and thanked Madame Tablier for bringing her 'lucky charm'.

'Commissaire?' Marcel was eager to get away.

Lapierre sighed heavily. 'I do not see why not.' He looked at Valérie as he began to rise, the plan had failed, the look said, we still have no evidence.

'Do you not want to hear how it was all done, Henri?' Valérie said while cuddling her dog. 'I think you will find it enlightening.'

'You have evidence?' he asked, sounding dubious.

'We do, don't we, Richard?'

This took Richard somewhat by surprise but his response was immediate. 'We do!' he replied, hoping that that was indeed the case.

'Top-up, old man?' Martin hovered at his shoulder with a fresh jug.

'Yep. And best keep them coming!' he whispered.

'Drinks all round, old girl!' Martin called over to Gennie. 'Looks like we're in for the long haul.'

Marcel retook his seat between his mother's wheelchair and the Commissaire. Madame Tablier preferred to remain standing behind her sister and Oriane. Opposite was Richard, next to Agnès Valadon who sat a little apart from Lennard Bridille. Felipe Santos sat even further apart but with the whole Fournier family, including the children, who for once were quiet, their roles presumably at an end. Bizarrely, Rolande Roy was a good ten metres away leaning on a wheelie bin, while Martin and Gennie hovered like clerks of the court. It was quite a crowd and it might take some warming up.

Valérie stood and handed Passepartout to Richard, which dented his confidence somewhat. That was his role, was it? He knew little of the whys, and the wherefores, but he was handy with a pooch. He took a defeated sip of his cocktail.

'It was Richard, who first identified the killer,' she opened dramatically, causing Richard to cough and take some half-hearted nods of congratulation from the vast minority. 'Look,' Valérie continued, 'here is your killer!'

Everyone turned to look at a defiant Marcel Bouchard, who met their eyes without a hint of remorse.

'Well, that was quick!' Gennie said with a slight disappointment.

'Wham bam, thank you, ma'am!' Martin added.

'All around you, that is the real killer.' Valérie swept her arms wide, taking in the street, the floral displays, the church, the fake Lavoir and, in the distance, L'Auberge Cuistot. 'La Chapelle-sur-Follet destroyed its own inhabitants.'

Richard had got used to this theatrical side of Valérie and loved it; it was pure cinema. The great detective dismantling the case for the suspects, chorus and audience alike, but even so, he felt she had gone off at a hell of a pace with this ethereal condemnation of geography, and that she needed to bring the audience with her a bit more.

'What Valérie means is that La Chapelle, and its standing, became an obsession with people, a competitive, unhealthy obsession.'

Everyone turned to Richard with the same look, which was 'yes, thank you, we're not idiots.' Even Fabrice Fournier, or whatever his name was, rolled his eyes.

'Top-up?' Martin whispered.

'Just leave the jug, I reckon,' was his morose response.

'I think it all started very well,' Valérie continued. 'All of the original La Chapelle committee, Florian Bouchard, Duval Cuistot, Christophe de la Cour, Agnès Valadon and Lennard Bridille, wanted the same thing. To put La Chapelle on the map. They, you,' she turned to Madame Valadon and Lennard Bridille, the latter of whom looked like he was smarting about being last on the committee billing, 'worked so hard. You all, as the Americans say, bought into it. The *Jardin Remarquable* status, the first in France ever given to an entire village, was the icing on the cake. It did not matter that it came from a corrupt minister who saw an opportunity for himself, it was a great honour and it made La Chapelle famous.'

'World famous!' Lennard Bridille added unnecessarily.

'Yes, monsieur.' Valérie rounded on him. 'And that is where the troubles began. Getting to the top is one thing, staying there requires a different set of skills.'

'We still worked so very hard,' Agnès Valadon offered quietly.

'Of that there is no doubt, madame but...'

'...but whereas you worked hard to open up La Chapelle to France,' Richard was determined to interrupt where he felt he actually knew something, and added sarcastically, '*and to the world* you then worked equally hard to keep the world out.'

This time everybody looked at him as something more than the dog handler. He was right.

'I don't know how it first happened,' Valérie continued after a sip of water. 'Perhaps this minister, Bernard Janvier, approached certain members of the committee, or perhaps certain members of the committee approached the minister. In the end, it does not really matter. Perhaps Janvier's ex-wife knows?'

The group turned to look at Oriane Moulin who shrugged. 'I do not know,' she said. 'Corruption and greed are like magnets, they attract one another.' Richard liked that, it reminded him of the kind of epithet that Charlie Chan films used to excel at.

'Or maybe,' Valérie's tone changed and became more mischievous, 'it was you who engineered this magnetic attraction and you have returned to claim your fortune?'

The reaction was immediate. Lapierre banged the table and shook his head, Felipe Santos stood, his eyes flaming and Rolande Roy nearly slipped off his bin. Oriane just smiled playfully, she may well have said, 'Stand down, boys!' à la Marlene Dietrich such was her command, but it was exactly the response Valérie had been looking for. And it was not lost on the three men either, the sudden realisation that they had each been played by a beautiful and manipulative woman.

'But Madame Moulin is here on official business,' the Commissaire said, keeping it formal.

'Did she tell you that?' Valérie asked, the genuine sympathy in her voice probably the most hurtful thing for the Commissaire.

'I was shown an official document.' He was determined not to back down.

'You were also shown a highly valuable property portfolio that was apparently controlled by Madame Cuistot. That was also false. Both were created by Oriane Moulin and passed to you on your assignations, Henri. I think Richard and I interrupted one of these at Patàpain.'

Lapierre looked embarrassed as Madame Cuistot went through a flustered pearl-clutching routine, protesting her innocence before she was becalmed by her sister. If Oriane felt any guilt at her actions and upsetting the woman sitting next to her, or even towards the three men she had obviously used, she certainly didn't show it as a little smile danced nastily on her lips.

'Why would I bother to do all of that?' Oriane asked, affecting a sense of boredom like a classroom rebel.

Valérie thought about this for a moment while everyone hung on this battle of wills. Only Richard, Valérie and Oriane herself knew how important the outcome of it was. At least, he assumed Oriane knew. She had changed since Valérie had begun, the veneer of comradeship had gone, the warmth she had shown to others had iced over revealing a nerveless, callous individual.

'Only you know why, Oriane,' Valérie concluded with a smile. 'You play games, you get bored, you manipulate for the sheer pleasure of it. It is why you are most certainly not here on *official business*, sorry, Henri. No government agency would trust you. You were a liability then, and you are a liability now.'

Oriane Moulin didn't respond to that, but nor was she defeated. Instead she looked Valérie square in the eye and smiled, her fake warmth having returned in a flash. 'Poor Valérie,' she said. 'You lost so much and you cannot forget.'

Richard didn't like that at all, but felt it wasn't his place to intervene and the rest of the group felt the same, now turning their heads towards Valérie as though this were a tennis match and Oriane had her running back after a successful lob.

'Forget? No. I do not want to forget.' She returned the smile though hers was more genuine, Richard could see that. Valérie didn't do games. 'But I move on. What were we taught? Compartmentalise, box it up, make it work for you later. Revenge is too emotional and you will make mistakes.'

'I must have missed that part of training,' Oriane chuckled.

'No, no. You were there. But you are flawed and that is why you cannot be here on official business; it is why I am.'

Valérie's overhead smash hit the line at the back corner of the court. Game, set and match.

'Oriane Moulin.' The Commissaire rose to his feet. 'I am arresting you for the murders of Duval Cuistot and

Christophe de la Cour. You may remain silent and so on…'
Lapierre's embarrassment meant that his heart wasn't in the
arrest, he had been duped.

Richard poured himself another drink.

Chapter Thirty-Six

Oriane Moulin stood slowly, tossed her hair back and held out her wrists unapologetically for the handcuffs.

'Oh, do sit down, Oriane,' Valérie's tone was harsh. 'I know you are not the murderer! I also know why you pretended that Marcel attacked you. You feared for his safety, you had convinced yourself that your ex-husband, Janvier, was behind the murders, that he was wiping out everyone who knew of his corruption before his comeback and you feared for Marcel. You were wrong, your judgement flawed.'

The other woman smiled sardonically and sat as she had been told to do while a predictable rumpus went up around the table, everyone asking what on earth was going on. Lapierre sat down too, humiliation piled on humiliation, and Richard felt for the man.

'Listen, can we just get on with my arrest?' It was Marcel Bouchard who interrupted. 'My mother is very ill and I'd like to take her home.' He stood up again but Lapierre grabbed his arm and sat him back down, an action which made him feel a bit better about himself.

'Well, if it isn't Madame Moulin, then we know it's Marcel. Why all this nonsense? I've got things to do.' Bridille was also trying to reclaim some dignity in the situation.

'What do you have to do, monsieur? You do not do any gardening yourself, you delegate and dictate and you huff and puff, but what is it you do?'

'He is the life force of the village!' Madame Valadon shouted angrily. 'The heartbeat.'

Valérie looked with sympathy at them both. 'I think not,' she said quietly. 'Let us go back to the original committee. Somebody wants to kill the committee off, why? Who gains from that? The obvious answer is someone else on the committee itself. This tontine idea where the last survivor takes the spoils.'

'But they have all been targeted,' Lapierre stated.

'They have,' Richard had this one, 'but not all of them successfully, meaning another committee member could, if you like, fake an attack on themselves to push blame elsewhere.' Lapierre's face told Richard he was not happy that it was Richard who had explained this. 'Sorry.' Richard muttered into his drink, cursing his Englishness.

'I believe,' Valérie continued, 'that Florian Bouchard, Duval Cuistot and Minister Janvier came to an agreement. Because of the *Jardin Remarquable* status the price of property in the village had soared, and a lot of existing inhabitants who had been frozen out of the decision-making or who did not want to be a tourist attraction took advantage and sold. Who bought these properties? The committee. And with what money? The money that Janvier's ministry had set aside for the new estate that is so neglected and cheap, and quite probably dangerous.'

Felipe Santos leant towards Lennard Bridille and a shocked Agnès Valadon. 'You bastards! Our families couldn't stay with us because of you. My son got pneumonia!'

'No, monsieur. That was not Monsieur Bridille or Madame Valadon, nor even Christophe de la Cour. It was Bouchard, Cuistot and Janvier. I think Lennard Bridille found out what had been going on, and going on under his name too. They used you as a front, did they not, monsieur? They used your, sorry to say this, your snobbery to build a wall around La Chapelle. You were very eager to ensure that only the right people were allowed to live in La Chapelle. You all agreed "no children", but the criteria narrowed all the time. What you did not know is that *they* owned the property, not the village.'

Bridille lifted his chin. 'Cuistot got drunk one night and told me. "We'll cut you in, Lennard," but they never did. Florian was furious of course.'

'So you began to kill them off, one by one?' The Commissaire ventured tentatively. 'This is the tontine that you mentioned, madame, actually quite illegal in this instance, but the surviving committee member inherits the lot.'

'No, Henri, not quite.' It's fair to say Lapierre was having an off day.

'Monsieur Bridille continued his policy of strict control.' Richard took up the story while Valérie took another drink. 'Hence the Fournier family here, all actors.' The fake-Fourniers all shuffled uncomfortably.

'I thought I recognised you!' Martin pointed at Monsieur Fournier. 'I've definitely seen you in something.'

Monsieur Fournier went bright red and said hurriedly, 'I was young and I needed the money!'

'Well, it's one of our favourites, isn't it, Martin?'

Richard raised his voice to reclaim some focus. 'They were obviously not going to move in, this was all for show, for the visit of the new minister. It was never going to work!' He was on a roll. 'I mean, I ask you, who could be called Garland and yet never have heard of Judy!' Everyone looked at him for an explanation which he was adamant he wouldn't give. 'Lennard Bridille decided that he would carry on the scam, but it would be solely in his own name. How did you do it, monsieur? How did you get the money?'

Lennard Bridille looked around the village, still his chin jutted out with pride and he held Agnès Valadon's hand, surprising her. 'I told Cuistot that I would inform the police if he and Florian didn't sign over some property to me. They did, and once I had one sold, I had the money to buy others. He had some in Madame Cuistot's name…'

'That is why you signed some documents last year, madame.' Valérie confirmed to a clearly bemused Madame Cuistot. 'And that is why the renewal of the *Jardin Remarquable* status was vital to you, monsieur, to pick up where those who had betrayed you had left off.'

Commissaire Henri Lapierre had had enough. 'All of this I understand, madame. The snobbery, the closed community, the fraud, but you told me before that whoever committed these murders wanted to destroy La Chapelle. In that case, it cannot be Monsieur Lennard Bridille!'

'It certainly wasn't Monsieur Lennard Bridille!' Agnès Valadon gripped her new man's hand tightly, and was unlikely to let go.

'You are correct, Henri.' The Commissaire visibly brightened, finally having scored a hit. 'I am just showing you how much has been going on in this tiny village. All of what you see around you, the beauty, the care, the love, it was hiding so much more and not just two rival groups of property fraud, or government corruption, but as we know, murder.'

Once again the entire group started talking animatedly amongst themselves.

'Has she been watching your films, Richard?' Gennie asked, sitting down. 'She's certainly developed a flair for the dramatic!'

'I'll say!' Martin agreed.

'Yes, maybe I'm starting to rub off on her,' he replied proudly, then immediately, at the same time as Gennie, 'not now, Martin.'

'At first I thought it might be Madame Cuistot,' Valérie began, which prompted Madame Cuistot to almost faint.

'Why?' she wailed.

'Because you had the motive, madame. You adored Marcel, and thought his parents terrible people.' Richard looked at the ailing Liliane Bouchard, who appeared to register extra pain at this. 'You despised your husband because he did not want children. La Chapelle became a symbol of everything you are and disliked. On the surface so warm and welcoming, but also childless. You blamed the committee for that.'

'It's true,' she said quietly. 'But I didn't kill anyone.'

'No, but your sister Madame Tablier thought you had, and claimed to be the murderer herself, using your motives to act on your behalf.' Madame Tablier, still standing, tapped her sister's shoulder in a gesture of solidarity.

'It was not helpful, madame,' Lapierre said a little too pompously.

'Like *you* were ever going to find the truth!' she replied venomously.

'Then I thought maybe Felipe Santos, he had motive.' Santos stared at Valérie unsmiling. 'But no, it didn't feel right. The same with Monsieur Roy, who also had the motive of losing his family, which Oriane preyed on so as to use him as her eyes and ears. Very clever, "nobody ever notices me," isn't that what you said?' Roy brushed away some imaginary dirt at his feet. 'But again, no.'

'Eyes, ears and broom-wielder,' Richard noted bitterly.

'So it was Marcel Bouchard all along then!' Lapierre was losing patience and had taken too many defeats.

'Yes, Henri. Our killer hated this village. It represents a life of sadness, a life ruined, opportunities lost, loneliness and despair but all, all of it realised just a little too late to do anything about it.'

Marcel Bouchard stood once again, taking his place at the handlebars of his mother's wheelchair, one hand gently resting on her shoulder. Madame Bouchard herself was trying to manipulate something on her controls but didn't have the strength to lean forward and do so.

'You are right, madame.' Marcel was forcing himself to speak. 'I hate this place. I had no parents as such, no friends, no life. I saw my parents throw everything they had into this sham and ignore me and I felt that it should end. It should end for good. I killed my father, tried to kill my mother. I killed Duval and de la Cour. I wired the plug on Lennard Bridille's stupid machine and loosened the nuts and bolts on the bell. Can we go now, please?'

There were tears in his eyes and it was obvious that he really did hate everything and everyone around him, that he blamed them for his loneliness and despair.

'It isn't quite true that you had no friends, is it, monsieur? You had one.'

Madame Cuistot was again quietly weeping at the sight of her beloved Marcel breaking down in front of her.

'That is true, I am sorry, Tata,' he said to the crying woman, moving towards her and kneeling at her side. 'I love you as if you were my mother.'

'Then why did you try to kill her, too?' Richard asked, picking up on Valérie's thread and making his way to the side of Marcel's stricken, struggling mother.

Marcel Bouchard bowed his head. 'Sorry,' he said, now crying himself but offering no explanation. 'I'm so sorry.'

'The truth is you did not, did you?' Valérie smiled at Richard who was bending down to see what Liliane Bouchard was trying to do with her controls.

'He didn't do it either? Why do people keep owning up to it?' Martin asked, shaking his head. 'This is like the end of *Spartacus*!'

Richard would have appreciated that but he was busy trying to help Madame Bouchard who was fighting for something. 'Is this the button you want?' he asked, but she couldn't reply. 'The voice thing?' he flicked a switch.

Liliane Bouchard's metallic voice crackled into life. 'My boy is not a murderer,' she said. 'I am!'

She fell back into her wheelchair, utterly spent by her efforts. Marcel quickly moved back to her and tried to turn the machine off, but Valérie stopped him. 'Please, monsieur,' she said, and that was enough as she tightened her grip.

With great effort Madame Bouchard continued. 'It was my plan all along. I saw last year how sad my son was, how sad and unhappy we had made him. Later, when he came back for Florian's birthday and was ignored, it broke my heart.' Tears streamed down her face. 'I planned it all. Duval's lawnmower, Christophe's eau de vie. It was I who wired Lennard's gutter cleaner and I who was in charge of the bell installation. All the people who had helped to ruin my son's life.'

'But why me?' a tearful Madame Cuistot asked. 'I love your son.'

The tears came hard down Madame Bouchard's face now and she appeared to spasm in pain. 'I know, I know and I hated you for that. I should have loved him the way you do.'

'And you poisoned yourself and your husband?' Valérie prompted, sensing time was of the essence.

'I did. We were supposed to die on the crossing, but my calculations were wrong. I hated that Marcel became a suspect and I begged him to tell the police about me, but he would not do it while I was alive. Madame Cuistot, my dear friend, you brought my boy up so well.'

Valérie let go of Marcel, who went to hug his mother, who was spent and had once again slumped back into her chair.

An officious Commissaire Henri Lapierre stood up and inevitably brushed his moustache. 'Madame Liliane Bouchard, I am arresting you for the murders of…'

Richard put his hand gently on the policeman's shoulder. 'Let it go, I think, mon ami,' he whispered. 'She can't hear you anymore.'

Chapter Thirty-Seven

Even two days later Valérie was still checking Wikipedia to see if there was any change on the slate message boards. It had become a habit, though Richard sensed there was more to it than that. Unless of course she was regressing into a teenager and just couldn't put her phone down, but then Richard didn't see Valérie as an avid TikTok influencer; he strongly doubted that was how the bounty hunter, covert assassination world operated. All hashtag 'middle of the forehead' and all that. It didn't sound right.

He was in a good mood. He still had no money, was on the cusp of divorce and Lana Turner had inexplicably stopped laying, but Madame Tablier was back – he could hear her stomping around upstairs – Valérie would feel more settled now that Oriane Moulin wouldn't be in her thoughts every day, and he was going to become a grandad. He had never given any thought to how something like that might make him feel, but it felt comforting. He had always been, according to Clare, an 'old person' even when he was young; well, he was now growing into that in an odd way. Though he hadn't told Valérie, the moment hadn't been right for that level of domesticity.

'Still no change,' she said, finally putting her phone down and reaching for her coffee.

'I don't know what you expect to find,' he said, eating what he considered a well-earned bacon sandwich under the disapproving but no less gluttonous eyes of Passepartout. 'Surely it's all over now? Poor Madame Bouchard. I say poor, she killed three people and nearly four others… but she's dead.'

Valérie sat down opposite him. 'You are assuming that it was she who was manipulating the Wikipedia site.'

'Wasn't she, then? She had all the equipment around her, and up until the last few days when Marcel limited her access to it in case she confessed, she was certainly capable.'

Valérie snorted dismissively, not of Richard's theory but of Madame Bouchard. She had far less sympathy for her than Richard did, though he'd be hard-pressed to explain why he had any sympathy for her in the first place, the woman was clearly a maniac, but were her motives all *that* bad?

'She was certainly capable!' Valérie repeated angrily. 'More than capable. Anybody who can grow E. coli bacteria from the excretion of someone else's food poisoning is very capable indeed!'

Somehow her use of the scientifically acceptable noun made it worse, and Richard secretly passed the remains of his bacon sandwich to Passepartout under the table.

'So who else was doing it then? The Wikipedia thing, not the… erm…'

She looked at him intently. 'Oriane Moulin,' she said quietly. 'You said yourself that it was a wide spectrum of quotes: Cicero, Audrey Hepburn, Godwin of Wessex. So I think more than one person was changing the signs.'

'And you think Oriane, Madame Moulin, was doing it as part of her plan to cause chaos?'

'Yes, I do.' She looked into her coffee. 'And Audrey Hepburn was deliberate. She knew I was nearby and she would have done her research on you. It was a trap for you, I think.'

Richard knew that he should feel alarmed, threatened even. But nobody else had ever done any research on him before, at least not to his knowledge, and certainly not as a trap. It was oddly uplifting, especially now the danger had passed. Even so, he felt obliged to change the subject before Valérie ripped the handle off her coffee mug.

'And when did Marcel realise it was his mother then?'

Valérie brightened a little, also happy to be on less contentious ground. 'That was easy. When the Commissaire told him about the plug on Bridille's gutter cleaning machine. He had brought it over with him, but he was here for one day and his mother probably offered to adapt it for him. Remember, he got his skills from her.'

'And the Duval, Bouchard, Janvier fraud. How did you know?'

'A lucky guess. It had to be something like that.' She smiled guiltily. 'It was worth a try!'

'An educated guess, let's say.' He smiled back at her and shook his head in admiration. 'We saw and heard all of the same things yet you worked it out way before I did, or even could have done.'

'Maybe,' she replied. 'But you saved my life, Richard. We are a good team, are we not?'

Inevitably, before either could add to the moment, Madame Tablier came trudging down the stairs, looking weary, irritable, on the verge of expletives and, as a result of all three, utterly delighted to be back.

'I need a new mop,' she said, clattering her metal bucket like a deranged percussionist.

The moment lost once again, Richard sighed and smiled at the same time and Valérie got up to get a refill. 'I'm not sure we can afford one,' he said, more jovially than he probably should have. 'I have to buy my ex-wife out, and unless she's prepared to take fresh eggs as a deposit, I don't know how I'll do that.'

Madame Tablier sniffed and pursed her lips. 'Here,' she said, reaching into her apron pocket. 'I forgot. I need to give you this.' She passed him a long white self-sealed envelope.

A resignation he thought, *she didn't hang around!*

He took the envelope nervously and opened it, catching Valérie's concerned eye. He pulled out an official banker's draft cheque. It was for the sum of two hundred thousand euros. He looked at her with confusion.

'It's made out in my name,' he said, bewildered.

She squeezed the mop into the base of the bucket as though wrestling a python, and without looking at him she said, 'Duval Cuistot left me La Manoir de Saint Sulpice and I sold it to that berk Bridille just in time.'

'Yes but…' Richard tried to intervene.

'I don't have a bank account,' she said, verging on aggression. 'Take what you need, put what's left aside for me and I'll ask you when I need something.'

'But, Madame Tablier…'

Valérie rushed around the breakfast bar and gave the old woman a hug before she knew what was happening and could fight back.

'Now, stop that.' She shook herself down and looked at a dumbfounded Richard. 'Consider it an investment,' she said grandly. 'There's going to be some changes around here. Firstly,' she looked him right in the eye like the cold-eyed businesswoman she now was. 'Firstly,' she repeated with menace. 'I want a new mop!' Richard breathed a sigh of relief. 'Secondly, she's out!' She hoisted a thumb in Valérie's direction adding to the shock both Richard and she were already under. 'You're not operating at full capacity and you've got that big house over there doing nothing, just you rattling around in it on your own. Time she moved over there with that dog of hers.' She turned to Valérie. 'I'll start cleaning your room this afternoon, probably dog hair everywhere!' And with that she went outside, slamming the door behind her and a look on her face like she would happily fight a cyclone.

'Thank you,' he said simply, before a silence fell on the room.

It was Valérie who spoke first. 'What do you think, Richard?' It was not often he had heard nerves in her voice.

She wouldn't have heard nerves in his voice as at that moment, he was utterly incapable of speech. He tried to speak and in his mind, as usual, he had grand words but all that came out was a kind of high-pitched whine, like a broken whistle. He knew he had to do something though and he fumbled in his pocket for his keys, and then grandly, ceremonially, removed his door key and presented it to her.

She took it gratefully, smiling at him and then somewhat ruined the moment by declaring, 'You do know I do not need a key? I could break in any time that I wanted to.'

He laughed. 'It makes it sort of official,' he said, trying to keep a steady tone.

The door behind them opened suddenly. 'I'm not disturbing anything, am I?' Oriane Moulin strode confidently into the middle of the room, a look on her face that suggested she knew her timing was awful for Richard and Valérie, and thus perfect for her.

'Why…' Valérie began.

Oriane spoke over her. 'I just wanted to say goodbye, before I left. You were so right, Valérie, what you said.' Valérie's look of suspicion changed into something else, a solid unease. 'It really is important to move on,' she sashayed back towards the door. 'If you can that is.' Her voice hardened horribly. 'If you can.' She leant out of the door and beckoned to someone out of sight. 'Do come in.'

A tall, well-dressed man came nervously around the door frame. Improbably he had an eye patch, a badly scarred face, a pronounced limp and yet, despite all that, he still looked good in a roll-neck. Richard looked at Valérie who was white as a ghost, which is exactly what she thought she was now seeing. The man approached slowly and held out a gloved hand for her to shake. She took it unconsciously and a look of confusion crossed the man's face. In his hand was the key that Richard had just given to Valérie.

'What is this?' he asked, his throaty voice sounding painful.

Valérie shook her head, unable to take her eyes off him. It was Richard who spoke, and for once reluctantly channelling Humphrey Bogart. 'That?' he said quietly, reeling off the last line of *The Maltese Falcon*. 'Oh, that's the stuff that dreams are made of.'

Also available

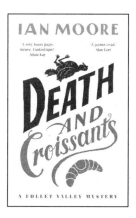

Death and Croissants
(A Follet Valley Mystery 1)

Richard is a middle-aged Englishman who runs a B&B in the fictional Val de Follet in the Loire Valley. Nothing ever happens to Richard, and really that's the way he likes it.

One day, however, one of his older guests disappears, leaving behind a bloody handprint on the wallpaper. Another guest, the exotic Valérie, persuades a reluctant Richard to join her in investigating the disappearance.

Richard remains a dazed passenger in the case until things become really serious and someone murders Ava Gardner, one of his beloved hens... and you don't mess with a fellow's hens!

OUT NOW

Also available

Death and Fromage
(A Follet Valley Mystery 2)

Richard is a middle-aged Englishman who runs a B&B in the Val de Follet. Nothing ever happens to Richard, and really that's the way he likes it.

Until scandal erupts in the nearby town of Saint-Sauver when its famous restaurant is downgraded from three 'Michelin' stars to two. The restaurant is shamed, the town is in shock and the leading goat's cheese supplier drowns himself in one of his own pasteurisation tanks. Or does he?

Valérie d'Orçay, who is staying at the B&B while house-hunting in the area, isn't convinced that it's a suicide. Despite his misgivings, Richard is drawn into Valérie's investigation, and finds himself becoming a major player.

OUT NOW

Also available

Death at the Chateau
(A Follet Valley Mystery 3)

Richard Ainsworth's French B&B has been taken over by a production company shooting a historical film at the Château de Valençay. But everything grinds to a halt with the sudden passing of an actor under suspicious circumstances.

To get to the bottom of things, Valérie d'Orçay and Richard offer catering services to the hastily resumed production. There they discover that the vanity, duplicity and murder of an eighteenth-century French court is nothing compared to that of a twenty-first century film set, with more heads yet to roll.

OUT NOW

About the Author

Credit: Richard Wood

Ian Moore is a leading stand-up comedian, known for his sharp, entertaining punditry. He has performed all over the world, on every continent except South America. A TV/radio regular, he stars in Dave's satirical TV show *Unspun* and Channel 5's topical comedy *Big Mouths*.

Ian lives in rural France and commutes back to the UK every week. In his spare time, he makes mean chutneys and jams.

He is also the author of two memoirs on life in France contrasting with life on the road in the UK. *À la Mod: My So-Called Tranquil Family Life in Rural France* and *C'est Modnifique: Adventures of an English Grump in Rural France*.

Acknowledgements

There is a small town not far from us that is a *Jardin Remarquable*. That is, I hope, where the similarity ends with my creation of La Chapelle-sur-Follet. However, it is a source of magnificent inspiration for horticulturalists, gardeners, and crime writers with a slightly warped imagination. I salute whoever it was who came up with the idea.

First thanks go to my wife Natalie, not just for the usual propping me up stuff, but for being my gardening and plant expert, fact-checking my hopeless lack of knowledge in the area.

To the wonderful team who make this all possible, I am as always eternally grateful. My agent Bill Goodall and all at Farrago Books: Pete Duncan, Rob Wilding, Matt Casbourne, Josie Cassaglia, Daniela Ferrante and the sales team who have been magnificent. I also reserve a special thanks to my wonderful editor and friend, Abbie Headon. How she retains so much information on the series is beyond me and I write the stuff!

I'd like to thank everyone who has read the series so far. I find it a world I like to inhabit when I'm writing and it is so pleasing to know that there are others out in the world who just like to escape for a bit too. It means everything.

Note from the Publisher

To receive background material and updates on further humorous titles by Ian Moore, sign up at farragobooks.com/ian-moore-signup